## BITTERSWEET LONGING

Sherry paused at the door and gave her an appraising look that suddenly changed. Niki felt as if he could see right through her clothes, and she took a step backwards. "Don't ever under-estimate yourself, Miss Owen," Sherry said softly. He put a finger under her chin and tilted her head up. "You are a beautiful woman, you know." He let his fingertip glide over the base of her chin, then went out.

Niki sat down again and stared at the closed door. She had never felt so vulnerable in her life. She turned toward the mirror, and pushed the heavy, dark hair from her face. She had never thought of herself as pretty.

She ran her fingertip over her chin where Sheridan had touched her, then ran her finger over her lips. He had called her a beautiful woman. It was the first time anyone had called her that. Instead of getting ready for supper, she went to her bed and did something most unlike her—she crawled into bed and hugged the pillow. Then she began sobbing for no reason at all.

DANGEROUS GAMES                    (0-7860-0270-0, $4.99)
by Amanda Scott

When Nicholas Barrington, eldest son of the Earl of Ul-
combe, first met Melissa Seacort, the desperation he
sensed beneath her well-bred beauty haunted him. He
didn't realize how desperate Melissa really was . . . until
he found her again at a Newmarket gambling club—being auctioned off by her father to the highest bidder. So,
Nick bought himself a wife. With a villain hot on their
heels, and a fortune and their lives at stake, they would
gamble everything on the most dangerous game of all:
love.

A TOUCH OF PARADISE          (0-7860-0271-9, $4.99)
by Alexa Smart

As a confidence man and scam runner in 1880s America,
Malcolm Northrup has amassed a fortune. Now, posing
as the eminent Sir John Abbot—scholar, and possible
discoverer of the lost continent of Atlantis—he's taking
his act on the road with a lecture tour, seeking funds for
a scientific experiment he has no intention of making.
But scholar Halia Davenport is determined to accompany
Malcolm on his "expedition" . . . even if she must kidnap
him!

# SHERRY'S COMET

## Juliette Leigh

Zebra Books
Kensington Publishing Corp.

http://www.zebrabooks.com

For my father who will always be with us. *We meet and the angels sing . . .*

ZEBRA BOOKS are published by

Kensington Publishing Corp.
850 Third Avenue
New York, NY 10022

First Printing: April, 1998
10  9  8  7  6  5  4  3  2  1

Printed in the United States of America

# Prologue

Sherry heard the noise when the firing started, and then the sound as the bullet whizzed by him. He had been shot at enough times to know when a bullet was meant for him, and this one had *Sheridan Devlin* written all over it. Without thinking, he grabbed Farnsworth and catapulted from the saddle over a thick bush. Farnsworth's spectacles flew through the air, and his portly body slipped sideways. Sherry fell on top of him as Farnsworth grunted.

"I say, what are . . . ?" Farnsworth began, but Sherry clapped a hand over his mouth and rolled on the ground to take cover under the bush.

The horses skittered, and Farnsworth's nag stopped, confused. Sherry's horse, Traveler, looked around for the man who had recently become his friend. Sherry risked leaping from behind the bush and smacking Traveler on the rump, yelling at the horse as he dived for cover behind a tree. It wasn't a moment too soon, as another bullet slapped into the trunk, spraying bark. Sherry cursed himself for being a fool as he watched Traveler break through the woods, crashing through the underbrush. That he didn't mind, but Traveler had Sherry's pistol and shot in his saddlebags as well as his rifle in its saddle sheath.

The rifles across the road roared again, entirely too close this time. Sherry left Farnsworth on the ground and crawled on his knees to the bush to try to see what was going on. Farnsworth sat up, confused, and looked around strangely. "I say, Devlin, why did you shove me down? I've lost my spectacles." He got to his knees and began feeling around on the ground.

"Get down," Sherry hissed, hearing voices in the thick woods across the road. Whoever was there was coming in for the kill, no doubt convinced that no return fire meant he and Farnsworth weren't armed.

Farnsworth paid no heed. He was still looking for his spectacles. "Why did you shove me from my horse?" Farnsworth said indignantly. "I wouldn't lose that horse for every deer in the forest."

"Deer?" Sherry peered around a covering of leaves that were dripping from the fog and mist. *God, everything drips fog and mist in this country,* he thought. "Whoever that might be isn't here for a deer, Farnsworth. Those shots were aimed at us."

"Ridiculous. This is England. That might be what you're accustomed to in the colonies, but I assure you that sort of thing simply doesn't happen here." He gave Sherry a condescending look, then ducked his head behind the bush as three shots rang out and glanced off the trees to their left. Sheridan glanced at the plump vicar he had met by chance on board a ship he had taken from Spain to England. "Does that convince you, Farnsworth? Do you see what I mean? There were three shots together. One hunter might have aimed at a deer and mistakenly shot at us. But three . . . no." He shook his head and glanced over at the road to Wynwoode, where Traveler had stopped and was standing. "Damme," he muttered, "I'd rather be shot myself than risk Traveler." He looked again as Traveler began to walk down the road, away from him. "At least I don' think they can see him. If we can just get . . .'' He stopped as Farnsworth interrupted him.

"Just look what's happened. It'll take forever to get new spectacles." Farnsworth held up bent wire frames and crushed lenses. "As to your comment—why would anyone shoot at us?" Farnsworth asked practically. "You're new to the country, and I hardly think any of those American savages would be here. All we have to do is identify ourselves."

"Sshh." Sherry waved him to silence, trying to peer through the leaves. The back of his neck was prickling—a sign he had learned to trust when he was in the woods in Virginia. "I see two of them although I can't make out the faces," he whispered. "That means the third one is trying to get behind us. We need to split up."

Farnsworth wheezed. "Nonsense. You may do what you wish, but this isn't the frontier. I'm going to identify myself and clear this up." He gave Sherry a disgusted look and stood up, waving the ruin of his spectacles. "I say there, whoever you are," he began, then looked quite surprised as a rifle cracked and a stain of red appeared on his waistcoat front. He turned to look at Sherry, but his face went blank before he could say anything, and he fell heavily to the ground. The leaves of the bush fluttered and then closed over Farnsworth as if he never had been.

Sherry looked around. The only weapon he had on him was a knife. Still, he wasn't waiting around to see if he, too, was a case of mistaken identity. Quickly he scuttled through the underbrush with the expertise born of long practice scouting the frontier across the Blue Ridge and Cumberland Mountains. He wriggled on his stomach under a bush and slid down a hill. He could hear the men who had been shooting creep warily up to the place he had been, then heard their disgusted shout when they discovered no one. He leaped to his feet and ran as fast as he could, cursing the boots he had bought in London. The soles were slick and twice he fell on the wet leaves.

At last he saw the big bay, reins tangled in a bush beside the road. He grabbed the reins free and leaped on the horse's back, bending low to miss the branches as the horse ran. He gave the horse its head, praying that there were no sudden holes or cliffs around. He had no idea what the country was like.

He rode hell-for-leather until the big horse was lathered, then stopped and walked the horse to cool him. He was sure he hadn't been followed. He would have heard or seen something if he had. He had watched for enough Indians to know the signs.

After the bay was cool, he wiped him off with his hand and patted his nose. "Good boy, Traveler." Sherry hadn't meant to do anything but hire a horse, but when he had seen this one for sale in London, he couldn't resist. The horse was cheap because, according to the owner, no one could handle him, but Sherry had never seen a horse he didn't love and couldn't manage, so he bought him on the spot and spent the better part of a week making friends with him. It had worked.

The horse had been named the Black Pearl according to his former owner, but Sheridan couldn't bring himself to call such a magnificent animal Blackie, and Pearl certainly didn't fit a stallion either, so he had taken to calling the horse after the pony he'd had as a boy in Virginia. "Good job, Traveler," he whispered, as the horse huffed into his hand, the warm breath filling Sheridan's palm.

He patted the horse's neck and remounted, pulling his pistol from the saddlebag and putting it in his waistband, then taking his rifle from its leather sheath and checking the priming. He was going back to see about Farnsworth. Sherry was sure the pudgy vicar was dead, but he had to make sure—he couldn't just leave him there. He wanted something else as well—he hoped to try to find out why someone would shoot at a stranger in England.

The woods were quiet now, and Sheridan found Farnsworth's nag beside a fence that enclosed a pasture of fine, deep green grass. He took the reins, and the horse fell into step behind Traveler. Sherry slowed Traveler to a crawl and guided the horse with the pressure of his thighs and knees. He wanted his hands free to use his pistol and rifle if he needed to.

Sherry stopped and dismounted a distance from the curve in the road. He could see the fresh wound in the tree trunk made by the bullet that had so narrowly missed him. He waited, tensed, the way he waited at home to see if Indians were in the woods. Then he began to move silently, gliding from one tree to another, always watching. He circled the spot and convinced himself that no one was there. Then he went over to the bush where Farnsworth had disappeared and parted the thick leaves to look under it where the hapless vicar lay.

Farnsworth was indeed dead, his broken spectacles still clutched in his hand and his last papers on marigold breeding slipping from his waistcoat pocket to get their edges soaked with blood. Sherry left Farnsworth for a moment and looked around. There was a set of tracks all around the bush that didn't belong to him. *One man only,* Sherry thought as he squatted to inspect the footprints. Whoever had been here to look had been sloppy and hadn't looked under the thick leaves where Farnsworth fell. He must have thought that Farnsworth had managed to escape as well.

Sherry left Farnsworth and went out into the road. There were three sets of tracks, all of them overlapping as though the men with the rifles had moved around and searched the edges of the road, but hadn't gone into the surrounding woods. The tracks showed that the men had turned and gone back into the woods where they had been hiding. Sherry followed the tracks for a few steps, but then the ground became rocky, and he lost the trail.

Going back to the scene, Sherry frowned as he thought about the last few days. There had been, he thought, at least one other attempt on his life—or maybe it had been an attempt on Farnsworth's. He didn't know that much about the man other than the fact that he seemed to be the mildest and meekest of men, concerned only with his marigolds. Sherry had met Farnsworth on the ship bringing him from Philadelphia to London and had been fascinated by the man's attempts to breed a white marigold. Sherry cared nothing for marigolds, but he thought Farnsworth had detected a pattern in breeding and was

curious how that might be applied to horse breeding. He had
persuaded Farnsworth to accompany him to look at Wynwoode.
He had even omitted a visit to the solicitor in London so
Farnsworth could hurry—the man had to be back at his living
in a small place called Dean Abbey before long. Sherry didn't
like lawyers anyway, so they had headed into the country,
bound for Wynwoode. Just outside Wrexham, they had stayed
at a small inn. During the night, the place had burned, and
when Sherry tried to open the door, it had been firmly bolted.
He had managed to wrap himself and Farnsworth in a cloak
and get out a window through the flames. At the time, he had
thought it an accident, in spite of the innkeeper's ranting that
someone had deliberately set the blaze. Now, as Sherry looked
through narrow eyes at the woods that seemed so quiet and
ominous, he thought perhaps the innkeeper had been right. He
remembered what his father always said about Indian attacks—
"If you can't fight your way out, and you're not sure what's
out there, disappear if you can." Sherry thought a moment,
and then decided to disappear.

He went back to the bush and picked up Farnsworth, grunting
at the heavy weight of the pudgy vicar. Then he put Farnsworth's body carefully in the road, taking the papers on marigold breeding from his pocket. He went through the pockets
carefully, taking whatever might identify the man as Farnsworth. Then he took some papers that identified him as Sheridan
Devlin and placed them neatly in Farnsworth's pocket. "I know
you don't have family, Farnsworth," he said to the body, "but
I promise I'll make this up to you. I'll see that you're put in
Dean Abbey with all ceremony. I promise." He walked to his
horse, then hesitated. He pulled a silver signet ring from his
finger and walked over Farnsworth, trying it on the vicar's
fingers. It barely fit the little finger. Sherry hesitated—his father
had given him the signet ring, a copy of the heavy gold one
he wore occasionally. His father had been in Philadelphia and
had gotten one of the famous silversmiths there to make it,
and it was a perfect copy. Sherry almost took the ring off
Farnsworth's finger, then shrugged. Another copy could be

made if he was unable to get this one back. The ring would be the final proof that the body in the road really was Sheridan Devlin.

Sherry put Farnsworth's papers into his own pocket and mounted Traveler. He hated to leave Farnsworth's nag, but there was no other way. He decided that he'd hide up the road a way, and if Farnsworth wasn't discovered in an hour or two, then he'd come back and try something else.

He had only gone a quarter of a mile or so when he heard someone coming and moved Traveler into the woods. It was a farmer in a cart filled with children. A woman sat beside him, and they were all singing as they rolled along. Evidently, Sherry thought, the farmer was taking his wife and family to the village. It was perfect.

In just a few minutes, Sheridan Devlin would be officially dead.

*June 22, 1819*

*To: Mrs. Mary Reade Devlin, Lady Wynford*
   *Sheridan's Quarter*
   *Charlottesville, Virginia*

*From: Messrs. Cromartie and Bradbury, Solicitors*
   *London*

*My dear Lady Wynford:*
   *I hope this letter finds you well and I do apologize for the address above, but I was not sure how to send this letter so it would get to you as speedily as possible, considering that it took almost a year for our last letter to reach you. Also, I do apologize for perhaps being overly explicit in the following, but I wish to make myself perfectly clear.*

   *As you know, our firm wrote your husband, Wyatt Sheridan Devlin, two years ago to inform him that his older brother, Richard Woode Devlin, Lord Wynford, had expired without living issue and that the estate of Wynwoode would pass to your husband as next of kin. We requested that Mr. Devlin—Lord Wynford—come to England for the purpose of claiming the estate and also asked that he come by our office and show proof of identity. We have been informed that he did, indeed, come to England, but he did not come by our office. Therefore, we were unaware that he was in the country and were unable to provide direction for him.*

   *I regret to be the bearer of bad news, and deplore the fact that there is no way to soften the blow. It is my unfortunate task to inform you that your husband, Lord Wynford, has met with a fatal accident on the road outside Wynwoode. I talked at length to the magistrate at the local village, Alderhill, and was informed that your husband did not suffer at all. Evidently he was accidentally shot by someone in the forest who was hunting deer. His*

*death was instantaneous, and I wish to emphasize again
that he did not suffer.*

*In view of the distance to his family home in Virginia,
I had no choice but to have his remains interred in the
family chapel at Wynwoode. If it is any comfort to you,
he now rests there with his parents, his brother, and his
brother's children.*

*I offer you my sincere condolences and wish there were
more I could do for you. You have not only my sympathies,
but those of the entire village of Alderhill. Each person
there was looking forward to the return of your husband.
At the funeral service, the church was full, and several
remarked that Lord Wynwoode had much changed since
he went to the Americas many years ago. He will be
much missed.*

*On another point, I realize that property in no way
makes up for your loss, but there will be a fair settlement
of the estate, I assure you. I will be forwarding particulars
and any moneys due to you as soon as the legal aspects
of this are untangled.*

*This may seem like an unseemly moment, but in order
to get the affairs of the estate in order, I need to know
if your husband, the last Lord Wynford (Wyatt Sheridan
Devlin) had any issue, particularly male. As you know, the
two sons fathered by the previous Lord Wynford (Richard
Woode Devlin) were killed in a carriage accident some
time ago, so the legal heir to Wynwoode will be your
children or any other issue of the last Lord Wynford
(Wyatt Sheridan Devlin). If he had no issue, the estate
and its assets will go to the next of kin, the surviving
child of his sister, Mrs. Elizabeth Devlin Jackson. This
claimant, James Ethan Jackson, has, as I had planned
to inform Lord Wynford had he stopped by our office,
been living at Wynwoode off and on for several years.*

*I regret the need for haste in this matter, but I need
your reply as soon as possible as Mr. Jackson has several
arrangements that depend on his status and needs to*

*clarify his position. I am also sure, that if Lord Wynford had male issue, you would wish to ensure that the rightful heir stepped forward to claim such an excellent estate as Wynwoode.*

*Again, my condolences on your great loss. The whole village has mourned the opportunity to have your husband in their midst. We can only console ourselves with the fact that he has gone on to greater rewards than those here on earth.*

> *Sincerely yours,*
> *Martin W. Bradbury*
> *Cromartie and Bradbury, Solicitors*

# Chapter 1

Miss Anika Owen raised her head slightly and peered through the grass and across the remains of a rock wall. "Are you sure he's here?" she whispered. "I don't see anything."

"Of course I'm sure. I told you I saw him this morning. He looked terrible." Robbie peered around his stepsister. "Be careful—those horrid men may be here, too. We've got to do something, Niki." He absently scratched the ears of a large, rangy hound who was liberally splashed with black and white spots. "Blazer and I came over here this morning and heard two men saying that they had to get rid of him."

"What were you doing here?"

Robbie gave her an angelic gaze. "Blazer and I come over here every day and bring the poor thing an apple. This morning, there were two men in the pasture, and we had to hide behind the fence, just like now. I was listening, and I heard one of them laughing and saying that someone—it sounded as if he said Creevy, but I'm not sure—someone had beaten the horse too hard and now he's only good for glue. We can't let that happen." He paused, and his voice cracked. "There he is, Niki!

Just look at him.'' He stuck out his hand and pointed, knocking down part of Miss Owen's unruly black hair with his finger.

"Ow!" She jumped and snatched at her hair, but Robbie was quicker. He clapped his hand over her mouth. "Quiet, Niki," he hissed. "We'll be hanged if we're caught, you know."

"Hanged?" She looked at him with wide eyes as he untangled his hand from her hair.

"This *is* stealing a horse, isn't it? That's a hanging offense." He nodded as he peered again through the bushes. "There he is! Niki, if we don't save him, he's going to die! Just look at him!"

Miss Owen shoved a tangle of hair from her eyes and parted the grasses as best as she could. The sight she beheld almost made her cry. The horse was standing in the middle of the field, looking around as if in a daze. He wasn't that thin, but was bony enough to appear sick and downcast. Worse, his coat was rough with sores and scars. He walked slowly as though each step caused him pain. From his configuration, Niki could see that he was a thoroughbred and had once been a magnificent animal. He deserved better.

"You're right, Robbie," she said slowly. "We've got to save him." She turned and looked at her brother. "It isn't stealing if you're trying to help, I wouldn't think. After all, we're just trying to save him, not take him. If we can rescue him and make him well, perhaps . . ." She hesitated, still having trouble calling Robbie's father Lord Larch, "Papa." He had asked her to, and she found she loved him dearly, but it was still too new. "Perhaps we could get your father to help us."

Robbie looked at her in alarm, "We can't do that. He'd make us give Comet back, and then those men would kill him for sure."

"Comet?"

Robbie looked up at her with large eyes. "That's the horse's name. I heard one of the men call him that one day when I was hiding behind the rocks."

Niki frowned at the implications. "They could have harmed

you if they had discovered you, Robbie. You shouldn't have been here.''

''I had to be here, don't you see? Comet wouldn't have a friend if it wasn't for me.'' He paused a moment. ''Isn't it sad, Niki? With a name like that, he must have been able to run like the wind.''

Niki looked back at the horse as the animal took painful step after painful step. His right front foot seemed to cause him great pain. ''Look how he's hurt, Niki,'' Robbie said, looking up at her again. ''We have to help him, Niki, we *have* to.'' Robbie put his hand on hers.

Niki couldn't resist the plea in his eyes. ''You're right, Robbie.'' She sighed. ''Lord Wynford probably doesn't want him anyway, or he'd treat the poor thing better.''

''That's what I thought, too.'' Robbie nodded in agreement, his red hair bobbing and falling down into his eyes.

Robbie turned and leaned against the rock wall that served as a boundary marker. ''I have it all figured out. I've even discussed it with Cam, and he agrees with me.''

Niki's dark eyebrows lifted. ''You told Camden?''

Robbie nodded, oblivious to her concern. ''I needed advice. I even brought him here to see for himself—the same way I'm doing you.'' He picked a stalk of grass and chewed on it thoughtfully. ''Cam suggested that we keep him at the old barn in the back woods. No one ever goes there, and since there are three of us involved, we can go check on him one at a time and no one will miss us.''

''The old barn?'' Niki hadn't lived at Breconbridge long enough to be able to place everything. ''Do you mean the one in the far corner of the estate? That's a long way.''

Robbie nodded again. ''That's why it's perfect, don't you see? Cam says that there's pasture there and everything. No one ever goes there.''

''If we took the horse, we couldn't let him out to pasture. Someone might see him.''

Robbie thought about this for a moment. ''No one would,'' he said with finality. ''Besides, after Cam and I—and you,'' he added quickly, "get through with him, no one will recognize him anyway."

Niki frowned. "I don't think it will work, Robbie."

Robbie jumped to his feet. "Are you a coward, Niki? I thought better of you than that." He pointed to the horse, who was trying to eat some grass, hobbling across the field on his lame leg. "Look at the poor thing. Uh-oh." He quickly dropped to his stomach behind the wall. "Someone's coming." He peered over the rocks and caught his breath. "It's the men who were here talking this morning. There's another man with them. I think it's the man Wynford has looking after his horses."

Niki pulled herself up to peer through a broken rock that made a hole in the fence. "Get down here with me unless you want them to spot that red hair," she whispered to Robbie. He slid down and scrunched up beside her, looking through the hole. There were three men coming into the pasture. They were too far away to hear what they were saying, but Niki could clearly see that one of them was the leader, telling the others what to do. He was heavyset, short, and had a swarthy complexion. Worse, he had a cruel, harsh expression. To her horror, the men walked up to the horse and looked at it quickly, then put a halter on it. The horse trembled as they ran hands across its back, touching the sores. Then, to Niki's amazement, the men threw a blanket on the horse and tried to saddle it. As soon as the weight of the saddle settled on its sores, the horse shied and tried to step away. The swarthy man jerked on the halter and lifted a whip. The horse was promptly beaten— unmercifully, Niki thought—with the whip, blood showing where the man hit. The horse tried and tried to move away, making strangled noises, but the other two men held it fast. Finally the men were able to saddle the horse and the swarthy man mounted. The horse tried to go through its paces, but it kept limping and stumbling. The man got off and beat the horse again. "Did you bring your rifle?" he called to one of the other men.

"No. Do you want me to go get it?" the man called back.

The swarthy man shook his head and pulled off the saddle

in disgust. "No, we'll all go together, and then you can come back and finish off this excuse for a horse. I told Jackson that he was done for." He handed the saddle off to the other man and began walking toward the gate, his voice carrying back to Robbie and Niki. "I'll leave the halter on him so you can take him to the woods and shoot him. Bring it back when you've finished." The men's voices faded as they went through the gate and walked back toward the big house. Robbie and Niki stayed hidden for what seemed like forever until they were sure the men were out of sight.

"We have to do something now," Niki whispered. "Now!"

Robbie nodded and stood, looking at the horse, his voice almost breaking again. "I was going to try to tame him and then ride him over to the barn. I thought I could tame him and get him to trust me in five or six days."

Niki stood up and ran for the road where there was another gate. "We don't have five or six days, Robbie. We don't even have five or six hours. Those men will be back inside an hour, I'm sure. We'll have to try to get him out of the pasture and take him to the barn ourselves. Come on."

Robbie glanced back towards Breconbridge. "Should I go get Cam?"

"There isn't time. Didn't you hear what they said? They'll be back with a rifle in just a few minutes. Come on!" She ran back, grabbed Robbie's hand, and pulled him toward the road and the other gate. Disregarding her dress, she pulled at the gate, throwing the slats down and rushing into the pasture.

"Good boy," she crooned, warily approaching the horse. "Oh, Robbie, look at the poor thing. He's all bloody." She held out her hand and the horse stepped backwards, afraid of her. "Don't be afraid, boy. I'm going to take care of you." She spoke in a soft singsong, and moved up to the side of the horse, gently touching his neck. "See if you can get the halter, Robbie. We've got to hurry."

Robbie moved on the other side and took the halter. Together they started leading the horse to the gate. The horse looked at the slats and balked. It took both of them to coax him through.

Once in the road, Niki looked down toward the little village of Alderhill. The road wasn't the main road to the village, but was used frequently by farmers as a shortcut. "We're going to have to go through the woods," she said to Robbie. "We could be seen if we keep to the road. Help me." She tugged on the halter, and they managed to get into the woods. Just as they got out of sight, Niki looked back and saw one of the men topping the rise above the pasture, a rifle crooked in his arm. "Hurry, Robbie, hurry. They'll be looking for us in a minute."

Robbie looked at the horse's back. "We could get him to the barn in no time if we could ride him."

"Well, we can't. We've got to try to walk him there and hide him before anyone discovers he's gone." She paused and looked around. "I don't know what to do except try to hide him. I've never stolen a horse before."

There was a chuckle from behind a nearby tree, and Niki whirled to face whoever was there, but saw no one. "Who is it?" she gasped. "Get ready to run, Robbie," she whispered as she put herself between Robbie and the tree. Blazer was no help—he flopped down on the ground and began wagging his tail.

"No need to run, I assure you." A stranger walked from behind the tree, smiled at them, then walked past them into the woods again. In just a moment, he returned, leading a magnificent bay.

"What a horse!" Robbie exclaimed, touching the horse's darker mane.

The stranger smiled, the corners of his blue eyes crinkling. "Meet Traveler, a most excellent bay," he said with a laugh. "You'll have to make the rest of the introductions yourself."

"I'm Robbie—Robert Beaumont of Breconbridge and this is my dog Blazer, and this is my . . ." Robbie stopped as he glanced at Niki and saw her look of alarm. He rounded on the stranger and stepped back. "And who are you?"

The stranger laughed again, then listened to shouts coming from across the road. "Just say I'm the man who heard your remarks about stealing a horse. I take it those noises are coming from the owner?'' He walked over to the horse. "And is this your prize?'' He ran his fingers down the horse's side and looked at the blood on his fingertips. "Good God. Did you do this?''

"No, they did,'' Niki said, tugging on the halter. "And we're not really stealing him. We're trying to save him. They were going to shoot him because he wouldn't do what they wanted. They beat him.''

"So I see.'' The stranger glanced from his bloody fingertips to Niki, then listened for a moment to the sounds across the road. "People like that don't deserve horses, do they? Where are you taking him?''

"Don't say anything, Robbie,'' Niki said, stepping backwards and reaching out for her stepbrother. Robbie closed his mouth with a snap.

"For God's sake,'' he man said impatiently, swinging himself up into the saddle of his horse, "I'm trying to help you. The only way you're going to get that horse away from here is to lead him, and you'd better do it in a hurry. From the sounds of it, they'll be here in a few minutes.'' He leaned over and held his hand out. "Do you want to get on with me and let Traveler lead the horse to wherever you're going? I have no intentions of turning you over to any authorities.'' He chuckled. "In fact, I suppose I've just turned myself into an accomplice to horse thievery. What would my father think?''

Niki paused a second as the voices from the pasture sounded closer. She reached up and grabbed the stranger's hand. He hoisted her in front of him, then reached out for the lead. "Climb up behind me, Robert Beaumont. Traveler can manage the three of us.''

Robbie scrambled up, and the stranger headed for deeper woods as the sounds of the pursuers got closer. He didn't stop until they were well away. He didn't say a word and even quieted Robbie when he began to talk. "We need to be quiet until we throw them off the track,'' he whispered.

He had his arm around Niki and she felt very strange. She had never been this close to a man before, not even the few

times she had been kissed at dances. This man she didn't even
know was molding her body to his and the feel of the horse
beneath her was quite unlike anything she had ever felt. His
arm was around her tightly, and his hand splayed across her
ribs, pinioning her. She felt herself begin to blush as strange
thoughts crept into her mind. Her body was strangely comfortable, even in this cramped position, but with every jolting step
the horse took, she was aware of the feel of the man's body
next to hers.

Finally, just when Niki thought she was going to explode
from all the strange sensations, the stranger stopped. "I think
we've left them behind," he said, and Niki noticed for the first
time his strange accent. He wasn't from here at all.

He held Robbie's arm as Robbie slid down to the ground
beside Blazer, then he handed Niki down carefully. He dismounted and smiled at them, a quick smile that disappeared
as he turned his attention to the stolen horse. Expertly he ran
his hands over the horse, then bent and picked up the hooves
one by one. He put the last hoof down carefully and turned to
face Niki and Robbie.

Niki had turned her own attention to the man as he examined
the horse. He was well dressed in a blue coat, a cream shirt
and stock, brown breeches and boots. His skin was tanned as
though he spent a great deal of time out of doors. He wasn't
exactly handsome, but was striking, with an open face and fine,
clear, blue eyes. His hair was almost two colors, dark blond at
the roots and almost flaxen where the sun had bleached it. It
was slightly curly and he wore it longer than most of the
men Niki knew. One troublesome curl kept falling across his
forehead, almost reaching his eyebrows. Niki smiled as he
shoved the hair back, exposing an eyebrow that had a pointed
arch, giving him a devilish look. Only one eyebrow was arched,
the other was curved. As the stranger had moved to feel the
horse's legs and hooves, the strand of hair fell down again. He
shoved it back once more.

When he stood to face them, Robbie smiled at him. "Do
you think he'll be all right? Did we do the right thing?" Niki

had noticed how the stranger's expression changed when he smiled, how his whole face became open and friendly, but now he looked almost murderous. There was no smile there now.

"Yes, you certainly did the right thing. Whoever did this to this animal ought to be whipped until he's shredded," he said, his expression deadly. "I can't imagine treating anything like this."

"That's why we had to save him," Niki said. She paused a second. "Thank you for helping us. We'll take him from here."

"And do what?" The stranger wheeled and looked right at her, his blue eyes cold. "This animal needs care. Do you think you can provide that?"

"I happen to know a great deal about horses." Niki glared right back at him, lifting her chin much as her aristocratic Spanish grandmother always did. Her brown eyes met his blue ones.

"I'm sure you do. But look at this." He picked up the horse's front hoof. There was a particularly ugly gash almost all the way around the leg. The edges were torn and puckered. The wound had gotten infected, and the smell was strong. "This is going to take daily care or else you'll have to be the ones to shoot him just to put him out of his misery. If you're trying to hide him, are you going to have that kind of time without letting someone else know?"

Robbie drew back, his face greenish. "He's right, Niki. We can't do it ourselves. Not even with Cam helping us. If anyone finds out . . ." He paused and looked, if possible, a shade greener. "You know what will happen."

"What did you plan to do with him?" The stranger leaned against a tree, keeping an eye on his own magnificent bay.

"We were going to hide him in an old barn at Breconbridge." Niki blushed as she realized how stupid their plan sounded. "We didn't have any idea what to do with him after that."

The man nodded. "He was, at one time, an excellent horse."

"A thoroughbred," Robbie said, patting the thin flanks. "He'll look like his old self when we nurse him back to health."

"I think he might." The stranger looked assessingly at the

horse and checked its teeth. "He's got some age on him, but the lines look good." He turned and looked at the two of them. "As it happens, I'm in need of a place to stay right now, and I'd be glad to watch after him in exchange for a spot in the barn. I'll just be here a few weeks, but he should be on the mend by then."

Niki stared at him. "Are you a deserter?"

He threw back his head and laughed, a joyous laugh that made everyone want to laugh along with him. Niki found herself giggling rather than being embarrassed. "Lord, no. I'm a stranger in these parts, but I have my reasons for lying low. I'm no deserter and no criminal either, so you can rest easy on those points." He glanced at the horse. "Or at least I wasn't a criminal until I met up with the two of you." He grinned again.

"We'd be happy to have you stay in the barn and look after Comet," Robbie said. "Wouldn't we, Niki?"

"Well . . ."

He ignored Niki's hesitation. "Thank you. I accept your kind offer. Now, we'd better be getting this horse—what did you say the name was—Comet? We'd best be getting Comet to a barn and giving him some water and some feed. I hope you have both there." He intercepted their guilty look at each other and sighed. "Somehow I think this may be a larger undertaking than I first imagined." He laughed again. "Shall we go, Robert Beaumont of Breconbridge and Miss . . . Beaumont?" The last word was a question.

Niki hesitated, then realized he would discover her identity anyway if he wished to do so. "No. Miss Owen. Miss Anika Owen."

He paused, then gave a small bow. "How do you do, Miss Owen. It's a pleasure to make your acquaintance." Niki gaped. His manners would pass in Carlton House if need be. "And your name, sir?" she asked.

"My name?" He seemed somewhat surprised. "I'm . . . I'm . . . My name is John Smith."

Niki looked at him, but he didn't meet her eyes. "Of course,"

she said, as he swung her up into his saddle and put Robbie
behind her. He gathered up the lead and the reins for Traveler
and grinned up at Niki.

"Of course. Call me John if you wish." He glanced around
the woods. "Which way?" Robbie pointed, and they set out,
John Smith leading them and whistling tunelessly through his
teeth as he walked.

"I've got it!" Robbie exclaimed as John Smith stopped and
looked at him. Robbie smiled down at him. "You're from the
Americas."

He grinned at them and bowed again, then broke into his
infectious laugh, his blue eyes dancing. "Of course I am, Robert
Beaumont of Breconbridge and Miss Owen. John Smith of
Virginia at your service."

# Chapter 2

Niki sat silently on Traveler while "John Smith" led them through the woods and over the country, following Robbie's directions. "Tell me," Smith said with a smile that Niki schooled herself to ignore, "are the two of you usually in the business of stealing horses, or is this an aberration?"

"Oh, an aberration, to be sure." Robbie signaled for Smith to stop Traveler, and he hopped down to walk beside him. "We were just afraid Comet would die from mistreatment. Then this morning, we discovered that they were going to kill him. I think we did the right thing."

Smith looked gravely at him, as though talking to an equal instead of a boy. "I think you did the right thing, but the courts may have a different view." He paused and looked at the two of them. "There must be absolutely no inkling that we've done this, or we'll all be in the suds. Pardon me, Miss Owen, but that's as apt expression as any, and I think you know full well what I mean."

"I do." Niki sat primly on Traveler and refused to look at him. John Smith was a bad one, she knew. The only reason he could have fallen in with their scheme so readily was if he was a horse thief himself. She had to alert Cam somehow—tonight both John Smith and Comet would disappear. She was sure of it. "I certainly don't intend to bruit it about, and I'm sure Robbie won't either."

Robbie nodded, picked up Traveler's reins, and began walking. "I'll never tell. I don't fancy seeing you at the end of a rope, Niki." He turned and grinned over his shoulder at her. "Or me either. I don't think Father would like that above half."

"We're agreed then." John Smith fell in behind Robbie and Blazer, whistling tunelessly again. Soon he was telling Robbie tales of his explorations along the frontier and wild stories of the rich grass in a place called Kentucky. According to Smith the grass was so lush that horses could almost get lost in it. Niki gritted her teeth as she saw Robbie glance at Smith with the beginnings of a bad case of hero worship. Lies, all lies, she wanted to shout—the man had to be a thief. Anyone else would have immediately turned them over to a magistrate, or at least tried to convince them to return Comet.

She glanced at Comet as John Smith dropped back to touch the horse's flanks gently. They stopped a moment as Smith put his hand under Comet's nose and waited a moment. Comet breathed into Smith's hand, and then Smith seemed to whisper to the horse. "What are you doing?" Niki asked.

Smith looked up at her innocently. "Just making friends. I believe Comet can use a few friends for a while." He ran his fingers down the horse's neck. "He was once a beauty, I think. Perhaps he will be again." He grinned at Niki. "Then you'll have a prize on your hands, and you'll have to decide again what you're going to do with him. His owner might want him back alive and sound."

"Perhaps to sell?"

"Perhaps." Smith gave her an enigmatic look and went back to Traveler's head, touching Traveler as he walked by. The horse picked up the pace again and they went on through the woods. Niki glanced at Smith as he walked, leading Comet. He had to be planning to take Comet, clean him up, and then resell him. That was the only answer. Tonight, she would find

Cam and expose the man. John Smith had saved them, it was true, but it was for his own purposes. The man was clearly a rogue and an opportunist.

They had crossed the road again—cautiously, with Smith looking each way before he allowed them to cross—and had circled around the house to reach the back field. Niki felt the sun on her arms and face and wished she had worn a bonnet. Sunburn was going to be almost as difficult to explain to her mother as their long absence. Either way, as Smith had put it, she and Robbie would be in the suds.

The barn was, as was everything on Breconbridge, in good repair, and it was a simple matter to get the door open. Comet seemed to realize the barn was a safe shelter and went right into a stall. Robbie grabbed a bucket and went to get him some water while Smith unsaddled Traveler and put him in an adjoining stall. "I gathered that you weren't very prepared, but do you think there's any grain around? Any medical supplies?" he asked Niki.

She shook her head. There was hay, of course, and grass outside, but nothing else there except empty buckets for water. And there was certainly nothing that might cure the sores and welts on Comet. "We hadn't really planned to take him today, and we weren't ready. Robbie planned to spend five or six days making friends with Comet, and I suppose we'd have gotten the barn ready in that time."

"Sometimes plans won't wait until everything's ready," he said cheerfully, putting his saddle over the wall of an unused stall. He rummaged around, looking for a brush and currycomb. "Where's the water supply? I'll want to wash him off first thing, and try to see how bad those welts and sores are. If we can make do tonight, tomorrow I'll go into the village and buy some supplies. What's the name of the place—Aldershot?"

"Alderhill," she said absently, then the implications of his comment hit her. "Tomorrow? You'll be here tomorrow?"

He turned and looked at her, his blue eyes clear and guileless in the gloom. "Of course. I told you I'd stay for a while. I need to . . ." he paused and groped for words, "do some things here anyway."

"I'm sure you do." Niki wasn't quite successful at keeping the sarcasm from her voice. Smith looked at her and started to reply when Robbie came bouncing into the barn. "Here's one bucketful," he said. "I'll go get some for Traveler. Will we need anything else?"

"Not tonight," Smith said. "I'll get some things tomorrow. Just show me where the spring is, and I'll wash him off later." He glanced around. "Is there a room for a groom here in the barn? That will be fine for me."

Robbie nodded and showed him the small room at the front of the barn. The room was clean, although sparsely furnished. There was a washstand with a pitcher and bowl, an old mirror, a small table with two chairs, and a narrow bed. There was a straw mattress on the bed, but nothing else. Smith shook it. "I've had worse," he said cheerfully, as Blazer sniffed all around the room. Apparently satisfied, the dog flopped down beside the bed and yawned. "I feel like doing the same thing, Blazer," Smith said with a grin, bending to rub Blazer's back, right between the shoulder blades. Blazer stretched contently. Smith stood and turned to Niki and Robbie. "Why don't the two of you get back home before someone thinks you've been kidnapped or fallen by the wayside. If I know parents, there'll be a hue and cry for the two of you if you stay away much longer."

"Besides, I'm hungry." Robbie felt his stomach as they walked back into the main part of the barn. "Aren't you, Niki?" He turned and looked at Smith with round eyes. "We don't have anything for you. Would you like us to bring you something?"

Smith shook his head. "No. I have food in my saddlebags. Just don't let anyone come back here unless you tell me, so I can hide the horse." He looked back at the stall, where Comet seemed to have made himself quite at home. "I'll try to soak his hoof some and clean him up." He paused and walked over to the stall, absently scratching Comet's head. "Why did someone do this to him, do you know?"

"Racing." Niki spat out the word. "Don't get me wrong, Mr. Smith, I love a good horse race, but some unscrupulous people do things to horses and people to try to change the outcome of a race. Comet belongs to Mr. Jackson over at Wynwoode. Jackson—he's Lord Wynford now—is in London most of the time, and maybe he doesn't know what's going on, but it's common knowledge that the men at Wynwoode mistreat the horses there."

Robbie nodded and jumped in excitedly. "Cam says that they don't race fair. He's never said that Jackson was involved in anything shady, but he did say that there had been talk."

"Now, Robbie, we don't know that. All that may be gossip. Even Cam said so." Niki gave him a severe look.

"I'd bet it's true." Robbie's mouth set in a stubborn line. "Where there's that much talk, something must be there. At least that's what Cam said." He turned back to Smith. "Cam knows everything about racing."

"Oh?" Smith said, nodding.

Robbie nodded back. "Everything. I brought Cam to see Comet, and he thought he'd seen the horse at a track somewhere. He said that Wynford knew that Comet was a goer and could take anything on the track, but he could gull people by having Comet look like a broken-down old hack. Anyway, Cam said the mark would put up a big amount, thinking any horse could beat something that looked like Comet, but then Comet would win easily and Wynford pocketed the winnings."

"Uummm. I've heard of such." Smith ran his hand over Comet's neck, knocking off some mud. "The two of you had better move along. I don't want anyone out here looking for you."

Robbie had to restrain himself from being too exuberant and contented himself with shaking Smith's hand. "We'll be back as soon as we can," he promised. He whistled for Blazer and started out the door. "Come on, Niki."

Niki paused a moment. "Good day, Mr. Smith." She hated to say it, but she had to. "And thank you very much for your help."

He smiled, and Niki had to make herself look away from his blue eyes. "Not at all, Miss Owen. I'm glad I could help. Both you and Comet."

Once outside, Robbie and Niki decided to circle back through the woods and come out behind the house, so no one would know where they'd been. "Isn't it wonderful that Mr. Smith came along, Niki?" Robbie asked, almost dancing. "I was so afraid, and I prayed someone would come to help us. All at once, there he was." He looked seriously at Niki. "Do you think I should put something extra in the collection on Sunday? Just by way of thanks?"

"Probably." Niki sighed as they slipped in the back door. If Robbie thought that John Smith was heaven-sent, there was no point in mentioning her fears to him. Still, Robbie was going to be crushed tomorrow when both John Smith and Comet disappeared. Maybe Cam could help her.

"Anika Marie, come here at once. And bring Robert with you."

When her mother spoke in that tone and called her by her full name, Niki knew that there was trouble. "We're in the suds," she muttered, as Robbie looked up at her with big eyes. He grinned at her. "And you're the world's worst liar," he said. "We're in for it now."

Lady Larch was sitting with her embroidery. She glanced at Niki and a look of horror crossed her face. "Whatever have you doing?" she gasped. "Just look at yourself!"

Niki took advantage of the invitation to look at herself in the drawing-room mirror. It was worse than she had feared. The skin on her face was pink, and her unfashionable olive complexion would be even darker by tomorrow, she knew. There were muddy smudges on her neck and the bodice of her gown from where she had leaned against Comet. There were grass stains on the bottom of her once-pristine white gown. Worst of all was her hair. It had gone every which way, tumbling down from its pins, and had acquired a few twigs and leaves from their ride through the woods.

"We've been in the woods," Robbie said, as Niki groped for a plausible story.

"I can certainly see that," Lady Larch said. "Whatever have you been doing?"

"We've . . we've . . ." Niki groped for words.

"We've been digging for treasure, Mama," Robbie said solemnly, his expression resembling a choirboy from heaven. "I made Niki help me." He looked crestfallen and went to sit beside his stepmother. "We didn't find a thing and I just knew we would. Jem down at the stables told me that Robin Hood had buried some things there, and it was just waiting for someone to dig it up." He looked up at Lady Larch, his blue eyes as wide and guileless as John Smith's had been. "Do you think that's true?"

"Oh, my dear!" Lady Larch patted him on the head. "I'm sure Robin Hood left some treasure somewhere. But perhaps not here. Why don't you and Niki clean up for dinner? We're having a guest. A friend of Cam's has stopped by for a short while." She gave Niki a speaking glance. "A most proper friend." She gave Niki a speaking look, and Niki sighed. There had been several young men in and out of the house, but Niki hadn't really found any of them appealing. Still, Mama had been trying to introduce her to every eligible man this side of London—and the other side as well, much to Cam and Robbie's amusement,

"I have another surprise, Lady Larch went on, "I got a letter from dear Julia, and she writes that she and Sarah are coming day after tomorrow. Do try to plan some things for Sarah to do. Perhaps you should have some evening entertainment and invite some of the young ladies and gentlemen around the countryside."

Niki sighed. It was usually wonderful to see Sarah and talk to her, but not now, not when she had Comet and John Smith to worry about. She saw that her mother was getting ready to ask her something else and didn't wait to find out more. She fled the room, then turned and waited for Robbie, who sauntered out behind her. "Robbie, you prevaricator! You're going to need more than extra in the collection to make up for that Banbury tale about treasure and Robin Hood,'' she said firmly. "How could you tell such a story?"

"What would you have me do, Niki? Tell the truth?"

Niki was caught. Of course they couldn't tell the truth, not to anyone except Cam, of course. "Well, usually the truth is best. Remember that."

Robbie nodded. "Did Mama say that Cam had brought someone home to meet you?" An evil grin spread across his face and he looked like a redheaded imp. "Perhaps, Niki . . ."

"Don't say a word," Niki warned him. "I don't want to hear a thing from either you or Cam." She frowned at him. "Do you understand me?"

"Of course." Robbie looked up at her and smiled innocently. "Would I ever say a thing?"

"Certainly you would. And Cam would, too." She grimaced, recalling the last eligible her mother had invited to the house— Mayhew's son, Edward, who had appeared quite promising. Robbie had wandered in and pulled a mouse from his pocket, then tossed it right into Mayhew's lap. The poor man had been overtaken with sneezing and trembling, then had fled, his eyes watering. Niki had never seen him again.

"Does Cam's friend like animals?" Robbie asked, trying to keep his innocent pose.

"Don't even think of doing anything" Niki said as Robbie dodged when she swatted playfully at him. "I'm going to get something to eat," he said. "Do you want me to bring you something?"

"No. Yes. You imp." Niki grinned as Robbie headed for the kitchen and she went up the stairs to see about a bath and some clean clothes. It would take Shotwell a good hour to untangle her hair.

Shotwell was busy combing Niki's hair when Robbie came in, smuggling in some cold ham, two leftover scones, a jam tart, and some fruitcake. He had it all wrapped up in a napkin he had hidden under his shirt. It looked rather as if he was trying to abscond with a melon.

"Just look what I brought you," he said proudly, spreading the napkin and displaying the food. Niki fell on the food as if she hadn't eaten in weeks. In truth, she hadn't had anything since breakfast, and that was long hours ago. "Ooww," she muttered around bites of jam tart as Shotwell tried to comb her hair. Niki had inherited both her mother's curls and her Spanish grandmother's heavy, black hair. It made a pleasing combination to look at when it was dressed to perfection, but that was seldom, much to Shotwell's despair. "I'm going to cut it all off one day, Shotwell," she announced for perhaps the thousandth time.

"Then you'll look like a lad," Shotwell muttered, tugging at a tangle with her fingers.

"Nothing wrong with that," Robbie said.

"Nothing wrong with that if you're a lad, but ladies don't want to look that way. Now scat with you before I take the scissors to your curls." Shotwell had once been Robbie's maid, but had always wanted to be a lady's maid and was overjoyed to take the post for Niki when she came to Breconbridge.

Robbie made a face and shut the door behind him. "The devil's in that one at times," Shotwell muttered, trying the comb again.

"Oowww," Niki moaned around bites of her fruitcake.

Shotwell fussed and fussed with Niki's appearance before Niki finally decided there was little to be done with her hair. She cared little about what to wear and selected a blue-striped gown trimmed with blue ribbons and small blue flowers. The blue complemented her olive complexion and her brown eyes. The high waist made her seem taller and more slender. She wasn't really plump, she just wasn't thin. *Just average,* she thought to herself, as Shotwell fussed with a blue ribbon in her hair. "There," Shotwell said in triumph, "that does it."

"It looks wonderful," Niki said, not really looking in the mirror. She had long ago come to terms with her unruly, curly, black hair, even if Shotwell hadn't. She knew that, no matter how Shotwell pinned and tied her hair, it would be undone and curly within a half an hour.

Shotwell nodded approvingly as Niki stood up. "Everyone will think you're a beauty and you are."

Niki glanced at her. By "everyone," Shotwell clearly meant Cam's friend, whoever he might be. Niki really didn't care how she looked for Cam's friend—she was two years older than Cam, who was one and twenty and fancied himself a man about town. Niki thought the odds were good that his friend was the same. Niki grinned to herself as she went down the stairs, looking for her stepbrother. No doubt Cam was displaying some new article of clothing. He seemed to live at the tailor's lately, much to his father's annoyance. The last purchase had been a coat of a particularly hideous shade of green which had buttons so gaudy that Lord Larch had threatened to hang them in the garden to scare vermin away. Cam had been greatly insulted.

The door to the library was open, and Niki heard the clink of glass on glass. Supposing Cam to be there, she pushed open the door. "Cam?" she called softly. She wanted to talk to him about John Smith before Robbie did. For all his terrible taste in clothing, and sometimes in friends, Cam had a solid, practical streak. Niki was sure he would recognize John Smith for what he was. "Cam, I need to talk to you." She went inside the library.

The man who turned to look at her wasn't a schoolboy. Instead, the man who turned from the sideboard where he was pouring himself a glass of wine was much different. He was a little above average height, his complexion as dark as Niki's, and he had smooth, dark hair. His eyes were fine and were so dark they almost glittered. He looked at her and smiled. Then he raised his glass to his lips slowly. "To a lovely lady," he said and sipped. Then he smiled at her, showing a dimple in the side of his cheek. He was quite the handsomest man Niki had ever seen.

# Chapter 3

The handsome stranger smiled at her, and Niki caught her breath. For the first time in her life, she found herself without words. Finally, she stammered out the obvious. "H . . . h . . . how do you do?"

She felt a movement in the doorway and turned to discover her stepbrother Cam walking in behind her. "Good evening, Miss Owen," he said, smiling and draping his arm around her shoulder. Since the day Niki had first come to Breconbridge, Cam had always acted as if she were his real sister, telling her at once that he'd always wanted a sister.

"Good evening, Honorable Camden Beaumont." Niki smiled up at him, reached up and squeezed his hand, and breathed a sigh of relief. Cam could be counted on to put anyone at ease. He propelled her on into the library and, moving his lanky form to stand beside her, took her hand and smiled down at her. "Gil," he said to the man sipping his wine, "let me introduce you to my sister, Miss Anika Owen, the loveliest lady at Breconbridge." He glanced around. "Better not let Mama hear that, had I?" He chuckled. "Niki, this is a friend of mine, Gilbert Martin, Viscount Alston. He's Lord Clare's heir and let me tell you, they've got stables you wouldn't believe. There must be a dozen horses there descended straight from the Godolphin Barb and Byerley Turk.'' He paused for breath, his long, lean face almost glowing. ''Not to mention the ones descended from Eclipse. I wish you could see them.''

Alston raised his glass slightly. ''Perhaps that could be arranged. I know I'd enjoy having someone as enchanting as Miss Owen at Piquay House for a visit.''

Niki felt herself blush, worried that Cam had practically forced Martin to invite her to Piquay House. ''Thank you very much. However, I must warn you that Cam has a tendency to be overenthusiastic at times, so we usually listen to only half of what he says.'' She smiled at her stepbrother with affection.

''And always the wrong half,'' Cam said, folding himself up onto a very uncomfortable chair. Cam was tall, well up into six feet, and very thin. His clothing, no matter how carefully tailored, always looked as if he had slept in it, and his cravat was always in the process of coming untied. His hair was as red as Robbie's and was his despair. Whichever way he wanted it to go, it went the other way. He had recently tried to have it trimmed into a fashionable ''windswept,'' and it looked rather as if one of those terrible storms her Spanish grandmother called a *tronada* had hit his head. Hair went in all directions. Cam was not at all handsome, but he had laughing green eyes and a sweet disposition. Niki found that after five minutes in Cam's company, she always forgot how he looked and was captivated by his humor and his company. ''Sit down, Niki,'' he said, ''and tell me what you've been doing today.''

Niki sat. ''Oh, Robbie and I did some things together,'' she said, watching Alston put his glass casually on the table and sit down elegantly. He looked every inch a fashion plate, from his gleaming boots to his snug breeches that molded to his rider's thighs to the black coat that was shaped so closely across his shoulders that it seemed painted on. In contrast to Cam, Alston's cravat was perfectly tied and every hair was carefully arranged in smooth, seemingly careless disarray. He was so perfect that Niki found herself staring at him. He smiled at her as if he was aware of exactly what she was thinking. She blushed again and concentrated on what Cam was saying.

"I've invited Alston to stay a few days at Breconbridge to try to convince him that I'm a fit owner for a colt he has." Cam's eyes sparkled as he talked, and he gestured with his hands to illustrate his points. "Niki, I swear this is the sweetest colt in the kingdom. He's of fabulous stock—goes all the way back to Eclipse, and you know what a racer he was! Besides, you know how Eclipse was described—the fastest chestnut that ever raced—and I think this colt will be the same. How could he miss?" Cam leaned forward and clasped Niki's hands in his. "Listen to this—his dam traces her lines back to Waxy. Think of it, Niki! This horse could be the best of all time!"

Niki laughed. "I don't think I'm the one you need to convince, now am I?"

Cam dropped her hands and looked gloomy for all of thirty seconds. "No, I've got to convince Father, but I think I can do it. Alston is along to help me. Perhaps you could . . . ?"

"Don't apply to me," Niki said in mock horror. "You know I could never do it. If anyone could convince Lord Larch, it would be you." Niki laughed again and stood. "If you'll excuse me, I really have some things to do. I'll see you gentlemen at supper." She dropped a small curtsy toward Alston and moved to the door, pausing there to look back at Cam. "Oh, by the way, Cam, I believe, uh, Robbie wanted to see you about something. If you have a few moments, you might want to look in on him and see what he needs."

Cam waved his bony hand at her. "Probably wants me to help him dig for treasure. I've already heard about the Robin Hood story. Robbie's up to something else, I'm sure. I intend to dodge that one."

"I think you should see him."

"All right, all right. Brotherly love and all that." Cam grinned at her, and she went on out the door, relieved. She didn't close the door entirely behind her, but leaned up against the wall, waiting for Cam. Still, she couldn't help hearing what Alston and Cam were saying.

"Lovely girl, isn't she?" Cam asked. Niki blushed again. Cam was all but throwing her at Alston. How could she look the man in the face if Cam kept this up?

"Yes, she's lovely." Niki heard the clink of a glass and reasoned that Alston was pouring himself more wine. "Any fortune?"

"Oh yes," Niki heard Cam answer negligently. Cam was careful with his funds, but money meant little to him. "Eight thousand a year from her father's estate, I think, as she's an only child. More from her grandmother when the old lady sticks her spoon in the wall. I don't know how much."

"Interesting," Alston said thoughtfully.

Niki heard a noise. "I'm going to go see what that scamp of a brother wants. Do you want to meet with Father and me after supper to talk about the colt? I'd like to get this settled as soon as possible."

There was another clink of glass on glass. "Of course. I plan to visit nearby tomorrow, so perhaps you could go with me. I promised Jackson I'd go to Wynwoode and look at some horse-flesh he has there. He's been negotiating with us for a horse or two. Now that he's the heir to the title and estates, he should be able to meet the price."

"Wynwoode?" Niki could almost feel Cam's amazement. "I didn't know that. Thought some American chap was going to get it all. Jackson was pretty bitter about it, last time I heard him talking about it at Tattersall's."

"Something must have happened. I saw him yesterday as he was leaving London to come here. He told me then that he was the heir now. A good bit of money involved, I believe."

Niki moved farther down the hall as the door opened slightly. Cam stood profiled there, still looking back into the room at Alston. "It won't do him any good, then. From what I've heard, Jackson's always spent money like water. He'll go through it within five years at most, no matter how much it is."

Alston's laugh was smooth. "I'm counting on it," he said.

Cam turned to come out the door and opened his mouth when he saw Niki, but she put her finger over her lips to quiet him. He stuck his head back inside the library. "Don't think me rude for leaving you to the library and the wine, but I'd better check on Robbie before he goes to bed. I'll see you shortly." Alston murmured some answer, and Cam came on out in the hall. Niki grabbed his hand and led him to the small green drawing room down the hall and shut the door behind her.

"Cam, that was all a hum about Robbie. I need to talk to you."

Cam raised his eyebrows and sat down heavily. "Intrigue isn't like you, Niki. Has anyone insulted you? Are you in any kind of trouble?"

Niki sat across from him where she could see the door. "No, well, yes, I suppose you could say that I—we're in trouble. It's just that Robbie and I—well, Robbie and I could hang for horse stealing."

Cam's eyebrows shot up under his hair. "Horse stealing?"

Quickly Niki began telling him what they had done, but Cam interrupted her. "Comet?" He nodded. "Robbie told me what was going on, and I agreed that taking the horse might be the only way. I didn't really think of it as horse stealing."

Niki frowned. "We took him, and he didn't belong to us. I think that would qualify as stealing in any court." She paused. "That's only part of the problem, however. There's Smith."

"Smith?" Cam's expression was blank. "Who's Smith?"

"I wish I knew. Smith is obviously an alias. When I asked him what his name was, he hesitated and then told me he was called John Smith. John Smith of Virginia."

"Captain John Smith?" Cam couldn't resist a chuckle. "Did he have Pocahontas with him?"

"This isn't funny, Cam. Robbie and I took Comet and Smith to the old barn, and I think Smith will run off with the horse tonight."

"Whoa, whoa! You're confusing me. Why don't you tell me the whole story, right from the beginning. I knew Robbie was talking about this, but I thought it was way off in the future and might never happen. Why now?"

Niki sighed and started her story at the beginning, telling Cam everything up to the point where she and Robbie had left John Smith in the barn with Traveler and Comet. "And you say he was riding a magnificent thoroughbred? A gypsy like that?"

"Yes." Niki nodded. "He had to have stolen that one as well, Cam."

Cam made a steeple with this fingers and stared at it thoughtfully. "Well, I'd say you had no choice with the horse that belonged—belongs to Wynford." He looked at her, frowning. "Actually, you had no choice at all but to accept this Smith's help. I'll try to ride over to the old barn right after supper and see what's going on. I don't want to send anyone, as I don't want a soul to know about this." He paused. "I wonder if I should take Alston with me? He knows horses up one side and down the other."

"Oh, my heavens, no!" Niki was surprised at her own vehemence and paused to begin again on a calmer note. "That is, Cam, I don't want anyone to know what we've done. Even Smith is one too many. The three of us need to keep this a secret. And"—she stopped and made a face—"Smith brought up a point I hadn't considered—what are we going to do with Comet when he's well again? We can't keep him, and we can't sell him. Providing, of course, that Smith doesn't solve that problem as well by running off with him."

"Good Lord, I hadn't thought ahead that far." Cam sat up and leaned toward Niki, all angles. "I suppose I was thinking that saving Comet was just a dream. I never did really consider the practical aspects of it."

"Neither did I. That's why there's no grain or medicine at the barn. And no plans for the future."

Cam grimaced. "No plans for the present either."

Niki sighed. "I'm afraid we've gotten ourselves into something here, Cam."

"Sshhh." He glanced up at the door. In just a second, Lord Larch came in. He looked just like an older version of Cam, and Niki thought him quite the most endearing man she had ever seen. He had accepted her as his own, and, although she couldn't yet think of him as her father, she loved him in a way she had never loved her distant father. "How are my children?" he asked, patting Niki absently on the head.

"Fine," they chorused together.

"And just what are the two of you discussing so earnestly?" he asked, smiling.

Niki and Cam looked at each other. They were saved from having to answer him by the arrival of Lady Larch, dragging Viscount Alston along with her. Lady Larch, as usual, chattered so much that no one else had to worry about what to say. With her practiced social eye, she placed Niki next to the viscount. To her surprise, Niki found him quite charming, although he was much friendlier than he had been before, and his face was slightly flushed. Niki wondered if it was one glass too many of Lord Larch's best.

Alston was the epitome of social London. He discussed the on-dits in London with Lady Larch, horses with Lord Larch and Cam, and fashions with Niki. Although he kept his wine-glass full, and Niki lost count of the glasses he had drunk, he was just as steady and affable at the end of supper as he had been at the beginning, although his color was even higher. Niki couldn't imagine how he could drink any more after supper, but, when she and Lady Larch went into the drawing room after a suitable interval, he was talking to Lord Larch, a glass of what looked like brandy in his hand.

"I'm amazed he can stand up," Niki whispered to Cam as she watched the Viscount down his brandy.

Cam chuckled. "Alston's capacity for spirits is legendary. He can drink anyone under the table and never show a single sign. He's the envy of half the bucks in London. The rest are too drunk to care." He paused, as Lady Larch sat down at the pianoforte and began playing. "I'm going to the barn as soon as everyone's in bed. I want to see if this Smith is still there. If he is, maybe I can size him up."

"I hope he is." She paused and though of something, then gave Cam an alarmed look. "Do be careful. The man may be a brigand for all we know,'' she whispered, as her mother motioned her to come sing, something Niki hated above anything. ''Do you think I could come down with a sudden headache?''

''Please do.'' Cam grinned at her. ''Having heard your singing, I think all of us would appreciate it. You may even swoon on my shoulder if you wish. Oh, wait—I forgot what a terrible liar you are. Look sad and I'll get you out of it.'' Niki tried to look forlorn. ''Not enough, but I'll try to do it.'' Cam winked at her and ambled across to the piano. He sat down on the bench beside Lady Larch and began to talk earnestly. In just a minute, he returned. ''I'm to take you up to your room so you won't fall,'' he said, grinning, ''and then we're all going to play cards since there's just four of us left. Probably whist.'' He offered her his arm and led her out the door. ''What I have to go through for you. This having a sister is a lot of work.''

''But you're glad to do it.'' Niki stopped on the steps. ''You don't have to walk me up. But will you wake me when you get back from the barn and let me know about Comet and whether Smith's there or not.''

''It'll be late—two in the morning, probably.''

''No matter. Wake me.'' With that, she left him on the stairs and went up to check on Robbie. He was sleeping already, looking angelic and innocent. For the first time in her life, Niki wished for a family or her own. She had decided when she was ten or twelve that she would never marry, because she thought all marriages were probably like her parents' marriage. True, her parents had been very much in love, but they were so absorbed in each other that there had been no time for a child. Her parents traveled everywhere together as her father made diplomatic trips for the Home Office, and they always left Niki with her Aunt Webster. Niki had been thoroughly ignored and had promised herself that she would never have a child to disregard and hurt. She saw her parents perhaps twice a year, so they never seemed like real people to her. She used to sit and look at other families and wish that she had parents like those imaginary people. It was only years later that she realized that those ideal families existed only in her mind.

Now that her mother had remarried, Lord Larch, Cam, and Robbie were more like a family to her than anyone else had ever been. She had recently thought about her decision not to marry, made so long ago, and had realized that she would like to have a family of her own. Still, she wasn't an ingenue any longer—she was three and twenty now, and the social seasons of flirting and becoming engaged had passed her by. There were no eligibles in sight, in spite of her mother's efforts. Perhaps, Niki thought, she could just be an aunt to Robbie's and Cam's families. She looked down at Robbie's sleeping face, his lashes soft on his cheek, and smiled. Being an aunt was a nice thought. She smoothed Robbie's covers and went on to bed.

It was almost six in the morning when Cam tiptoed into her room, looking very tired and muddy indeed. "I promised I'd come by, or I'd have just gone on to bed and tried to recover from this night. Thank God I don't have to meet Father until this afternoon. We're riding around some of the estate."

"Was Smith there?" Niki lit her candle and sat up on the edge of her bed, letting her feet dangle. Instead of getting her dressing gown, she wrapped up in a blanket that was on the bed.

Cam nodded. "He was there, and so was Comet. The man almost shot me."

"Shot you! Oh, Cam, I told you he was a common thief."

Cam shook his head. "No, he thought I was the common thief. I rode up to the barn, not really trying to be quiet, but not thinking about him having a pistol. I just wandered into the barn like an idiot, and he promptly put my lights out."

"Put your lights out?" Niki was confused. "Did you have a lantern?"

"No, but it probably would have been better if I had. The

man hit me on the back of the head with his pistol butt. I didn't know a thing until I woke up in one of the stalls, trussed up like a roast goose. Smith didn't come by for an hour or so, and by then I was too cramped to move.'' Cam grinned. ''He threatened to turn me over to the magistrates, and I called his hand on it. Told him that he'd be hanged for a horse thief if he did. After that, we managed to talk, and I finally convinced him that I was your stepbrother. I think he expected a suave man about town instead of a handsome fellow like me.''

Niki gave him a look and made a face at him. ''No doubt your tailoring dazzled him.'' She glanced down at Cam's green coat, which he wore with a purple-and-green-striped waistcoat. It looked livid in the early-morning light. ''So Comet was still there.''

Cam nodded. ''Smith had cleaned him up fairly well, and had soaked his hoof for a while. You and Robbie need to go up to the barn first thing in the morning and get a list of supplies. Smith said he didn't want to go into the village just yet.''

''So he is a criminal!''

''I don't know. After we got my identity established, I talked to the man a while. I rather liked him.'' Cam rubbed the stubble on his jaw thoughtfully. ''As for the John Smith name, I agree that there's something not quite right there, but the man doesn't seem like a criminal.'' He looked at her. ''Why don't you use a few woman's wiles to get his story out of him? I think he'd tell you.''

''Woman's wiles? What on earth are you saying, Cam?''

He laughed at her. ''Perhaps you're right. You can't lie, and your face shows every thought you have. Maybe Robbie could worm it out of Smith. Robbie's as tricky and turning as the road to Wales.'' He laughed. ''That Robin Hood story was classic. What inspiration!''

''If you can stop congratulating Robbie on his lies, perhaps you could tell me how we're going to manage to get over to see Comet daily, and what we're going to do with him after he gets better.''

Cam rose and headed for the door. ''That, my dear sister,

is a question with no answer. I think we're just going to have to play it by ear and hope everything goes well.'' He saluted her and picked up the boots he had put by the door. ''Had to tiptoe into the house,'' he said with a grin. ''Now I'm going to bed and no one had better disturb me. You be sure to go over to the barn and get Smith's list, then go to the village and get what he needs. Put it on my account.'' He grinned. ''I'm good for it.''

''This is going to be fun,'' Niki grumbled, covering her toes to keep them warm. The blanket barely reached her feet. ''I can see it now—'Mama, I need to go to the village for some ribbons and some medicine for a stolen horse.' ''

Cam chuckled. ''Let Robbie tell some story. As I said, you can't lie at all.'' He became serious. ''You'd better try to get that medicine back to Smith as soon as possible, as I'm sure he needs it. Comet needs to get some medicine on that hoof and those sores before they get infected. Perhaps you and Robbie can stay a while and help.''

Niki curled her feet back under her covers. ''And just how am I supposed to manage that? Mama informed me that she'd invited Mrs. Keene and Sarah to visit, and they're supposed to come today.''

''Nooo. Please tell me it's not true.'' Cam put his hand on his head. ''Sarah's fine, but not the repugnant Mrs. Keene.''

''The same, and yes, it's true, but that's not the problem. The problem is that I'll be stuck with entertaining Sarah Keene all day, all month if they decide to stay that long. How am I supposed to get away to the barn, much less to the village and back to the barn without my absence being remarked? After all, Sarah and I were in school together, and we're close friends.''

Cam grinned at her. ''If all else fails, go searching for Robin Hood's treasure. Or better yet, take Mrs. Keene and lose her in the forest.'' He went out into the hall, then stuck his head back inside, still grinning. ''Not a bad idea, that. It would make a full morning for you—eliminate Mrs. Keene, go to the barn, the village, and back again. Gilbert will be gone during the afternoon, so Mama can't get into her matchmaking, so you'd have time to spend with Sarah. I'm sure someone with your creativity and ingenuity could manage a few little tasks like that.''

He shut the door before Niki threw one of her pillows at him.

# Chapter 4

The day was perfect. It was sunny and warm, with just a small, sweet breeze blowing. It reminded Sherry of those wonderful spring days in the Shenandoah. Once, when he was in Kentucky, the breeze had been blowing like this, carrying the perfumed smell of the bluegrass. He took a deep breath and could almost smell it again. He turned and glanced at the horse standing near him. "Perhaps, Comet, my friend, you could come join us in Kentucky. You'd like that." Comet looked up at him and nodded, as though he knew what Sherry was saying.

Sherry peeled off his coat and tossed it over the top slat of a wooden fence that enclosed a small pen beside he barn. He stretched and enjoyed the breeze, then untied the collar of his shirt. The warmth of the sun felt good on his back, and he leaned against one of the rock walls of the pasture as he opened the small notebook he was carrying, He pulled out some folded sheets that he had carefully tucked in the front. They were the notes on marigold breeding that he had taken from Farnsworth, and he looked at them carefully, then put them on the grass beside him and got out his pen-and-ink case. His mother had

known how he liked to make notes wherever he was and had
given him the case some years ago for his birthday. It was
silver, and had his initials—WSD—engraved on the front. It
was a clever design which carried his ink, a knife for sharpening
quills, sand, and a spare seal. Sherry never went anywhere
without it. Now he opened it and, after sharpening his quill,
began to write in the small notebook. He heard a noise and
peered over the rock wall. Robbie and Miss Owen were coming
out of the woods, looking from right to left as though they
expected to be apprehended at any second. They were carrying
a basket.

Robbie spotted him first and ran up to the other side of the
wall. He put his foot in a cranny and tried to hoist himself up,
but the entire section of wall tumbled, along with Robbie.
"Robbie," Niki shrieked, "are you all right?" She ran up to
the pile of rubble, her hair flying, and reached for Robbie, who
lay limp among the rocks. Robbie turned his head and grinned
at her. "Fooled you, didn't I, Niki?" He scrambled to his feet.
"Didn't know that wall was that flimsy. It looks solid." He
wobbled as he stepped on a rock.

Sherry reached for Robbie to steady him. He then folded
his papers and put them away, along with his writing case.
"Appearances can be deceiving," he said mildly.

"What do you mean?" Niki looked at him, sensing another
meaning in his words.

Sherry smiled at her, that smile that lit up his whole face
and made it different. "Merely what I said. Must I always
mean something else, Miss Owen?" He glanced down at her
basket. "Have you brought the supplies for Comet?"

Niki handed him the basket. "Not for Comet. Cam is going
to gather up what you need and bring that later. Last night he
told me to get them, but when I looked at the list he gave
me, I knew that was an impossible task. So"—she blushed
slightly—"we brought these for you. Robbie and I thought
you might need a few things."

"Notably breakfast," Robbie said, reaching into the basket
and removing a biscuit, which he promptly began eating.

"Robbie, stop that! You've had breakfast, and this is for Mr. Smith." Niki removed the cover. "I apologize for what's here. It really isn't . . ."

"It's what we could steal without being caught." Robbie finished the last of his biscuit. "We were grabbing with both hands. Niki must have made five or six trips out of the breakfast room." Robbie peered into the basket. "The soap was Niki's idea. I really didn't think you'd need it."

"I need it." Sherry laughed as he put the napkin on the ground and spread the feast. There were boiled eggs, a cold piece of steak, muffins, strawberries, and a small jug of milk. "Thank you. How did you know I was starving?" he asked as he shared a muffin with Robbie.

"I own it was Niki's idea," Robbie said with a sigh. "I thought you'd live off the woods, but Niki said we had to feed you. Good manners and all that."

Sherry met Miss Owen's fine dark eyes and smiled at her. "Thank you, Miss Owen. Not many people would have thought of doing this."

Niki felt herself blush but was saved from having to answer by the sound of a horse coming from the woods behind them. She jumped up to shield Smith from view, then relaxed as she got a glimpse of a hideous purple coat. "Cam," Niki said with relief.

Cam dismounted near them and pulled a package from his saddle. He joined them and sat on the ground, folding his lanky frame as he sat. Sherry offered him breakfast. "If you don't mind, I will. I got out early to get what you needed, and didn't get to eat breakfast myself. I didn't want to let anyone know I was leaving, afraid they'd want to accompany me."

"Viscount Alston?" Niki asked.

Cam shook his head. "No, Alston never gets up early unless there's a race on. He drinks late and sleeps late." He looked at Sherry. "I don't quite know how to bring this up, but it would be better if you could simply go get what you need. I'm not sure I have everything. If you want to go into the village,

I'd be glad to give you some money to buy whatever . . ." He paused awkwardly.

"I agree with you. Then too, I will need to be away occasionally," Sherry said, looking at his breakfast rather than at Cam. "I appreciate your offer, but I have funds." He glanced over at Traveler. "What I would like to do is borrow a horse to ride into the village, if you could do it. I certainly can't ride Comet, and Traveler is the sort of horse one never forgets." He paused. "I hardly think an itinerant named John Smith would be riding such a horse."

There was an awkward silence. "That's true. I'll see what I can do," Cam said, rubbing his chin. "That will be difficult, to say the least. Papa always keeps up with his cattle, so I can't filch one from the stables." He looked at Niki. "Maybe you could say that Qadir is ailing and needs to be put to pasture for a while."

"I'll do no such thing!" Niki was indignant. "My horse is known all over this county, Camden Beaumont. Besides, Qadir is accustomed to having only me ride him. To my knowledge, he's never had anything but a sidesaddle on him."

"I believe I might attract more than a little attention if I rode into the village sidesaddle," Sherry said with a grin. "Never mind. Maybe I can buy a broken-down nag somewhere." He smiled at them and folded up the remains of breakfast. "Would you like to see Comet and perhaps help me with him for a while? He looks better already."

They went inside the dark, comfortable gloom of the barn. Niki loved the barn smells—hay and horse and years of saddle soap. She stopped to scratch Traveler lightly on the nose. He smelled her hand and looked at Sherry. "Go on and flirt with the lady if you wish, Traveler," he said. He smiled at Niki, his smile very white in the dark barn. "I warn you, Miss Owen, that he's a gigolo and a flirt. Incorrigibly so."

Niki laughed. "I have to take my chances with him, I gather." She paused before Comet's stall and stared, amazed. "Look at him! Robbie, come here."

Robbie came to stand beside her and they looked at the horse standing there. The sores were still there, the welts were there, and his hoof looked no better, but there was something about him that had changed. He was clean, and Smith had brushed him carefully, getting all the burrs from his mane and removing all the mud. But that still wasn't it—finally Niki realized what had happened. "He has his pride back, doesn't he?" she said softly.

Sherry came to stand beside her. "Yes, he has." He reached out and touched Comet's nose with his fingertips, softly. "I think he probably suffers from the sin of pride. Look at him." Comet arched his neck as Sherry scratched underneath his jaw. "I think, when he was in his prime, that he had much to be proud of. He's still quite a horse." Comet nuzzled his hand and made a snuffling noise against Sherry's skin. "He knows you're the person who will take care of him, doesn't he?" Niki said.

Sherry smiled at her again and opened the stall door. He took the lead and brought Comet out into the hall. He and Cam began putting ointment on the sores and welts while Robbie and Niki watched. "Robbie, go get a bucket of water so we can soak this hoof," Sherry said. Niki glanced after Robbie as he ran out the door and saw the sun high in the sky. "My goodness, it's midmorning," she said, scrambling to her feet. "I must get back. I promised Mama I'd be there when the Keenes arrived. I don't know what I'll tell her."

Cam grinned at her as he reached across Comet. "You can always tell her that you've been practicing to be Maid Marian. That would go right with Robbie's bouncer about Robin Hood's treasure." Niki stuck out her tongue at him and dashed from the barn as Cam began telling Smith about Robbie's inventive story. She could hear them laughing as she went across the field. Tomorrow, she promised herself, she would get Qadir out and ride over early. No one would remark it at all if she began riding early for exercise. She hurried through the woods, trying to get home before the Keenes got there. If she hurried, she thought, she might get to Breconbridge before they did. She was out of breath when she topped the hill behind the house. She paused as she caught a glimpse of a carriage pulled up in the drive at the front. It was the Keenes—she would recognize Sarah's slight form anywhere.

Niki started to run down the hill, but got tangled up in a creeping vine and lost her footing. Before she knew what was happening, she was rolling down the grassy slope and, to her horror, finally landed in the stream at the foot of the hill. The water was icy and took her breath for a moment until she managed to drag herself half in and half out of the stream. She floundered in the water a moment, then managed to climb from the water and get on the little bridge that spanned the stream. She was a ruin—her dress was drenched and muddy, she had watercress in her hair, and worse, someone was coming. There was nothing to do except walk toward the house. She assumed her most dignified look, scraped watercress from her face, and walked out to meet whoever was there.

To Niki's horror, as she approached the walker, she discovered that it was Viscount Alston. "Good morning, Miss Owen." He looked up and down her dress, and Niki realized that the thin, wet muslin was not hiding her body. "Allow me." Alston removed his coat and wrapped it around her shoulders. "I saw you take a tumble from the hill. Are you hurt?"

Niki shook her head. "Just wet. I need to get home and change as soon as possible."

"Of course. Allow me to help you." He offered his arm. "Ordinarily I prefer not to go walking this early," he said, as if he were having a conversation at court with a lady of quality, "but I found I couldn't sleep late this morning. I was up before ten, and with nothing to occupy my time, I thought I might walk around the estate. I have an appointment soon at Wynwoode, so I was just going back into the house." He smiled down at her. "Fortunate that I was here. You might have drowned."

"Yes, thank you." Niki was shivering, and she wasn't sure that the cause was her tumble into the stream. There was something about being this close to Alston that was unnerving, and wearing his coat was altogether too much. It smelled of him, and she could still feel his warmth through her sodden gown.

She concentrated on a noise she couldn't identify, and then realized it was the squishing of water in her thin kid slippers. Alston kept on chatting about inconsequentials while she prayed to reach the back door and get into her room without being seen.

They reached the back door and Niki turned. "Thank you, but I should go up by myself, I think."

"Of course." He looked right into her eyes, and Niki felt that the man was looking right through her. It was more disconcerting than being doused in the stream. She forced herself to look away and began to go inside when she stopped. "You'll need your coat," she said, removing it and handing it to him. "Thank you." The morning breeze hit her through the wet dress, and suddenly she felt naked. She took a step back into the house but not before she had seen Alston's appreciative gaze flick over her figure again.

He reached over and took his coat from her fingers. "Thank you, Miss Owen. I would be delighted for you to keep it until you get to your room if you need it."

Niki shook her head. "No, thank you. I do appreciate your coming to my rescue." She glanced at his coat, which he was still holding in his fingers. The coat was wet through in spots and was dripping at the bottom. The collar was drenched where her hair had soaked it. "Your coat is quite ruined," she said in despair.

"It gave its life for a worthy cause." He smiled at her again. "I trust I'll see you later, Miss Owen." He bowed slightly and backed away. Niki turned and dashed up the stairs, feeling guilty. She didn't know much about fashion, but that coat had been very expensive. Cam had mentioned that Alston went to only the best tailors and shops. She could never repay the man.

She was thinking of what to do to about Alston's coat when she rounded the top of the back stairs and careened into the hall. She stopped as she came face-to-face with Sarah Keene, who looked, as she always did, as though she had just stepped from a fashion plate. "My goodness, Niki, whatever happened to you?" Sarah smiled impishly. "Have you been out playing with frogs?'' Niki opened her mouth to give Sarah a set-down when her mother walked up, Mrs. Keene in tow. ''Anika, whatever has happened? You're wet and . . .'' Lady Larch looked at the dripping dress clinging to Niki's figure.

''I fell into the stream. Excuse me.'' Niki edged along the wall and fled into her room. Behind her, she heard Mrs. Keene talking to her mother. ''Really, Zoe, it's time to take that girl in hand. I realize that you were unable to discipline her while you were grieving, but it happens to be more than time to teach her how to be a lady. I'm sure my Sarah would be glad to give her some instruction. She hasn't even had a London season either, has she, poor dear? And it's much too late now.''

Niki gritted her teeth and turned to shut the door behind her as Sarah slipped inside. ''Pay no attention to Mama,'' Sarah said, shutting the door behind her. ''You know how she is.''

Niki nodded. She did indeed know how Mrs. Keene was. Sarah's parents were in trade, and her mother had been a cit, one of those who hoped to make a mark in society, but did not know how to go about it. Mrs. Keene had alienated half the ton with her lack of manners and had ruined more than one of Sarah's chances in the Marriage Mart. With her parentage, it was a wonder Sarah had turned out at all. In spite of them, it seemed, she was a sweet, mannerly young lady. She and Niki had met at school and become friends. Sarah wanted nothing more than to be married, and married well, but considering her background, it was doubtful, even though her father was incredibly rich and Sarah was his only child. Sarah smiled and rang for Shotwell. ''Let me help you with that gown. If we wait long for Shotwell, you'll catch your death.'' She began unlacing the gown in the back, chattering all the while about their trip.

''There,'' Sarah said, as Shotwell came into the room, stopping to gasp at Niki's appearance. ''I'll leave you to better hands.'' She smiled again. ''Just let me help you do this.'' She laughed as she reached up and removed a large clump of watercress from Niki's bushy, curly hair. ''I'll see you downstairs in a while.'' Sarah laughed as she left.

It took Niki over almost two hours to bathe and change her clothes. As it was, her mass of hair was still damp when she finally went downstairs, much to Shotwell's annoyance. Worse, her hair was curlier than ever and more unmanageable. Shotwell had done her best, however, and tamed it a little by tying a blue ribbon through it. The ribbon matched the blue flowers on Niki's dress.

Niki was starving. She and Robbie hadn't really taken the time to eat, as they had been busy trying to smuggle out food to take to Smith and because of her drenching, she had missed the midday meal. *Drat the man, anyway,* Niki thought. Her growling stomach was another thing for which she could blame him. She wandered back toward the kitchen, trying to find something to eat. Cook supplied her with some cold ham and bread. Niki wanted nothing more than to dodge her mother's questions as long as she could, so she took her sandwich and wandered out the back door. She needed to see Qadir and reassure herself that the gelding was all right. She had neglected Qadir lately and hadn't realized it until she had seen Comet. She went back inside the kitchen and filched two apples the cook had culled because they weren't as firm as required. She took the apples and headed for the stables.

Qadir looked up as she came in and his ears pricked up. She fed him the apples and stroked his nose. "You've been lonesome, haven't you?" she asked. He moved his head as though he agreed, Niki thought. She hadn't been riding in almost a fortnight. No wonder Qadir had looked dispirited when she first came inside and saw him. "This afternoon we'll go out," she promised, then went in search of a groom to leave instructions to have Qadir ready to ride within the hour. If she could, she thought, she really needed to take Mr. Smith something else to eat. It would be difficult to steal much from the kitchen, but the man had to have sustenance.

Niki went back inside and was caught by Lady Larch. For the better part of the hour, she was forced to sit in the drawing room and smile at Mrs. Keene. Robbie was off having his lessons and Cam, the coward, had sent word that he wouldn't be in until late afternoon. Niki pasted on a smile and sat beside her mother, nodding at Mrs. Keene. Sarah sat quietly across from her, working at her embroidery. She said nothing until Lady Larch mentioned that there would be another guest for supper—Viscount Alston. Sarah colored visibly. No one except Niki noticed it or the fact that Sarah stuck herself with her needle at the mention of the viscount's name.

Mrs. Keene looked at Niki sharply. "Working up a match, Zoe?" she asked bluntly.

Lady Larch only smiled. Niki looked again at Sarah. The slight flush was still on Sarah's porcelain skin and she bent her head over her embroidery, her blond curls helping to hide her expression. Before she thought, Niki tried to rescue her friend. "I was going riding, Sarah. Would you like to go with me?"

Sarah looked at her in amazement, her pale blue eyes wide. "Niki, you *know* I don't ride."

"She can't ride," Mrs. Keene said sadly. "I can't count the number of invitations the dear girl has had to decline because she can't ride. Mr. Keene engaged a riding master, but Sarah simply refused."

"Now, Mama," Sarah said, "we went over that with Papa, and I told him I simply didn't care for Monsieur Lemonte. He didn't ride much better than I did and knew nothing of sidesaddles." She smiled at Niki. "I do remember how much you love to ride, Niki. Do go on and enjoy yourself." She looked at Mrs. Keene. "It's all right with us, isn't it, Mama?"

With Mrs. Keene's and Lady Larch's blessing, Niki stood to go upstairs to put on her habit. The others began doing what Lady Larch and Mrs. Keene loved best—discussing London society, a topic that Niki neither knew about nor wanted to explore. Still, Niki stopped at the door when Mrs. Keene turned to Lady Larch and asked, "tell me, Zoe, does your charming neighbor visit often?"

"Neighbor?" Lady Larch was as confused as Niki was.

"Yes." Mrs. Keene nodded her head vigorously. "Mr. Jackson, or, as I suppose he is now, Lord Wynford. When I last talked to him at Lady FitzSmythe's rout, he told me that he expected to come into the title soon. It seems that the other heirs have all passed on, and Jackson is now the heir.''

Lady Larch looked blankly at Niki. ''Do you know of Lord Wynford, Anika? I don't believe I've met him. Does he attend the local assemblies?''

''I don't believe he has, Mama,'' Niki said. ''I do recall Cam saying something about him, though. I believe the title hasn't yet been settled on him, and he hasn't taken formal possession of the estate. I'm sure you can ask Cam for particulars.''

''That's it, Julia,'' Lady Larch said to Mrs. Keene. ''I'll ask Camden—he seems to know everything that happens around here.''

''Perhaps,'' Mrs. Keene suggested gently, ''Lord Larch might invite Lord Wynford into our company and make him welcome. That would be most neighborly.'' She turned and looked at Niki brightly. ''Lord Wynford is very fond of horses, Niki. Perhaps we could all take a carriage over one day and view his stables.'' She smiled and signaled to the footman to bring her a cup of tea.

Niki was so surprised that she stared at Mrs. Keene. ''Lord Wynford? I really . . .'' She intercepted a frown from her mother. ''Lord Wynford may not even be at home,'' she finished lamely.

''He said that he was coming here.'' Mrs. Keene sipped her tea and gave Sarah a significant look as the reason for the Keenes' visit became appallingly clear. Sarah blushed again, furiously this time.

''Never you mind, dear.'' Mrs. Keene patted Sarah's hand. ''I'm sure Lord Wynford will be here to visit if he's in the country. Who knows what may happen?'' She turned to Lady Larch. ''Tell me, Zoe, have you made any plans for Anika's future?''

Annoyed that she should be discussed like a piece of furniture, Niki excused herself and slipped out into the hall. *Poor Sarah,* she thought to herself, and sighed. There was certainly nothing she could do about Mrs. Keene, but she could filch some food for John Smith. She started toward the kitchen but stopped as she heard Lord Larch coming. She hurried up the stairs and rang for Shotwell to help her with her habit. She changed into her riding habit quickly, ignoring Shotwell's moans over her hair, and hurried down the back stairs to the kitchen. To her chagrin, Cook was still there, sitting at the table, eating. "I simply was not able to eat very much and wondered if you would mind wrapping up something for me to eat. I wanted to go riding and didn't want to get hungry." Niki kept her eyes carefully on a copper pot as she told the Banbury tale. Cook raised an eyebrow, but wrapped up a hearty snack in a napkin and gave it to her. Niki thanked her profusely, all the while staring at the toes of her riding boots. If this farce with Mr. Smith continued, she thought to herself as she walked to the stables to get Qadir, she was going to have to take some lessons in prevarication. Robbie was going to have to teach her how to lie properly. It was something she had never been able to do.

It felt good to get up on Qadir and out into the air. Niki had always loved riding, and even found that she was comfortable sidesaddle. She had heard that some women liked the comfort of riding astride, but she had always felt safe and at home sidesaddle. Qadir had never had any other kind of saddle on him. "Are you ready, Miss Owen?"

Niki turned to see Jem, the groom who always accompanied her. Jem had been one of the first people she had met at Brecon-bridge when she came to live there, and he loved horses as much as she did. Working with horses was sometimes difficult for him, as he had a crippled hand, one which appeared to have been crushed at some time in the past. Niki was curious, but had never asked him about it, and he had never offered to tell her. Right now, he was holding Qadir's reins loosely in his good hand, while his horse waited patiently, saddled and ready to go. "I'm ready, Jem," she said with a smile. "Let's have a good run, shall we? Qadir needs the exercise, and so do I." She felt the napkin full of food that she had intended to leave with Mr. Smith and realized that she was going to have to dodge the old barn where Smith and Comet were hidden. The last thing she needed was to have Jem come back to the stables at the main house, telling everyone what he had seen. Niki sighed and nudged Qadir on.

They had been gone for the better part of half an hour when Niki decided that Qadir was entirely too frisky and needed more exercise than a sedate lope. With a yell to Jem, she urged Qadir on, and the Spanish barb responded. In just a minute, they were flying into the wind, getting ready to jump the hedge that divided the pasture. Niki leaned forward to take the weight from Qadir's back and transfer it to the front, then shouted in exultation when Qadir cleared the hedge by an easy foot. Riding on Qadir was always an adventure when she let him have his head. She let him run part of the way across the pasture and then reined him in, turning him so she could get ready to clear the hedge on the way back. To her surprise, there were two riders beside the hedge, looking at her. They rode over to where she and Qadir stood.

"Miss Owen," Viscount Alston said, admiration in his voice, "I've never seen such bruising riding from a female. Where did you learn that?"

"In Spain, my lord," Niki said smiling at him. "I lived there for some years. That's where Qadir came from. He was a gift from my father." She stroked the horse's neck lightly.

"I wondered where such a superb piece of horseflesh came from," the man with Alston said. "I should have known that horse was Spanish. Arabian stock, isn't he?"

Niki nodded, looking at the man. He was dark and almost as handsome as Alston. He was of slightly above average height and sat his horse well, in perfect control of the large gray stallion he rode. He had short, fashionable, dark brown hair, dark blue eyes, and a thin, aristocratic face.

"Ah, Jack, do allow me to present Lord Larch's stepdaughter, Miss Owen," Lord Alston said. "Miss Owen, may I introduce Lord Wynford." He smiled strangely. "The *new* Lord Wynford, I might say."

# Chapter 5

There was nothing for it except for Niki to ride and chat with Wynford and Alston. Jem followed at exactly the right distance behind, neither too far to allow anyone to think Niki was alone, but not close enough to overhear the conversation. They rode in the direction of Wynwoode for a while, and, to her vexation, Niki realized that they were turning into the road that ran by the pasture from which she and Robbie had rescued Comet. "Wynford was just telling me that he had a horse stolen from here," Alston said, nodding toward the pasture. "A brazen theft in broad daylight."

"Really?" Niki couldn't think of anything else to say.

"Yes." Wynford glanced at the gate, which was still down. "The horse wasn't in health, so I believe that he's probably somewhere in the area. I don't think anyone could have ridden him far." He grimaced. "I have inquiries out and intend to prosecute to the limit of the law."

"Did you say that the horse was in poor health?" Niki asked, trying to act innocent and nonchalant. "Why not simply ignore the theft if that's the case? If the horse wasn't worth keeping, surely it will be more bother to prosecute than it would be worth.''

"It's the principle of the thing," Alston said. "Isn't that the way you feel, Wynford?"

"Indeed. If you let one horse thief get by, then everyone in the country thinks he can sample your cattle at will. Besides, I owe it to Comet. He won more money for me than any other horse I ever had. Just to look at him, you'd never know he was as fast as the wind.''

"Was that the broken-looking horse you bet against Williford last year?" Alston laughed. "A thoroughbred, of course, but he looked as if he'd be more at home pulling a dray cart than at a track. I didn't think he'd make it to the first turn.''

Wynford chuckled, and Niki shivered. It wasn't a pleasant sound. "Neither did Williford. If you recall, I won a nice little piece of property and a hunting box out of that. Comet overtook his horse in the second turn and never looked back.'' He laughed again. "Williford threatened me with legal action, but his father paid up.''

Alston nodded. "I recall." He gave Wynford a strange look. "Almost ruined the family, didn't it? By the by, I haven't seen Williford since then. What happened to him?"

This time Wynford laughed aloud, but the sound held no mirth. "His father shipped him off to the Indies to live until he learned to judge horseflesh.''

"He was just a green boy." Alston still had the strange expression on his face, but now it was tinged with disgust.

Wynford gave him a cool stare. "Now he knows better. Perhaps his father should be thanking me for assisting in the boy's education.'' There was a pause. "People who don't know the rules shouldn't play, should they, Alston?" His tone was low and amused. Alston didn't answer him, and Niki realized that there was an undercurrent between the two men. The stress between them was heavy.

"It's a lovely day for riding," Niki said, saying the very first thing to come into her mind, hoping to ease the tension.

"Indeed." Alston spoke lightly, but his face was tight. Before

Niki could reply, they rounded a bend in the road and saw the main house at Wynwoode in the distance. "Would you care to join us for some refreshment, Miss Owen?" Wynford asked.

Niki reined in Qadir and motioned to Jem to ride up beside her. "No, thank you. I've certainly enjoyed riding with you, but I really must return. Good day." She started to turn, but Wynford caught her reins. "I do hope we can ride again soon. Since becoming heir to Wynwoode, I've been remiss in visiting my neighbors. However"—he gave her an assessing gaze that gave Niki a chill—"I had no idea my neighbors were so charming or I would have been by sooner. I do hope you and your family will be able to visit Wynwoode now that I'm in residence."

"Perhaps we shall." Niki gave him the briefest of smiles and turned to Jem, nodding toward Breconbridge. Jem had eased her horse in front of Qadir when he saw Wynford grab her reins. He held his horse with his knees and put his good hand out to touch Qadir to quiet him. Niki was very glad of his presence. There was something very dangerous that she sensed in Wynford. With a nod and a smile, Wynford released Qadir. "I shall be looking forward to your acquaintance, Miss Owen," he said, as he and Alston went on their way to Wynwoode.

As Niki and Jem rode slowly back to Breconbridge, she wondered just what disconcerting element she sensed in Wynford's personality and could reach no answer. The man was civil, he had said nothing untoward. However, the tone he had used gave his words an entirely different meaning that filled her with unease. Wynford *seemed* polite and mannered. Still, he had seemed to take pleasure in his ruination of Williford, whoever he was. Niki could simply sense that the man had no scruples. She closed her eyes as she thought of what he had said about the theft of his horse, and she knew that he would do it—he would see that the persons who had taken Comet would hang. She felt physically ill.

Back at home, she went in the back way again so she wouldn't have to talk to her mother, Mrs. Keene, or Sarah. She had to find Robbie or Cam and needed to do it immediately. They had to do something with Comet. With Alston riding all over the place, it was only a matter of time until the horse—and Mr. Smith and their own involvement with the theft—was discovered.

Neither Robbie nor Cam was in the house or on the grounds. There was only one place that they could be, Niki reasoned. Quickly, she grabbed the napkin full of food that she had planned to take to Smith and slipped out the back, dashing over the small bridge and into the woods as fast as she could. She looked for Robbie and Blazer in the woods as she practically ran down the path. They weren't there and could be anywhere, but she would almost wager that they were at the old barn.

She had almost reached the clearing that opened into the pasture when she spotted Robbie's dog, Blazer, drowsing in a patch of sun. Robbie was right around the bend of the path, digging several holes. He looked up, surprised. "Blazer was supposed to bark if someone came." He frowned and put down his shovel. "We're on watch," he explained. "I'm glad it was just you." He collapsed against the base of a tree trunk. "Do you know, Niki, that this digging is hard work? Look at my hands." He held out red and blistered palms so she could see them. "I thought if I had to cover up by telling this bouncer about Robin Hood, I'd better dig some holes so someone would think I was really searching." He frowned. "Dratted hot work."

"Robbie," Niki said, sitting down beside him. "I just talked to Wynford, and he plans to, as he said, prosecute to the limit of the law."

"What does that mean?"

"That means that he intends to have the magistrates catch the person or persons who stole Comet and then he wants them hanged."

"Oh, Lord." Robbie looked distinctly green. "What will we do, Niki?"

She shook her head. "I don't know. We've got to tell Cam and see if we can get Comet away from here."

Robbie stood up. "Why should Wynford care? They were just going to shoot Comet anyway. That's what they said."

Niki stood and stepped over the shovel. "He wants to make an example out of this person, I gather. He thinks that if he doesn't, then everyone will try to steal from him." She picked up the shovel and propped it against a tree. "Is Cam at the barn, or do you know?"

"He's there with Smith. They've been working on Comet all day. That's why I'm on watch." He eyed the shovel, then ran to catch up with Niki. "I'll get that when we come back. I'm going with you." He looked at the napkin in her hand. "What's that?"

"Food for Mr. Smith." She smacked at his fingers as he tried to reach inside the napkin. "Not for you, you bottomless pit. We're going to have to figure out a way to feed Mr. Smith without taking food from the kitchen. Cook looked at me most strangely."

"We're going to have to figure out how to do more than that. I don't know how long I can keep up this Robin Hood story." He looked down at his blistered palms. "Not long, I suspect."

When they got to the barn, they let themselves into the warm, dusty gloom. Cam and Mr. Smith had Comet in the middle of the hall, and Niki hardly recognized the horse. He stood erect, an arch to his neck, and looked every inch a thoroughbred. She rubbed his neck and congratulated Cam. "Don't give me the credit," Cam said, laughing. "Smith's the one working magic. I've never seen such a touch with horses."

"Hardly." Smith glanced at the napkin Niki was holding. "That wouldn't be another picnic would it? I'm going to have to import a chef if I stay here much longer." He laughed and took the napkin from her hand, opened it, and shared with Robbie. "Many thanks, Miss Owen." He offered to share with her, but she shook her head.

"I'll try to smuggle out something else later," she said, then she turned to Cam. "We may not be able to hide Comet here much longer. I've just had a conversation with Wynford.'' She stopped as Mr. Smith choked on a crumb.

He stopped coughing and stared at her. ''With whom?'' he asked.

''Wynford. Lord Wynford of Wynwoode. The man who owns Comet.'' She went on to relate her conversation with Alston and Wynford.

''How long has Lord Wynford been at Wynwoode?'' Mr. Smith asked. ''I was under the impression that Wynford had died.''

Cam grunted. ''The older one did. That is, Richard. I heard there was some kind of heir in America or somewhere, but he was killed, so they say. This one—Jackson is his name, I believe—is the next in line. He's the son of the sister who married an army captain.'' Cam grimaced. ''Jackson didn't waste any time calling himself Wynford, did he?'' He turned to Smith. ''We can't let you get involved in this, Mr. Smith. I believe that Jackson will do what he says. This is our problem, and I won't have you strung up because of it. Thank you for your help, but you need to move along. We appreciate your help.''

Smith shook his head and folded the napkin carefully into a neat square, then smiled at all of them. ''Thank you for trying to save my neck, but I'm very involved anyway.'' He hesitated as he looked at each one in turn, then smiled, that smile that transformed his whole face and made his eyes seem even bluer. ''I suppose I need to confess, don't I?''

''It's good for the soul, you know,'' Robbie said, as Blazer sniffed around John Smith's feet and then flopped down in the sun.

''So I've heard.'' Smith pulled a bench over next to the barn wall and motioned for them to sit. Niki sat down and leaned back against the barn wall, hitting her bonnet. She reached up, pulled it off, and put it on the bench beside her. Cam sat next to the bonnet, while Robbie sat on some straw on the floor. Smith sat down on a box facing them. ''I suppose you've surmised that my name isn't really John Smith.'' He grinned.

"I should have been able to come up with something better, but I was taken unaware." He paused and looked at them. "Actually, I'm the heir from America."

Niki felt her jaw drop. Cam and Robbie did the same thing. "That's not exactly correct," Smith continued, ignoring their shock, "my father is the heir, but, about the time he received word that his brother Richard had died, he fell off a horse and broke his leg, so he didn't want to travel. He sent me over here to find out what condition Wynwoode was in and claim the estate." He paused. "We didn't really want the estate and hadn't planned on acquiring it. I recall that Father received a letter from Uncle Richard telling him of the deaths of his boys—my cousins. Father felt that Uncle Richard would probably remarry and sire more children. He also knew of Jackson, but only vaguely, as he had never met either Jackson or his father. I've heard him mention his sister, but it was strictly in terms of the bad marriage she made."

"So your real name is . . . ?" Niki let her words trail off.

He smiled that melting smile at her. "Sheridan Devlin at your service, Miss Owen. At the risk of being labeled as one of those unmannerly Americans who rushes his fences, I will tell you that my friends call me Sherry."

"I don't believe you." Niki blurted out the words before she could stop herself and clapped her hand over her mouth. "I'm sorry, Mr. Smith, I don't mean to contradict you, but we have no proof of this. You could be anyone."

Sherry sighed. "I know, but I assure you that this particular story is the truth."

"It was all over the village this morning when I went in to get those supplies—the heir had been killed by a deer hunter, almost in sight of Wynwoode." Cam regarded Smith seriously. "He was positively identified, I won't say how."

"I can tell you." Sherry nodded. "I put my signet ring on his finger, and a letter to my father from the solicitors in London in his pocket. I wanted people to think Sheridan Devlin was no more." He pushed back the lock of hair that had fallen across his forehead and looked at them. "That was no deer hunter and no accident. Someone tried to kill me, and it wasn't the first time, either. Someone did kill poor Farnsworth.''

''Farnsworth?'' Niki looked at him blankly. ''Who is Farnsworth?''

''He's the marigold breeder who was with me.'' Sherry paused. ''Actually, he's the vicar who was telling me about his theories on marigold breeding.''

''Marigolds?'' Niki looked from Sherry back to Cam. Cam shook his head and looked just as blank as Niki. Comet wandered over and nuzzled the back of Sherry's neck.

''Lonesome?'' Sherry asked him with a smile, and reached up to scratch the horse's nose. Comet made soft, huffing sounds as Sherry scratched him. Then he turned and stood patiently behind Sherry. ''Perhaps we had better hear the whole story,'' Cam said slowly.

Sherry began with the receipt of the letter from the solicitors and finished with discovering Comet, Robbie, and Niki in the woods. ''That's why I was planning to stay here. I needed to discover what was going on and why someone was trying to murder me. The only possibility is Jackson—who else would benefit? However, I need some proof. If I went to a magistrate with the story I've just given you, what do you think would happen?''

''Easy,'' Robbie said with a grin. ''You'd be chained and put in Bedlam.''

Sherry nodded. ''Exactly. Also,'' he said with a grin, ''if I get caught with this horse, I'll be hanged. Not a pleasant prospect either way, is it?''

''We may be hanged with you,'' Niki said slowly, looking at him, assessing him. ''Mr. Smith . . .''

''Sherry,'' he prompted.

''Sheridan, Wyn . . .'' Niki gave up. ''Mr. Smith, your story is almost too strange to be anything but true but . . .'' She paused and looked at Robbie and Cam. ''I had the worst feeling when I met Wynford. The man has no feelings, no conscience. I can believe that he would do whatever he needed to do to get what he wanted.''

Niki leaned back and hairpins slid from her hair. She tried to shove her unruly curls back into place, but it was impossible. With a sigh, she gave up and let her hair tumble down onto her neck.

"So you believe this could be true?" Cam asked. Niki nodded, and Cam smiled. "Good. I believe it as well." He turned to Sherry, smiling. "Now what, Smith, or rather, Sherry?"

"It seems to me," Niki said frowning, "that our first problem is to hide the horse. To do that, we're going to have to disguise him."

"I don't know what we could do." Cam glanced toward the barn. "You do know that we can't keep him here indefinitely. Someone will be over this way. You know Papa. He checks on everything." He sighed. "I don't know how we could disguise him—the horse, I mean."

"Dye?" Sherry looked at her and frowned. "That might be possible if someone doesn't look too closely."

"Dye." Niki's tone was decided. "Yes, that's the very thing." She grasped at a barely formed idea. "Cam, Robbie, that's it! Dye would do it."

"Dye?" Sherry and Cam said the word together as they looked at Niki in surprise.

Niki paused, the beginnings of a plan forming. "It's perfect!" she said, knowing she had hit on the very thing. "Cam, we'll dye Mr. Smith's hair . . ."

"Call me Sherry," Sherry said.

Niki ignored him as she put the pieces of her plan together. "We'll dye Mr. Smith's hair and dye the horse. That way we can disguise both of them."

"Why would I need to be disguised?" Sherry asked. "I can find out what I need to without anyone discovering me."

Niki shook her head. "Not so. You've been discovered. Didn't you say there had been one or two attempts on your life? No, you said yourself that you need to go to the village and out in the countryside so you can talk to people. You couldn't do that if you were recognized." She pinned him with a look. "There would be another attempt, I think."

"And this one might be successful," Robbie added.

Cam threw his arm around Niki's shoulders, scooting over and almost crushing her bonnet in the process. "You're right!" He grinned at Sherry. "A woman with a logical mind under all that hair. I call that a miracle."

"You're going to call yourself dead if you make another remark like that one, brother Camden." Niki scowled at him, shrugged off his arm, and rescued her bonnet. "Anyway, Cam, you could invite Mr. Smith to stay with you at Breconbridge for a fortnight or so. It would be the perfect base for him, and no one would suspect a thing. He could take his horse with him. No one would remark on a guest at Breconbridge having such a horse—or horses. He could have Comet there as well. Papa wouldn't remark on that."

Cam looked at her in amazement. "You're absolutely right, Niki," he said slowly, grasping the form of her plan. "It is perfect. He could dye Comet and bring him along, and who would ever think that a guest at Breconbridge would be harboring a stolen horse. For that matter, that a guest at Breconbridge wouldn't be everything he says he is." He grinned at her. "Just perfect." He looked at Sherry. "What do you think?"

"I don't think I can batten myself on you just like that." He shook his head. "No, I'll just find a nice, quiet inn and take a room."

"And what about Comet?" Robbie asked. "A magistrate might look at an inn for a stolen horse. You'd have a time keeping the dye on Comet, and the grooms at the inn might notice it. After all, you couldn't really care for Comet at an inn yourself the way you could at Breconbridge."

Niki leaned toward Sherry, her dark eyes sincere. "It's our only way out, Mr . . . Mr . . ."

"Sherry," he said.

"It's our only way out," Niki said again. "If Comet is discovered, you could always claim to have been duped in some way when you bought him. No one would question you if you were a guest at Breconbridge. However, if you were discovered and were at an inn . . ." She let her words trail off.

"Then it would just be my word that I'm really Sheridan Devlin against the word of whoever has charged me, wouldn't it? It would appear that I'd absconded with Comet."

"So you'll join us at Breconbridge?" Cam asked. "I think it will be the ideal solution. You'd have free rein to roam, and you most certainly would have access to more people than you would if you were not introduced around the county."

"Also," Robbie said, making a face, "you could even go to Wynwoode whenever you wanted to. Niki said that Wynford had invited her to visit. That would extend to all of us, I'm sure."

Sherry chewed on his lower lip as he thought, then pushed back his hair. "All right. If you're sure I won't be imposing on your hospitality."

"Imposing? Don't be absurd." Cam stood. "There's nothing Papa likes better than a house full of people. He'd have half of London here if they'd come to the country." He stretched, then sat back down. "We'll have to concoct some kind of story, won't we?"

"And purchase a large quantity of dye." Sherry frowned. "I'll get out this afternoon and see to that."

"Perhaps each of us should purchase some dye. It might be remarked upon if you bought such a large amount. I could even ask Alston to buy some."

Niki shook her head. "No, Cam, I know you like the man, but I feel that the fewer of us who know about this, the better. The four of us can go several places and buy small quantities of dye—black, I suppose—and no one will know. It may take us a day or two. I can go to Twyford and the village, and even as far as Caswell Dean. You could go farther afield."

"I think you're right, Miss Owen," Sherry said, giving her an appreciative look. "The fewer, the better." He pulled at a strand of his blond hair and grinned. "I just hope the dye all grows out before my mother sees me again. She'll go into a decline if she thinks the English climate has turned me into a brunet."

Niki smiled back at him, thinking to herself that he certainly did have a wonderful smile. "About our story . . ." Niki began.

They concocted a plausible story, they all agreed. There was no hiding Sherry's accent, so they decided to make him an American from Richmond in Virginia who was in England searching for excellent horseflesh to take back with him. "That's quite true, to an extent," Sherry said. "Let's say that I'm interested in racing stock. That should interest Jackson— or Wynford as he calls himself."

"What about your name?" Niki asked.

Sherry sighed. "I just don't care for John Smith, for reasons more than the obvious. Do you think I could get by with using part of my real name? I'd prefer to answer to something reasonably familiar."

Several possibilities were offered, with the group finally settling on a combination of Sherry's own name and that of one of his father's best friends, a Thomas Jefferson. From this point on, he was to be known as Thomas Sheridan, of Sheridan's Trace Farm between Richmond and Charlottesville. "I trust Wynford won't know exactly how much territory that encompasses," Sherry said with a laugh. "It sounds good enough." He paused, then rose and searched in his saddlebags for his pen case. Opening it, he scribbled a quick note. "My trunks are at this address. Do you think you might send for them, and I'll reimburse you when they arrive."

Cam glanced at the slip of paper. "You'll do no such thing, Sm . . . Sheridan. I'll take a day or so away from Breconbridge and go get them myself. That will also give me an opportunity to buy a quantity of dye." He glanced around. "Alston and Wynford had planned to go to the races in Ayleswood and had asked me go along. I'll simply decline, and that will give us, I think, three days to get this together." He stood up and grinned. "Niki, you're a genius."

Niki smiled primly. "I'm glad you recognize that. I'm very humble, as well."

Robbie grabbed her arm and jerked her onto the floor while Cam tossed Sherry's horse blanket over her head. Niki sat up, drew the blanket from her head, and looked at the two of them. "I happen to be an advocate of revenge, as well. I just want the two of you to know that. My turn will come." She stood and glanced at the small watch pinned to her bodice. "Oh, my goodness, I've got to get back before the Keenes and Mama miss me! Mrs. Keene is sure to comment on my absence." She turned to Robbie. "You, too. That Robin Hood story is going to wear thin, you know." She reached down and retrieved her bonnet as Comet nuzzled it curiously. "Another minute, and this would be dinner," she said, brushing the hay from it.

To her surprise, Sherry smiled and pulled the hat from her fingers. It was a lovely green, with a white feather. He finished brushing it off, and Niki noticed his fingers, long, capable, yet very graceful. He put the hat on her head and tied the ribbons under her chin. "My sister Martha always has trouble with the ribbons," he said, expertly smoothing the bow. "I've become something of a lady's maid. Of course, anyone who trails behind Martha is that, she leaves pieces of clothing here and there— her hat here, her gloves there, and can never find it all." He chuckled. "You'll have to meet her some time."

Niki touched the ribbons as he turned. No man had ever done such an intimate thing for her, and it had shocked her. It was one thing for Cam and Robbie—whom she regarded as brothers—to throw a horse blanket at her, but it was entirely another thing for this man to tie her ribbons, even though he seemed to think nothing of it. As she walked back to the house, Niki touched her chin where those fingers had touched her. Perhaps, she thought to herself, Americans were different. She had heard that.

Still, the sensations were strange to her. Not only had he touched her skin, but he had been close to her, oh, so close. She had looked right into his blue eyes and had been only inches from his smiling lips. It had been very—she cast around for a word and the best she could find was *unsettling*. But it had been more than that. Worse, at her own suggestion, this man was going to be at Breconbridge for weeks, and she would be around him every day. Her lips tingled slightly.

Close to him every day. Could she manage that? As she paused and looked at Breconbridge in the sun without really seeing it, she wondered. Sheridan Devlin was an attractive man.

*If,* she reminded herself as she walked toward the back of the house, following Robbie and Blazer as they ran down the hill, *if* that was who he really was.

# Chapter 6

The next days were fairly uneventful ones. Cam told the family he had suddenly discovered pressing business in London and had to go there for a few days. Alston and Wynford went off for the races at Ayleswood and decided to go look at some cattle at a farm in the Midlands. Niki stayed at home and chafed, worried constantly about being discovered. She and Robbie took turns smuggling food out to Smith—or Sheridan Devlin as he kept reminding them. Mrs. Keene remarked on Niki's wish for long, solitary walks, and Lady Larch felt obliged to try to fill Niki's days. It certainly made slipping away from the house difficult. Worse, Sarah was around her constantly, chattering about this thing or that. It seemed that Sarah's parents were determined to marry her off to a man in trade if Sarah had had no offers from a member of the ton by year's end. "I can't bear him, Niki," Sara moaned more than once. "Whatever shall I do?" Unfortunately, Niki had no answer.

Also, Mrs. Keene was doing everything possible to find a way to throw Sarah in Wynford's way. Niki tried to tell her friend that Wynford might be unsuitable. "I know he is," Sarah almost sobbed. "I met him in London and thought him coarse and vulgar.'' She hesitated. ''It doesn't matter, Niki, it doesn't matter at all. My affection is . . . is fixed, but he would never be seen with me, much less offer for me.''

Niki hugged her friend, but there was little she could say. Sarah knew well that marriage with the ton was largely a matter of connections, and most of them would starve rather than marry someone whose parents were in trade. Sarah's misery was so acute that Niki asked her mother if anything could be done. Lady Larch's answer was her usual one—when out of sorts, go shopping. Happily, she organized shopping trips to the nearby village and towns. It gave Niki the perfect opportunity to get the things she needed, although she was hard-pressed to slip away from Sarah on their shopping trips to purchase the dye. She was obliged to take Shotwell with her, so Sarah wouldn't dog her every footstep. Then, of course, there was the necessity of persuading Shotwell that the dye was really for Robbie and had something to do with creating a medieval siege machine like something Robin Hood would have used. She even managed to look in Shotwell's direction when she told this bouncer, but not right in the eyes. She was getting closer, but she wasn't nearly as good as Robbie at prevarication. That was changing, she thought to herself. On their last shopping expedition, she sighed as she carried her package of dye back to the coach, cautioning Shotwell not to tell anyone about it. It seemed that since she had become involved with Comet and John Smith—no, now he was Thomas Sheridan—she had made great strides in becoming an accomplished liar.

It was just as bad when she was at Breconbridge. There, she and Robbie still needed to smuggle food out to Smith—or Sheridan she kept reminding herself. It would be just like her to forget and call him Mr. Smith right in front of everyone. Robbie had taken to calling him Sherry, no matter how much Niki fussed at him. ''You're much too young to be calling him such,'' she warned Robbie one day when she handed over the rolls she had smuggled out of the dining room. ''You should always refer to him as Mr. Sheridan.''

''But that isn't his name,'' Robbie said with irrefutable logic, adding the rolls to the slices of ham he had hidden beneath his coat. "He told everyone to call him Sherry, and so I am."

"Well, you can't do it when he's here at Breconbridge. After all, he's supposed to be a stranger when Cam brings him here." She sighed and looked at the food. "That just isn't enough, Robbie. We've got to send him more."

Robbie glanced at the small pile of rolls and ham. "That will do, I suppose. He told me to bring it and leave it because he wasn't going to be there today." Robbie chuckled. "He had to go buy some dye, I think." He gave Niki an admiring glance. "By the by, Niki, that story you came up with about the siege machine was pure genius. I can't wait to tell Cam about it. Sherry said it showed real flair, and he certainly had no idea that you were a born liar. You always look perfectly guileless, he said."

Niki tied the napkin holding the food tightly. "I don't believe that's a compliment, Robbie," she said. "Off with you. I'll tell Mama that you're out digging again."

Lady Larch received this information with a smile. "Robbie has certainly been diligent in this search," she remarked to Lord Larch. The two of them had rather despaired of Robbie ever becoming serious about anything. "I'm glad to see him interested in something, even something so frivolous," Lord Larch had remarked. "It's a good sign." They all nodded sagely, and Niki forced herself to peer at her embroidery on the pretense of untangling a knot. That wasn't difficult. She had never been much of a needlewoman, and most of her efforts had almost as many knots as stitches.

Because of Sarah, Niki had only been able to go back to the barn a few times to check on Sheridan. In truth, Niki was almost relieved to put some distance between herself and the American. It had unnerved her more than she admitted when he had tied her bonnet for her. If he was as familiar when he was staying at Breconbridge, she had decided, she would have Cam speak to him. But, no matter how hard she tried, she couldn't get the image of the man from her thoughts—his smile, his blue eyes, the touch of his fingers on her chin.

It was annoying. She finally decided that the man, being an American, had no knowledge of propriety and simply didn't know he shouldn't do such. Still, there was that glint of mischief she had seen in his eyes and in his smile that seemed to say that he knew very well what he was doing, knew that he shouldn't be doing it, and just didn't care at all.

Cam was expected back on Friday, and Niki supposed that he would be bringing Sheridan to the house on Saturday. She had sent her purchases by Robbie to the barn to be hidden there. There had been no sign of Sheridan's trunks, so she thought Cam would probably bring them with him when he came. She sighed, thinking about it one sleepless night. She really wasn't sure she could carry such a deception off. What if she said something? What if she acted unnaturally? There were a dozen *what ifs*. The whole thing seemed to be getting well out of hand.

Alston returned on a Thursday in midafternoon. He and Wynford had gotten back late the night before, he told them, but he had spent the night at Wynwoode since the hour was so late. He spent a pleasant half an hour in the drawing room with the ladies. Mrs. Keene quizzed him unmercifully, while Sarah stayed bent over her embroidery, not saying a single word. Alston was polite to Mrs. Keene and was his usual charming self. He finally excused himself and left.

Mrs. Keene gave Niki a piercing look. "Is there a reason he's here?" she asked bluntly.

Niki looked at her in surprise. "He's a friend of Camden's," Lady Larch said firmly.

"Well, Zoe, if you ask me . . ." Mrs. Keene began, but Sarah interrupted her.

"Mama, please!" she said, throwing her embroidery down. To everyone's surprise, she ran from the room. Niki stood to go after her, but Lady Larch stopped her.

"Perhaps she needs to be alone for a while, Niki," Lady Larch said. "Give her some time."

Mrs. Keene sniffed. "The gel's been all up in the boughs since Mr. Keene told her that it was marry by year's end or else.'' She shook her head. "Girls today don't know what's good for them.''

Rather than wait for another lecture, Niki excused herself and fled in the opposite direction toward the library where she curled up with a new book.

She had gotten well into the third chapter when she heard a noise out front—a horse coming up to the front block. She thought it might be Alston escaping to Wynford. She moved her feet to a more comfortable position and began reading again. She hadn't read more than a paragraph when the library door opened stealthily and Alston slipped inside, quietly closing the door behind him. He was already over to Lord Larch's extensive collection of various whiskies and wines before he spotted Niki. "Don't tell me that you, too, are hiding from Mrs. Keene,'' Alston said ungallantly. He poured himself a stiff whiskey.

Niki laughed and realized she was curled up in a most undignified manner. She put down her book and sat up straight. "I've already done my duty there,'' she said. "Remember, I've been entertaining that formidable lady while you've been away.''

Alston shuddered and sat down with a fresh whiskey. "Do you mind if I fortify myself, Miss Owen?'' He sipped this one slowly.

"Not at all.'' Niki was casting around for something to say in the way of conversation when the library door burst open. Cam came in, slapping dust from his clothing with the backs of his gloves. Another man Niki had never seen followed right behind him. "Alston, how good to see you!'' Cam said, coming over to them. "I hope the Ayleswood races were good for you.''

"Wonderfully so. I made a packet.'' Alston looked up and sipped his whiskey. "Found some decent cattle on a farm nearby as well. I think Wynford is planning on buying some for breeding stock.''

"Wonderful. Perhaps you and Wynford can help Sheridan here.'' Niki almost gasped as Cam paused and reached behind him, taking the man's arm and moving him forward. "Thomas, this is Viscount Alston, a man who knows horses from one end to the other. You can depend on his advice.'' He smiled at Sheridan. ''Alston, this is a man you should know. He knows as much about horses as you do, I'd wager. This is Thomas Sheridan of Trace Farm, a plantation in the Americas. He's here to buy horses.'' Sherry stepped forward and Niki gaped, her jaw dropping. Cam kicked her shins as Sherry greeted Alston, and she remembered to shut her mouth. She couldn't believe the transformation. She would never have known Sheridan in a million years. His tanned complexion now complemented his dark hair. He had cut his hair as well, and it was arranged in something of an unkempt Brutus. His clothing seemed different as well. He was dressed in tan breeches, a white linen shirt, a waistcoat of narrow navy-and-tan stripes that had been embroidered with small burgundy flowers, and, the final touch, a navy coat that looked as though his broad shoulders had been poured into it. ''Sherry, let me present my stepsister to you. Miss Anika Owen, Mr. Thomas Sheridan.''

Niki looked right up at him, gulped, and acknowledged him. He smiled at her, and she noted that at least his smile was the same. She would *never* have known him. His blond hair was black, his sun-bleached eyebrows were black, a dark, glossy black that made him look rather sinister and dangerous.

''Are you here for long?'' Alston handed Cam his empty whiskey glass to refill as Cam poured a drink and handed it to Sherry.

Sherry sipped appreciatively at the whiskey. ''Scotch whiskey?'' he asked, lifting an eyebrow.

Cam nodded. ''Sherry's here for several months,'' he said to Alston.

''I'm trying to stock my plantation with some fine English stock,'' Sherry said, sitting and giving Alston a level look. ''As you know, we've been racing horses in the United States for years, but we've never reached the level of horseflesh, I think, that you have here. I hope to remedy that situation.'' He paused and smiled. ''Cam tells me that you have several fine horses for sale.''

"I do." Alston regarded him for a moment, obviously tal-lying up the cost of his clothing. "Of course, the price is steep."

"I expect to pay a steep price for quality. Cost is no object." Sherry sat back, quite at ease, and looking as if he belonged in the house. Niki kept waiting for something to happen, but nothing did other than that Cam and Sherry persuaded Alston to take them over to Wynford the next day to look at horses. The talk turned to the races at Alyeswood just as the clock in the hall struck. Niki jumped at the sound and decided it was time for her to leave. She couldn't sit around all day waiting for Cam or Sheridan to make a mistake. It was simply too difficult for her nerves. Instead, she decided to go take Qadir for a ride. She really needed to get out—if she stayed and listened to one more falsehood, she thought she would simply scream.

There was a strange horse in the end stall beside Qadir, and Niki paused. The horse was a glossy black and looked at her proudly, his neck arched and his tail held high. It wasn't until she looked in the stall on the other side and saw Traveler there that she looked back. She slipped inside the stall with the black and ran her fingers over him. The sores were healing, but they were still there. She could feel the ridges of the welts where he had been beaten. It was Comet. He nuzzled her neck, and she petted him, pulling a bit of apple from her pocket and giving it to him. She had brought Qadir bits of apple, but he would have to share them with Comet. She didn't think Qadir would mind.

Jem saddled Qadir for her. Over the years, Robbie had told her when she had asked, Jem had learned to make do without the use of his hand. He was a better groom, Cam had said, with one hand than most were with two. Niki had to agree.

When they got away from the house, Niki let Qadir have his head, and they went at a gallop across the fields and cleared a hedge. She waited a minute there until Jem could go around and catch up. Jem never took fences. Niki moved out of the field and into the small road that ran alongside the woods. It was seldom used by anyone, and she felt comfortable riding there. Jem followed her, and she had no fear. She rode for the better part of an hour, then returned to Breconbridge, feeling immeasurably better.

As she walked toward the house, she removed the hat that matched her habit. As she touched the ribbons to remove it, she was reminded anew of Sheridan's touch on her skin when he had tied her bonnet ribbons for her. However would she manage to be in the same house with the man for over a fortnight? A smile crossed her face as she mounted the steps to the door. *Sarah Keene.* Niki would simply throw Sarah at poor Sheridan. That was the answer. It would keep Sheridan away from her and would give Sarah a prospect.

Niki made a point of stopping by the upstairs drawing room on the way to change for supper. Sarah was there, idly turning the pages of a book of fashion plates. "Have you met Mr. Sheridan?" Niki asked, coming into the room.

Sarah shook her head and looked up. There were dark circles under her eyes. "No, Mama met him and told me he might bear further investigation."

Niki caught her breath. "Investigation? Have you heard anything?"

"No." Sarah looked up at her blankly. "I have no idea how eligible the man may be. Do you know anything of his prospects? Mama will probably be asking you or Camden about it."

"Oh." Niki let out her breath slowly. "That's precisely why I stopped by, Sarah. I can tell you that the man has excellent prospects. I don't believe he wants everyone to know since he's merely here on a buying trip, but he stands to inherit a large plantation and perhaps more." Niki was being scrupulously honest.

Sarah looked at her sadly. "It doesn't really matter, Niki. Tell Mama whatever you want. I don't care." She looked back at her book. "Perhaps it might be a possibility. Do people in the wilds of America care whether or not someone is in trade?"

"I really don't know about that." She had promised herself that she wouldn't stretch the truth—much, anyway. "Perhaps you could engage him in conversation after supper and find out.'' She smiled at Sarah. ''I really must go change. I'll see you at supper.''

Sarah stood and put down her magazine. ''I need to do the same.'' She paused in the hall as they heard the voices of the men in the library. They were laughing about something. Sarah glanced wistfully down the stairs, started to say something, then caught herself. ''I'll see you shortly,'' she said, turning into her room. *Sarah,* Niki thought to herself, *is certainly acting strangely.* She had never seen her friend this much in the mopes before. Just as soon as she could, she promised herself, she would give Sheridan a hint that Sarah would be an excellent— and wealthy—prospect. She felt quite satisfied with herself.

Everyone met in the drawing room before supper. Alston bowed over Niki's hand when she came in, and she could still smell the whiskey on him. She was the last one in the room. They were all there: Lord Larch, Mama, Cam, Mrs. Keene, Alston, Sarah, Sheridan, and finally, herself. Sarah was deep in conversation with Sheridan while Mrs. Keene beamed at them. Niki had to own that Sheridan looked presentable. Actually, more than presentable. He was wearing black, and with his black hair and brows he looked almost like a pirate. The cut in his brow that made it arch so appeared almost silver on his skin. Niki caught herself looking at him and forced herself to turn and talk with Mrs. Keene. ''I understand Mr. Sheridan is quite an eligible,'' that lady whispered to Niki.

''So I understand, but I have no details. Perhaps you should ask Cam later.''

Mrs. Keene pursed her lips. ''I'll certainly do that. A mother can't be too careful, after all.'' Niki was saved from having to reply by Lady Larch suggesting they go in to supper. Mrs. Keene moved quickly to keep Cam from escorting Sarah in, leaving the field open for Sheridan. Before Niki could edge up beside Cam, Sherry was at her side. ''May I, Miss Owen?'' he asked, quite properly, giving her his arm. There was nothing Niki could do except smile and take his arm. Still, she noted with satisfaction, Alston was taking Sarah in.

"You're looking quite the thing tonight," Sheridan said with a smile. "Remind me to tell you how fine you look in that color. What would you call it—bronze?"

"Yes." Niki smoothed down the bronze silk that was trimmed with ecru lace. The color set off her dark looks and dark eyes. She always looked better in deep, rich tones rather than the virginal pastels that everyone insisted she wear. "I chose it myself."

"I commend your taste," Sherry said. He leaned down slightly and dropped his voice to a whisper. "Now Miss Keene's . . ." Niki looked at Sarah and saw what he meant. Sarah had put on a rather muddy yellow dress that made her complexion look jaundiced. It was one of those fashionable pastels that Niki loathed. "Tell me, though, Miss Owen. Are you the one I am to thank for being favored with Miss Keene's company this evening? Her mother has all but put the young lady in my lap." Niki didn't answer him, but she felt herself blush. "Certainly not. Mrs. Keene, however . . ." She stopped and groped for the polite words.

"I thought as much," Sherry murmured, helping her sit. "I am familiar with mothers, I'm sad to say." He grinned again, and Niki found herself smiling back at him. One thing she had noticed about Sheridan—she always felt comfortable when she was talking to him.

The conversation, as Niki had known it would, turned to horses midway through the meal, and the topic was discussed in detail. She noticed that Sheridan discussed his "buying mission" with aplomb, smoothly covering every possible question. The man was as good as Robbie. Finally, Lady Larch rose, and the women followed her, leaving the men to port and cigars. Mrs. Keene fell in beside Niki as they went into the drawing room. "What did you discover?" she asked.

"About what?"

Mrs. Keene looked at her in exasperation. "About Mr. Sheridan's prospects? Of course, he's a mere mister, and it would be much better to have a title. Still, if he has a plantation and an excellent income . . ." She let her words trail off. "Perhaps

you should speak with Cam. He knows Mr. Sheridan well,"
Niki said.

"I'll certainly do that." Mrs. Keene went over to Lady Larch
and sat beside her while Sarah came to sit beside Niki. "I was
so embarrassed, Niki," Sarah whispered. "Mama was terrible.
She did all but tell Mr. Sheridan that I was hunting for a
husband. I fully expect her to give him an accounting of Papa's
finances tomorrow. Perhaps tonight." She shuddered. "I don't
know what to do."

"Perhaps Mr. Sheridan might be interested."

Sarah shook her head. "I think not. And then"—she looked
wistful again—"I don't know if I could ever care for him."

"Perhaps," Niki said with a smile, "you might fall in love
with him."

Sarah shook her head. "Never, Niki. I told you of my feelings." Her chin began to quiver as her eyes glazed with tears.
Niki reached over and put her hand on Sarah's. "I hope things
end as you wish them to. I really do, Sarah."

Sarah gave her a wavering smile. "I have you for a friend,
Niki. That's a great deal." She turned as her mother called to
her. "Perhaps I can keep Mama occupied tonight, and she
won't embarrass us all." She smiled at Niki again, impishly
this time. "A formidable task, isn't it?" Before Niki could
answer, Sarah hurried across the room to her mother and Lady
Larch. Niki went over to the doors that opened onto the gardens
and smelled the night breeze. The flowers were mixed with the
scent of new-mown hay, and the smell was wonderful. She
stayed there and enjoyed it while the others discussed fashions
and then, not wanting to lose the mood she was in, sat down
at the pianoforte and began to play, letting her fingers move
over the keys. She glanced up to find Sheridan leaning against
the piano, watching her.

"Don't stop," he said. "Mozart, I believe."

Niki nodded and began another. "My favorite musician,"
she said. "I don't do the music justice, but it speaks to me."

"I think you do very well, Miss Owen." He lifted his scarred
eyebrow and smiled at her. "You constantly amaze me with

your talents. You're a bruising rider, a talented musician, and, um, several other things. What other surprises are in store?''

Niki fumbled with her music, and it floated from the pianoforte. Sheridan bent and retrieved it, but she had stopped playing and was standing by the time he returned it to her. ''Why did you stop?'' he asked softly.

''Lovely music, Anika,'' Mrs. Keene said loudly. ''Do you have any Beethoven? Dear Sarah is always practicing her Beethoven. It sounds quite divine, I always say.''

Taking the cue, Niki handed Sarah the stack of music and moved away. To her—and Mrs. Keene's—chagrin, Sheridan moved with her, grimacing as Sarah began the Beethoven. ''I do see why dear Sarah is always practicing,'' Sherry muttered, sitting down next to Niki. ''She should do more.''

Alston came up beside them, a half-empty wineglass in his hand. He finished the wine and put the glass carelessly on a table beside the sofa. ''I must agree. It was lovely music, Miss Owen. Of course, I'm no connoisseur, but I thought it quite fine.'' He looked across her to Sherry, and the conversation turned again to horses. It seemed that Alston knew that there was some fine horseflesh at Wynwoode, and he invited Sherry to go with him the next day to view it. To Niki's amazement, Sherry seemed to hesitate a moment before he agreed. She had thought he would jump at the chance to see Wynwoode.

Before she could talk further to either Alston or Sheridan, Lady Larch set up the card tables and everyone sat for cards. There was much maneuvering on Mrs. Keene's part to get Sarah seated at the table with Sheridan and Alston. To Niki's amusement, Sherry couldn't quite hide the pained expression on his face as he sat down opposite Mrs. Keene. Sarah was on his right, opposite Alston. Niki was unable to see what transpired after that as she was seated with her back to the quartet, but she did notice that Cam, who was opposite her, smiled more than several times in amusement. Sheridan did not seem in a good humor when the party finally broke up and everyone went to bed.

Niki lay in her bed, thinking, and finding that her thoughts wandered more than not back to Sheridan. He had looked so different that she felt there was no risk of his being recognized, but there was something else, something she could not identify. Why had he been slightly hesitant to visit Wynwoode? Was there something there? Was the man really the person he said he was? For all they knew, he might have really been Farnsworth and had killed the real Sheridan Devlin. She dismissed that thought as soon as it flashed through her mind.

She sat up in bed and hugged her knees, wide awake now. That couldn't be, she thought. The man had goodness in him, she could sense it. Cam had accepted him at face value, as had Robbie. He must be the person he claimed to be. Lighting a candle, she tried reading, but it was no use, and the book was deadly dull anyway—a book of moral essays. She remembered the book she'd been reading in the library, a new, engrossing novel. That book and a glass of warm milk would be just the thing, she thought.

She slipped from her bed and put on her dressing gown, then picked up the candle. At the door, she stopped and thought a minute. She certainly didn't want to wake anyone else, and the candle might possibly do that. She could find her way around Breconbridge blindfolded and didn't need a candle. She put it back on the table and slipped out the door. Mama always had a candle lit at the top and the bottom of the stairs anyway, so there was enough light to see. Niki slipped down the stairs and wandered to the kitchen. The springbox there held a jug of milk, heavy with cream. She searched for a few minutes to find something to skim the cream into, then checked the stove to see if there were coals enough to heat the milk. By placing her pan almost on top of the leftover coals, she heated her milk to lukewarm and drank it on the spot, carefully putting everything away. Cook loathed a messy kitchen—Niki had discovered that through hard experience.

She went back toward the library to get her book, her bare feet making no sound on the floor. The floor was colder than she had expected, and she paused to rub one of her feet, propping herself with one hand against the wall. While she was standing there, the library door opened softly and someone came out, someone dressed in black. Someone with hair that gleamed a glossy black in the faint candlelight. Quickly Niki flattened herself against the wall, worried that her pale dressing gown would give away her presence.

She need not have bothered. Sheridan didn't look either way in the hall. Instead, he paused, pulled the door closed quietly, glanced down at a piece of paper in his hands, folded it, and put it carefully in his pocket. Then, without a backward glance, he went quietly up the stairs.

Niki waited until he was out of sight, then slipped up the stairs behind him. She rounded the landing at the top just in time to see him disappear into his room and shut the door behind him.

She bit her lip and wondered. Should she awaken Cam right now and tell him? Worse, what had Sheridan taken from the library? Had they played right into his schemes somehow? Had she and Robbie and Cam brought a thief into the house? She padded down the hall to Cam's room and knocked softly on the door, whispering his name. Just as Cam opened his door, Sheridan opened his. He was barefooted but had on his breeches and a shirt open at the neck. "Is something wrong?" he asked, stepping out into the hall.

"What the deuce?" Cam asked. He had on his dressing gown and had very obviously just awakened.

Niki stepped backwards. This was no time or place for a confrontation with Sheridan. She stuttered and said the first thing she could think of. "I . . . I must have been dreaming. Please excuse me." With that she fled to her room and shut the door behind her.

# Chapter 7

Niki didn't go to sleep until almost daybreak, her head full of unanswered questions. For every question she had about Sheridan, there was always the feeling she had that he was telling the truth, that he was really a good person. She tossed fitfully until she finally went to sleep at daybreak. When she did awaken about half past ten, she was groggy and had a headache. She sent for toast and chocolate to be brought to her room while she pondered how best to tell Cam about Sheridan's foray into the library after midnight. What could the man have taken from there? Lord Larch didn't use the desk there for his accounts, so there was no money there. What could Sheridan have found so desirable that he went skulking around the house at night to find it? She finished her chocolate and sat on the edge of the bed. Her head felt somewhat better, but there remained a dull ache behind her eyes. Still, she had to find Cam. She rang for Shotwell.

Later, she owned that she felt much better. Shotwell had insisted that she take a bath and rest a few minutes with a damp towel over her eyes. Actually, she had gone back to sleep then, all clean and warm and comfortable, and when she woke up

again, her headache was gone. Shotwell had laid out a dress
in a deep rose color, and it exactly suited Niki's mood today.
The only thing Shotwell hadn't been able to work her magic
on was Niki's hair. It was as unruly as usual, so Shotwell
tried something new. She piled Niki's hair on top of her head,
fastened it down with pins, then tied it with a ribbon. It looked,
Niki had to allow, quite fetching.

It was time for luncheon, and she knew Cam would be
there—he never missed a meal. She knew just where to find
him. Unfortunately, everyone else knew as well. Cam was
surrounded by the others, and Niki was unable to talk to him.
Mrs. Keene tried her most artful maneuvers, but somehow
Alston sat beside Sarah and Sheridan once again slipped in
beside Niki. Sheridan acted as though nothing had happened
the previous night.

"I thought you had declared yourself an early riser, Miss
Owen," he said cheerfully, unfurling his napkin. "Did your
dream bother you?" He seemed to place an emphasis on the
word *dream*.

"I have nightmares from time to time." Niki stared straight
at her plate. No better than he knew her, if he looked into her
eyes, he would still be able to see that she wasn't telling the
whole truth. "I prefer not to discuss it."

"Of course." He moved slightly as the footman came around
with some soup. "Jem pointed out your horse to me in the
stables. A fine animal. Arabian, isn't he?"

Niki glanced at him and raised an eyebrow. "Yes. He's a
Spanish horse, a gift to me from my parents. Papa said he was
of almost pure Arabian stock."

"I thought so. How did you father come by him?"

"We lived in Spain at the time." Niki's eyes clouded over
as she remembered. "As you know, my grandmother is half-
Spanish and we were living there with my relatives. Papa always
encouraged me to ride and made sure that I rode every day.
He gave me Qadir shortly before he died."

"I'm sorry." His voice was sincere. "I had no idea that I'd
be opening old wounds. Please forgive me."

"It's quite all right." Niki pushed some food around on her plate. "I've come to terms with Papa's death."

"Did you enjoy Spain?" He paused. "Good heavens! I'm trying to find another topic of conversation and here I'm returning to the same thing. I apologize."

Niki laughed at his expression. "Don't apologize. As I said, it's quite all right. Yes, I loved Spain. My grandmother is still there, and I enjoy visiting her from time to time. She's the one who gave me my name, Anika."

"It's a lovely name, although I own I've never heard it before." Sheridan looked at her and smiled. "Does it have a special meaning?"

"My grandmother told me that it was the Spanish version of Hannah. I have no idea if that's true or not, but I believe I'd rather be Anika than Hannah." She laughed.

"Either suits you, Miss Owen. Your grandmother chose well. I'd like to make her acquaintance someday."

"She seldom leaves her house and, of course, has never been to England. That's not to say, of course, that she's a recluse. Grandmother is a very independent lady, even though she's been quite successful in Spanish society. It's a very closed, very restrictive society."

"I know. I was in Spain for three months some years back. I can't say I cared very much for some of the customs, although the country was beautiful. My father sent me there to buy some horses."

"Speaking of horses, Sheridan," Alston said across the table, "don't forget that we're to go to Wynwoode this afternoon. I sent word over this morning to make sure that Wynford would be there and could show you some of his prizes. He's expecting us."

"That's excellent. I'm looking forward to it." To Niki's ears, Sheridan sounded anything but excited about the visit. She wondered why. It must, she decided, have something to do with Sheridan's late visit to the library and that scrap of paper he had so carefully pocketed. She had to get to Cam right after luncheon and talk to him.

It wasn't to be. Sarah smiled and took Niki's arm as she was leaving the dining room after luncheon and asked if Niki would go to the village with her to buy lace to edge a handkerchief. By the time Niki had agreed to go and dashed out into the hall, Cam was nowhere to be found. She even went out to the stables, only to have Jem tell her that Cam, Mr. Sheridan, and Viscount Alston had just left on their way to Wynwoode. When she came back inside, Sarah was waiting for her. "News about our afternoon excursion, Niki," she said with a strange smile on her face.

"Our excursion? Where?" Niki said blankly. "Oh, Sarah, I had already forgotten. You wanted to go to the village." Niki glanced around. "Is your mother going with us as well?"

"No, not to the village." Sarah took her arm, smiling, as though she had a secret all her own. "While you were out rambling around the stables, Viscount Alston returned to the house. He said a messenger had just arrived from Wynwoode. It seems that Wynford has invited all of us over there for tea this afternoon. Mama is, of course, ecstatic." She frowned and looked worried. "Lady Larch has already accepted, and I hope she can keep Mama from saying anything inappropriate."

"We're invited to Wynwoode? Today?"

Sarah nodded. "It seems that Wynford has been in charge of the place for some time and has made some great improvements there. Alston was sure we would find the trip worth our while." Sarah looked at Niki from under lowered eyelashes. "Of course, if you really do not have time to go . . ."

"We'll go," Niki said shortly. "Has Mama ordered out the barouche? The last time we planned to go anywhere, she forgot, and we were delayed the better part of an hour. We certainly don't want to ride over there on horseback, do we?" The image of Mrs. Keene bobbing along on the back of a horse made her laugh.

"Ride?" Sarah was aghast. "You know I can't ride, Niki." She paused. "Do you want me to tell a footman to order out the barouche?"

"No, I'll do it."

Sarah touched her arm. "Thank you, Niki. Thank you very much for everything." Sarah smiled again, the same almost-secret smile, and left before Niki could ask her anything else. Niki looked after her friend, wondering.

She had been correct—Lady Larch had completely forgotten to order the barouche. Niki gave instructions and glanced at the clock. She had a few minutes to go check on Comet before she had to get ready. She hurried out to the stables.

Jem and Robbie were in the back of the stables. Robbie was sitting on some hay, idly scratching Blazer's ears, while Jem was working on Comet's leg. "Ah, the man who did this should be horsewhipped," Jem was saying, placing the horse's foot carefully in a bucket of medicated water. "No call for such. I'm glad that Mr. Sheridan had the good sense . . ." He broke off as Niki bumped into a pitchfork handle and knocked it down with a clatter. Jem stood in front of the horse.

"No need for distractions, Niki. It's all right," Robbie said. "Jem knows."

Jem relaxed and smiled as Niki's horror registered on her face. "Jem knows?"

Robbie nodded and stopped scratching Blazer. The dog gave him an expectant look, then stretched out next to the hay. Robbie didn't notice. "Sherry and Cam said we needed to tell him. He's been helping with Com . . . Comment's care."

"Comment?"

Robbie looked around and whispered. "Well, we couldn't call him Comet, now, could we? Sherry said we'd call him Comment so he wouldn't get confused. Technically, his name is now Quick Comment."

"Comment for short." Jem nodded and stepped back to check on the leg.

"The dye washes off in the bucket," Robbie muttered. "Jem has to make sure he doesn't have a foot of a different color when he's finished. And, of course, we can't let the horse get in the rain." Robbie grinned at her. "This was the best idea you ever had, Niki. I wish I'd thought of it myself."

Niki quelled him with a look and went over to stroke Comet's side. "He's going to be beautiful, isn't he?" she asked, running her fingers through the horse's mane.

"That he is." Jem picked up a tin of salve and began applying it to the sore spots. "I hope he gets to America before anyone ever misses him. He'll be happy there."

Niki raised an eyebrow. "America? I had no idea that he had already found a home."

"Where else, Niki?" Robbie said reasonably. "We aren't going to return him, and we certainly can't keep him here forever. I think America is just the place. Sherry says that the grass grows as tall as a man there." He glanced at her dress. "What are you doing here at the stables, anyway? You're not going riding in that, are you?"

"No, I just ran down here for a few minutes before we left. We're going to Wynwoode for tea."

Robbie jumped up and grabbed her hand. "I want to go, too! There may be other horses we need to save."

Niki clapped her hand over his mouth. "Quiet, urchin. Do you want to be dangling at the end of a rope? You can't go, and we definitely are not going to rescue any more horses. I'll tell you all about it when I return."

"Promise?"

Niki promised and went back to the house. She decided against changing clothes, but did allow Shotwell to try to tame her hair again. Then she filled the minutes until it was time to leave in the library, checking everything she could think of. She could find nothing missing or even out of place. Whatever had Sheridan taken? There had to be a way to find out.

The ride to Wynwoode was uneventful, even boring. Lady Larch and Mrs. Keene prattled on endlessly about fashions, balls, and routs, none of which interested Niki in the slightest. Sarah sat, looking off to one side, a dreamy expression on her face. She wasn't hearing a single word, Niki thought. She wished the same was true for herself. She had to listen to Mrs. Keene prose on about the fact that Niki's choice of deep, rich colors was unfashionable, how her chipstraw bonnet trimmed with rose ribbons and cherries was last year's style, and, worse, convince Lady Larch to take Niki to London posthaste to buy new clothes and bonnets. "I really don't care for shopping," Niki said as Wynwoode came into view. It was almost a pleasure to watch Mrs. Keene gasp and fan herself at such a heresy.

Although she had been some time in the area, Niki had never visited Wynwoode. The sons who were Lord Wynford's heirs had died just before she arrived, and the house was in deep mourning at the time. Lord Wynford himself had died before the family ever visited. She was surprised at the house. She had expected a large, gloomy pile of rock, but instead, Wynwoode was golden stone. It had been enlarged over the years, and she could discern several different styles. The left wing seemed to be Elizabethan, while the main part of the house was more modern. It could be, she reflected as they walked to the front, a happy, pleasant place. Right now, most of the upstairs windows were closed, the curtains drawn.

"It needs a woman's touch," Mrs. Keene whispered loudly as they went inside. Niki knew immediately just which woman Mrs. Keene had in mind.

The men were waiting for them in the drawing room. Lord Wynford welcomed them and rang for tea. He asked Lady Larch if she would mind pouring, and an hour or so was spent in pleasantries as they drank their tea and chatted. "I plan to reopen Wynwoode and have some social functions," Wynford said, "as soon as it's possible. Of course, you know that the heir from America was found dead, so entertaining publicly is out of the question for a while. However"—he smiled at Lady Larch and the others—"I hope we will be able to have some private occasions until that time. Perhaps you would honor me by coming to supper here next week."

"We would be delighted," Mrs. Keene said promptly. She turned to Lady Larch. "I know I can speak for you as well, Zoe."

"Of course." Lady Larch was always polite.

That done, the party went outside for a short tour around the grounds. Niki wanted to see the barns and stables, but evidently Wynford had decided that women would not want to view such. She had to be content with touring the gardens, which were sadly weedy, and looking out at the fields, where she saw several horses. They all appeared to be in excellent health.

Cam fell into step beside her and pointed to a glossy horse in the nearest field. "Wynford plans to race that one in the next Brecon races. How do you think he'll do?"

"The horse or Lord Wynford?" Niki asked as the others laughed.

"Both of us, I hope." Wynford fell into step on the other side of Niki and took her arm. "I think the horse has a good chance of winning. He's directly descended from the great winner Waxy, and I think he may take most of the races this year." He frowned slightly. "I certainly hope so, at any rate."

"Aren't you afraid to enter him in a local race such as the Brecon?" Niki asked. "He might get hurt." She paused a second, looking at the horse. "What is his name?"

"Waxworks. I wanted to get in a little of his ancestry with the name." He waved his hand in the direction of the horse, and Niki saw that he wore several rings, among them a silver signet ring. "As for his being hurt—that's a chance I'm willing to take to make sure he gets some experience. Besides"—he smiled down at her and Niki felt cold all over—"I want to show him off to Mr. Sheridan. He's expressed a great deal of interest in Waxworks."

"He's a beautiful horse." Niki sincerely meant it. But then, Comet had been beautiful at one time as well. What had made Wynford mistreat Comet so? Even if he were using the horse to dupe marks at races, as Cam had said, wouldn't he have made more by racing him legitimately? It was puzzling.

Everyone left Wynwoode together, Alston, Cam, and Sheridan riding beside the barouche to Breconbridge. While Cam and Alston kept up conversation, Niki noted that Sheridan seemed most subdued. He rode most of the way with a frown on his face, silent. He wasn't even paying attention to where he was going, she noticed. If Traveler hadn't been an excellent horse, Sheridan probably would have headed toward Ayleswood and not known it.

At Breconbridge, Cam was the one who cornered Niki outside her room as she went in to dress for supper. "Niki, whatever was that sham about nightmares last night?" he asked, too loudly.

"Sshhh." She put her finger to her lips and motioned Cam inside her room. "I wanted to talk to you last night," she said in a low voice, closing the door behind them, "but I couldn't."

"Is this proper?" Cam took a look at the closed door. "After all, we may be like brother and sister, but we aren't really . . ."

"Cam, we're family. Anyway, I wanted to talk to you about Sheridan, and I couldn't think of a thing to say once he came out of his room." She paused a moment. "Did you notice that he was dressed at that time of night?"

Cam shook his head. "No. Was he?"

"Yes, he was." Niki gave him an exasperated look. "And what's more, he had just come from the library." Quickly she told Cam exactly what she had seen the night before. "I searched the library this morning and could find nothing missing. I can't imagine what that piece of paper was."

Cam shrugged. "Maybe a reading list. That's logical."

"Be serious." Niki sat down in the small chair in front of her mirror as Cam seated himself in the big wing chair she sat in to read.

"I am serious. Niki, I believe the man. We've talked at length about his background. He knows things that no one else would know about the family."

"Such as?"

Cam hesitated. "Such as the fact that his uncle, the heir, was the one who was in gambling trouble, but Sherry's father took the blame and went to the Americas. I'd heard rumors, of course, but didn't know for sure.''

"So his father left under a cloud?"

Cam nodded. "It seems Richard, the heir, cheated at cards and was called on it. Sherry's father was in on the game as well and knew such a scandal on Richard's head would kill their father. He took the blame, fought the duel—deloped, by the way—and went to Virginia." He paused. "He never saw his family again. Richard kept in touch and tried to get him to return once old Lord Wynford died, but by then, Sherry's father was successful in America and stayed there."

Niki worried at a stray strand of hair that had escaped from Shotwell's pins, twisting it around her finger. "I don't know, Cam. I want to believe the man, and I did. But last night bothers me. Anyone wandering around at that time of night is up to no good."

"And what were you doing at that time of night?" Cam asked with a grin, standing. "Getting ready to abscond with the silver?" He turned to the door. "I'm going to solve this mystery for you, Niki. I'm going to ask the man."

Niki jumped up. "Don't you dare!" Cam merely smiled at her and went out of the room, closing the door behind him. Niki heard him knocking on Sheridan's door on the opposite side of the hall. It was only a few minutes until someone knocked at her door. She thought about pretending she wasn't there, but that was the coward's way out. "Come in," she called.

Cam came in first, followed by Sheridan. Sheridan had evidently been in the process of getting ready for supper as he was dressed much as he had been last night, in breeches and a loose shirt. Today, however, he did have on his boots, and his cravat had been hastily—and not very well—tied. He held a piece of paper in his hands. Without a word, he handed her the paper.

It was paper from Lord Larch's desk, the foolscap Larch

used for short notes. On it, in bold strokes, was a rough map. Breconbridge was clearly noted on the left while Wynwoode was carefully sketched in the center. "Lord Larch showed me his maps of the county when I arrived, so I could identify the farms around on my, ah, horse-buying trips. I went back last night to make a map of Wynwoode, so I would know the boundaries. The main purpose of my trip is to find out about Wynwoode and report to my father."

Niki felt her face redden. "I do apologize, Mr. Sheridan. It was absurd of me, but between your nocturnal trip to the library and your subdued behavior, I didn't know what to think."

He smiled sadly. "I suppose my behavior today was suspect. My father told me much of Wynwoode, always with sadness. He loves Virginia, but part of his heart will always be here. It was a strange experience for me to see the places he'd described." He paused and his face hardened. "And to see everything belonging to someone else."

"I understand, Mr. Sheridan, and I apologize for doubting. You must think me very foolish."

He sat down opposite her and smiled. "It's Sherry, if you recall. And no, I don't think it was foolish. As you pointed out to Cam, you have only my word that I am all I say I am. I appreciate your caution, Miss Owen. If, at any time, you have a question, please ask me, and I'll do my best to give you an answer."

Niki nodded. "Did you get any answers at Wynwoode today, Mr. Sheridan?"

"Sherry," he said again.

"I really can't call you that, Mr. Sheridan. It just wouldn't be proper."

He chuckled. "All this English propriety befuddles me. Very well, Miss Owen, I'll settle for Mr. Sheridan. I suppose that's close enough." He smiled at her, and Niki was struck once again at how very nice his smile was. He unconsciously shoved back the stray lock of hair that had fallen over his eyebrow—

a black lock, this time. "Actually, I got an answer or two, but I discovered many more questions." He paused as Cam pulled up a footstool and folded himself onto it, his knees almost reaching his chin. "I do think that perhaps Jackson, or Wynford as he styles himself now, is the man who tried to arrange my demise. He's the only one who would benefit." He grimaced slightly. "I can't possibly describe my feelings when I saw him wearing my ring today."

"The silver signet?"

Sherry nodded. "My father gave me that. He has the original in gold. Uncle Richard sent it to him right after his two sons died. There was no message, no letter, just the ring in a box. Father knew that Richard felt he should have it as he was the heir now. He wrote Uncle Richard and offered to return it, but Uncle Richard wanted him to keep it. He begged Father to come to England. My father was preparing for his trip when the letter came saying that Uncle Richard had died. I think my father cared very much for his brother—I'm sure Cam has told you the story of . . . of . . ."

"He told me," Niki said quietly.

Sherry nodded. "When Father found out that Uncle Richard was dead, he went on a tear across the fields and took a fence that his horse didn't make. As I told you, he broke his leg, and that's why I'm here."

"Thank goodness you are," Cam said. "Your father could well be dead by now if he had come."

Sherry nodded. "But we still have to prove that it was murder. I owe poor Farnsworth that much. If I declare myself—and remember I have no proof at all now—then Father would be declared Lord Wynford, but his life would certainly be in danger. Jackson wouldn't be called to account, but I think he would try to regain the title. I sense that much in him. I don't think he'd let anything come between him and the comfortable living he feels is his."

"I think you're correct," Niki said, "but how do we prove he's the one who tried to kill you?"

Sherry shook his head. "I have no idea." He leaned forward

and spread his palms downward. "If either of you have any schemes, please let me know. Otherwise, I thought I might simply stay around here and try to discover something. I thought if I could somehow find out about Jackson's illegal racing and betting, I might be able to stumble onto something that would implicate him in the murder plans."

Cam looked up at Niki suddenly. "Niki, my girl, I noticed Wynford looking at you today and contriving to spend some time with you. Perhaps you could encourage him somewhat and discover a clue for us."

"Absolutely not." Sherry's tone was harsh. "Jackson's a dangerous man, Cam. I don't want to put Miss Owen in danger."

"What possible danger could there be around here?" Niki asked. She wrinkled her nose. "The only problem I see is that I can't tolerate the man. I find him quite . . . quite . . . slimy."

Sherry laughed. "Quite an apt word, Miss Owen. I would have to agree." The smile faded. "However, when it comes to you encouraging a man such as Jackson, I can not approve at all. Jackson has no scruples and could . . . could possibly put you in harm's way. I don't want you involved."

"I am already involved, Mr. Sheridan." She looked levelly at him. "Furthermore, I would like to see Wynford discredited, more for Comet's sake than anything else."

Sherry threw back his head and laughed. "Put me in my place, didn't you, Miss Owen? Not for me, but for Comet." He stopped laughing and looked at her face as though searching for an answer. "I know you can take care of yourself, Miss Owen, but Jackson would know ways . . . things . . . He's a dangerous man."

"I fully realize that, Mr. Sheridan. I would like to remind you that I am three and twenty. I feel sure I would be in no danger from Lord Wynford."

Sherry shook his head and threw up his hands. "All right, I give up, Miss Owen." He looked at her with a grin. "But promise me that you'll be careful and take no chances whatsoever. Don't be alone with the man, not even for an instant."

Niki lifted an eyebrow. "As I said, I am quite capable of taking care of myself, Mr. Sheridan."

Cam reached out and took her hand.

"I think Sherry's right on that count, Niki. Always have one of us around."

"I'm sure I'll discover a great deal that way." Before they could protest, she rose. "Now, gentlemen, if you'll excuse me. I need to get ready. In case you didn't know, Mama invited Lord Wynford here tonight for supper, so I need to look my best."

Cam rose and pulled at her hairpins, tumbling her hair in a mass around her shoulders. "That shouldn't be too difficult, pet, since there's no competition. You could wear sackcloth if you wanted to, or even look like Blazer."

"You're going to be in the doghouse with Blazer if you keep that up." Niki put her hands on her hips and frowned at him. Cam laughed and dashed out the door before she could say anything to him. She turned to Sherry. "You're going to have to take that incorrigible in hand and teach him some manners."

Sherry laughed again. "Manners? Me teach someone? My mother would love to hear that one. As for what he said, I can't challenge him—I happen to agree." He paused at the door and gave her an appraising look that suddenly changed. Niki felt as if Sherry could see right through her clothes, and she took a step backwards. "Don't ever underestimate yourself, Miss Owen," Sherry said softly. He put a finger under her chin and tilted her head up. "You are a beautiful woman, you know." He let his fingertip glide over the base of her chin, then went out.

Niki sat down again and stared at the closed door. She looked down at herself to make sure that she still had her clothes on. She had never felt so vulnerable in her life. The worst part was that she couldn't describe how she felt. She turned to the mirror and pushed the heavy, dark hair away from her face. She had never thought of herself as pretty. Her mother, all blond, and china-doll pretty was beautiful. Niki didn't look English at all. She looked Spanish like her father—dark hair, dark eyes.

She ran her fingertip over her chin where Sheridan had touched her, then ran her finger over her lips. He had called her a beautiful woman. It was the first time anyone had ever called her that.

Instead of ringing for Shotwell and getting ready for supper, she went to her bed and did something most unlike her—she crawled into bed and hugged the pillow. Then she began sobbing for no reason at all.

# Chapter 8

Shotwell outdid herself, Niki thought. She had chosen for Niki a dress of deep green, trimmed with ecru lace. Shotwell had put her hair on top of her head but had left a curl or two hanging to soften the look. Niki thought she looked much older than her three and twenty years, but Shotwell assured her that she looked perfect.

Wynford looked elegant as well. It was the first time Niki had seen him out of his riding clothes. His tailoring was unmistakably London, and was all the latest style, Niki was sure. Alston was much handsomer, but that wasn't the difference between him and the other men there. Wynford had a quality she couldn't define, but didn't like. There was just something about Wynford, she decided, looking at him as he and Alston chatted with Sheridan before supper. Sheridan looked much different as well. He, too, was dressed impeccably and seemed much more at ease than he had been. He left the group and drifted over to Niki.

"I hope you've changed your mind," he said, sitting beside her. "About trying to discover something from Wynford."

"Certainly not." She smiled at him as Sarah walked toward them. "I fancied we had settled that point."

"Miss Owen, I've thought about this and you simply can't . . ." He paused as Sarah came within earshot and sat down across from them. "If you'll excuse me," Niki said with another smile at Sheridan, "I really need to help Mama welcome our other guests." She smiled at Sarah. "If you would entertain Mr. Sheridan, Sarah, I would more than appreciate it." Sheridan scowled at Niki as she wandered over to Alston and Wynford and began talking. When it was time for supper, she quickly smiled at Wynford and he immediately offered his arm. Niki felt she was making progress, although she was woefully unversed in the ways of flirting. She had seen enough done in London to know the general methods, but she had never practiced. *This is,* she thought grimly to herself as she smiled brilliantly at Wynford, *as good a place to start as any.*

At supper, Niki sat between Wynford and Sheridan, but she ignored the American and concentrated on Wynford. Sherry kept trying to distract her, but she was determined to talk to Wynford. She gradually steered the conversation around to horses. "I'm certainly looking forward to seeing Waxworks in the Brecon races," she said casually. "Have you selected someone to ride him?"

Wynford nodded. "I've had Creevy working with a boy I brought in from London. That's another reason for the local race—I want the boy to get some experience with Waxworks before we move on to the larger races."

"Creevy?" Niki frowned slightly.

"My trainer," Wynford said, turning to her and smiling. "Perhaps you've heard of him. Ned Creevy, perhaps the best jockey ever to ride. I'm fortunate to have him."

Niki smiled in what she hoped was a flirtatious way. "I'm sorry, but I don't know the name. I was in Spain when I was young, then in the country for several years after that, living with my aunt, so I really didn't know what was going on in London."

"I understand." Wynford smiled brilliantly back at her and

touched her arm briefly. Niki had to steel herself not to pull away. Instead, she tried to look encouragingly at Wynford. "I wouldn't expect a young lady to know what was going on in the racing world. It's rather specialized. It's surprising enough to me to see that you're such an excellent rider. An unusual thing for a woman. Most women don't ride well at all. Many say it's the sidesaddle, but I think it's a question of anatomy."

Niki smiled to hide the fact that she was gritting her teeth. The man was insufferable. "Interesting. My Uncle Webster taught me how to ride. We lived in Spain at the time, and he had a stable full of spirited Spanish horses. It was quite an experience."

Wynford leaned toward her slightly. "Oh? Do they still live there and have horses?" He tried for casual and missed. He was almost salivating at the prospect of finding some excellent Spanish horses.

"No. My uncle died, and Aunt Webster moved to England. At the time, my parents were in Turkey. My father was with the diplomatic service, and he and Mama were away most of the time. That's why I lived with my aunt and uncle."

"What did your aunt do with her horses?" Wynford didn't seem extremely interested in Niki's relatives, but the horses were another matter.

"She sold them before we moved from Spain. My uncle had loved them so that it caused Aunt Webster pain every time she saw them. Besides, she really couldn't care for them, and the Spanish help didn't want to move to England." She paused. "I really don't blame them."

Wynford looked at her in surprise. "You don't like England?"

Niki smiled at him. "Of course I like it. It's just that I spent a great deal of my life in Spain and loved it. It is very much different there."

"I've heard." Wynford nibbled at his fruit before he spoke again. "I can't conceive of living anywhere other than here. I had relatives in America, and, from all accounts, they seemed to like it there. My uncle told me that the country was wild and uninhabited. I can't imagine anything worse." He smiled at her and his hand slid up her arm to her elbow, where he gave her a slight squeeze. "I find the charms of England quite enough."

Niki smiled back at him and tried to keep from cringing. She wasn't particularly successful and bumped into Sherry's arm. He glanced down at her and caught her agitation. With a brief smile at her, he leaned over and commented on Wynford's remark about America. Niki was surprised, but realized he must have been eavesdropping on the conversation. Sherry spent the rest of the meal talking about the wonders of America and the frontier. Niki found herself edging away from Wynford and toward Sheridan. He seemed so solid and warm. She took herself in hand and made herself stop. If she was going to discover anything from Wynford, she was going to have to endure being around him.

After supper, it was a relief to go into the drawing room away from the men for a few minutes. Even Mrs. Keene was better than Wynford. "I trust you enjoyed yourself," she said icily. "Here I thought you had set your cap for Alston. Little did I know."

Niki couldn't resist. "I enjoyed myself immensely," Niki answered with a smile. Mrs. Keene flounced off to the pianoforte, where she encouraged Sarah to play until the gentlemen came into the room. Lady Larch then decided on cards, so there was no opportunity to speak further with Wynford in a private way. However, before he left for the evening, he invited Niki back to Wynwoode to visit. Mrs. Keene came up to them, Sarah in tow. "We'd be delighted to return for a visit," Mrs. Keene said as Sarah blushed and gave Niki an exasperated look. "I can think of nothing more interesting than a horse farm, and I'm sure Sarah can't either," she said to Wynford. "Sarah just adores riding, you know."

"Perhaps we can ride tomorrow, then," Wynford said, bowing slightly in Sarah's direction as he took his leave. Mrs. Keene looked satisfied. "Viscount Alston and I had planned

to ride, but he tells me that he has business in the village and
will be away."

Sarah clutched Niki's arm as soon as Wynford was out the
door. "Mama has insisted, Niki," she moaned. "You've got
to show me how to ride in the morning."

"Riding well will take more than a half an hour of instruction,
Sarah," Niki said. "I can't possibly do that. Tell your mother
to come up with some excuse."

"You know Mama." Sarah was near tears. "Could I come
down with spots? A headache."

"Don't worry, Sarah," Niki said with a sigh. "I'll think of
something."

"I knew I could count on you, Niki." Sarah clasped her
arm.

"Mama has this notion that Wynford will offer for me if
. . . if whatever." She paused. "At least his background is
unsavory enough so that he couldn't throw mine in my face."

"Sarah!" Niki gasped. "How could you say such a thing?"
She peered at her. "Is Wynford the man for whom you have
an attachment?"

Sarah stared at her, wide-eyed. "Good heavens, Niki! How
could you say such a thing!" She stalked off to talk to Cam
as Sherry came up beside Niki. "I trust your evening was
worthwhile," Sheridan murmured beside Niki. "Did you learn
anything?"

Niki made a face at him. "I thought you were hanging on
every word, Mr. Sheridan. Was I wrong?"

He offered her his arm and led her to the sofa. "You were
wrong, Miss Owen. I did have to converse with your mother.
After all, she was on my other side." He grinned. "Fortunately,
she found Alston's conversation about London fashions much
more to her taste than my offerings about society in Williamsburg." He glanced around to see if anyone was around
them who might hear. "Did you discover anything of note?"

She shook her head. "No. The only thing he told me was
that his trainer was someone named Creevy. Do you know of
him?"

"No. Cam might. I'll ask him later. Did Wynford ask to further the acquaintance?"

She nodded. "He invited me over to tour more parts of the farm tomorrow. There was also the suggestion that we might go riding during the afternoon." She grinned. "Mrs. Keene practically forced him to ask Sarah to ride. Now Sarah wants me to teach her to ride in the morning."

Sheridan laughed out loud. "Mrs. Keene must be asking Cam to do that as well. That's why Cam is cringing. I don't blame him." He paused. "Would you mind if I went along to escort you tomorrow morning? I'd like to meet this Creevy. He wasn't around when we were there."

"Wynford said that Creevy had been working with a young boy from London who was a new jockey. They're going to use the boy in the Brecon races."

"An unknown? That's odd. I would have thought they'd be using someone with some experience. Hmmm. A good night's work, Miss Owen." He smiled at her.

"Thank you, sir. I hope you see that I was right."

He rose and bowed slightly. "I do hope you'll excuse me, Miss Owen," he said with a lazy smile. "I didn't get a tremendous amount of sleep last night, so I believe I'll go to bed." He made his excuses to the others and left, Cam edging to the door right behind him. As soon as Cam left the room, Sarah came over to Niki. "I don't know whether to be relieved or not. Mama asked Cam to teach me to ride, and he said much the same thing you did," she said. "Mama insists that there can't be much more to riding than sitting on a horse and telling it where to go. She fails to see why you won't help me."

"Because I simply do not wish to be the cause of you breaking your neck, Sarah," Niki said. She smiled at Sarah and patted her hand. "Don't worry. I said I'll think of something."

"You always do." Sarah went with her to bid their mamas good night.

The next morning, Niki was up early, dressed in her habit, ready to take Qadir out before breakfast. To her surprise, Sherry was already in the breakfast room, eating. "You're later than

I thought you would be," he said, helping her sit. "Do try the bacon—it's exceptional."

"I should say the same thing about you." Niki reached for her coffee.

He grinned at her. "That I'm exceptional?"

"Heavens no. That you're later than I thought you would be. I assumed that you'd be at Wynwoode by daybreak."

"I needed to talk to you about camouflage. That's you." He paused in mid-bite. "When we're there, do you think you could distract Wynford—I hate calling him that—while I try to talk to the jockey? If he's a young boy, he might tell me something and not realize it."

Niki sighed. "I'll try. Despite most men thinking that women are born flirtatious, I sadly lack practice. And as for Wynford— you'd better call him that or you'll forget yourself. What would you rather call him?"

He laughed and grinned at her, his blue eyes wicked. "The litany would bring you to blush, Miss Owen. Trust me on that."

"I can well imagine." She finished her coffee and got up. "I must be on my way. I wanted to take Qadir out for a gallop this morning."

"I'll go with you." He finished his coffee and followed her out the door. "Quite a fetching habit, Miss Owen," he said appreciatively, watching her go out the door in front of him. "Thank you, Mr. Sheridan," she said with a raised eyebrow.

"And you said you lacked practice." He chuckled as she stalked off toward the stables.

Qadir and Traveler were ready for a brisk run, so Niki and Sherry gave them their heads. Jem followed on his horse, but Qadir and Traveler left him behind before they had gone far. The two horses galloped over the fields, easily clearing the low hedges. Finally, Niki nudged Qadir to the higher fence and took it easily. Sheridan followed her, then galloped toward the woods, taking a ditch without pause. Not willing to be outdone, Niki came right behind him. They rode at a furious pace on a small track through the woods and headed up a rocky hill.

Sheridan pulled up on top of the hill, which overlooked a

well-kept farm. He paused and pulled the small map from his pocket. "Where have you led me, Miss Owen? We seem to be here, I think"—he pointed to the map with his finger— "so that should be the back side of Wynwoode."

"I don't know. I've never been there from this side. I haven't ridden here before." She looked down at the farm, quiet in the early morning. "Should we go down there now? We could circle around and go right up to the front."

"I intend to—after I've looked around here a little. This is the farthest point from houses around, so if there's anything to hide, it's here." He looked at her and grinned. "Are you with me?"

Niki ignored him and put heels to Qadir. She was over the hedge and into the pasture before Sheridan caught up with her. They rode around for the better part of an hour and saw nothing that looked suspicious. There were several horses, but they looked well cared for and healthy. Niki and Sheridan were just about to circle around to the main road leading to the house when Sheridan stopped suddenly and grabbed Qadir's reins. "Look there," he said pointing. "What's that?"

Niki followed his gaze. Several men seemed to be herding two horses into a closed wagon. One of the horses seemed almost unbroken. It was a large gray, unmistakably a thoroughbred. The other seemed dispirited and went into the wagon without hesitation. "Reminds me of Comet," she said. "No spirit at all."

Sherry nodded. "I asked around about Wynford's racing methods. People were reluctant to talk about him, and then I got one man to open up at the tavern. I didn't learn much except that the man had lost about everything he had to Wynford. He was bitter and felt he had reason, although he didn't go into detail. I thought I might try him again later. I might learn something there."

They watched as the workers finally cornered the gray and got him loaded. The wagon moved away slowly, headed not for the main house, but for the road. "Taking them to market, I suspect." Sherry nibbled at his lower lip for a moment.

"Would you consider going back to Breconbridge with Jem? I'd like to follow that wagon and see where it's going."

"We left Jem somewhere behind, in case you hadn't noticed. It would be just as bad for me to go back home unaccompanied as it would be for me to go up to Wynwoode alone."

"You can't go to Wynwoode alone," he said decisively. "I'll take you back and find Jem. He can take you home." He looked at the dust the wagon raised on the road. "I just have a feeling about that horse. If anyone had a horse like that gray, he'd keep it and race him. There has to be something going on."

Niki started to protest, but knew there was no use. Grudgingly she turned back to find Jem. They had gone almost halfway to Breconbridge before they found him. He was frantic. "I thought you had been hurt, and I'd missed you," he said.

"Jem, you know I ride better than that."

"Accidents happen." Jem couldn't keep the worry out of his voice. Sherry explained that he was going to follow the wagon and left them. Following Jem's directions, he cut across country, riding at a good clip across the hill to intercept the road farther up.

"I take it that Mr. Sheridan has told you everything?" Niki turned and headed Qadir toward the road. "Including what Robbie and I did."

"That he did." Jem said nothing else. He didn't need to. "I know it was wrong, but we had to do something to save that horse."

"I would have done the same." Jem spoke quietly, but there was an undercurrent to his words. "I just hope there's no others." Niki nodded, and they rode on in silence, Niki thinking about the possibility of other horses. At the road, she turned Qadir toward Wynwoode. "We need to get back to Breconbridge," Jem said. "Those were Mr. Sheridan's orders."

Niki shook her head. "Wynford invited me to visit. It wouldn't be polite to be this close and not visit him, Jem." Jem frowned, but followed her closely. He clearly disapproved. To his immense relief, when they was almost to the front gate of Wynwoode, they caught sight of Cam. He rode up to her, his cravat askew, and his hair obviously uncombed. "Thought I'd go riding," he said with a guilty flush. "Alston and I were supposed to go, but he had some business." He lowered his voice. "I think his father sent a solicitor to meet him at Lisway. Alston must be in the suds on some front."

Niki's eyebrows rose. "I rather thought Alston was his own man."

"He is to a point, just like the rest of us. However, his father controls the purse." He looked behind him as if someone were there. "I left early, so I could get over here and see their morning routine," he explained briefly.

"Before Mrs. Keene got up?" Niki couldn't resist. Cam's ears turned as red as his hair. "Drat it, Niki, I don't want to offend the woman, but to ask me to teach Sarah to ride before breakfast . . ."

Niki laughed. "Mrs. Keene told Wynford that Sarah loves to ride. Perhaps I can think of something to rescue you."

"I wish you would." He looked around. "Where's Sherry?"

Niki told him what they had seen and that Sherry had followed the wagon. "He thought they might be taking the horses to market."

"To the races at Wilmay, I'd think," Jem said. "There's a fair there today. Not a big fair, but plenty of local folks will be there."

Cam nodded. "More money changes there than one would realize. Farmers always like to bet on horses." He glanced at Jem. "Wouldn't you say that most of the horses there will be local horses?"

"I think so." Jem frowned as he thought. "Small places like that don't attract much in the way of outside horses. Most of what's there should be homegrown."

"Then the gray will take everything," Niki said. "Anyone could see that. He was a superb horse."

"If anyone dares to run against him." Cam looked around. "We'll just have to wait for Sherry's report when he gets back." He smiled at Niki. "In the meantime, let's beard the lion in his den, shall we?'' He urged his horse to a gallop down the long avenue leading up to Wynwoode. Not to be outdone, Niki urged Qadir after him. They were neck and neck by the time they reached the house.

Wynford walked up to them as they stopped, and he took Qadir's reins. ''Well done, Miss Owen. Another quarter mile and you'd have been well ahead!'' He held his hands up to help her dismount and it seemed to Niki that he held her waist just a fraction too long. Cam had dismounted and come around to join her before Wynford let her go. Wynford gave the reins of the horses to a groom with instructions to cool them and rub them down. Then he held out his arm to Niki. ''I hoped you might come early, so I had the cook ready a late breakfast. As soon as I saw the two of you riding up, I sent word inside, so things should be ready shortly.''

Since it would have been the outside of rude to refuse, Niki had to go inside and have breakfast again. Thank goodness she hadn't eaten much before she left Breconbridge. They sat and ate an excellent breakfast. ''I brought a cook from London as soon as my inheritance was certain,'' Wynford told them.

''So everything has been settled?'' Niki asked, looking at him over a cup of chocolate. By her calculations, the American heir had been dead only a few days. Wynford would hardly have had time to get in touch with the solicitors, much less find a cook and install him at Wynwoode.

''Oh, yes. As soon as the American heir was identified and the magistrate brought a finding of death by accident, everything was released to me.'' He glanced around. ''Of course, I had been more or less in charge for several years. After Uncle Richard's sons were killed, he was never the same. He kept to his room and left things to me.''

''That was certainly sad.'' Cam buttered a muffin. ''Carriage accident, wasn't it?''

Wynford nodded. ''They were going to school. No one was ever quite sure what happened, but it seemed that a wheel came off the carriage and they took a nasty tumble into the river.''

''What about the driver and groom?'' Niki wasn't really

interested, but felt she should say something. She really wanted to get outside and see if she could see any more abused horses.

There was a slight pause. "The driver was killed. The groom, poor man, evidently was injured or killed immediately. He was presumed drowned, although no body was ever recovered. Uncle Richard, of course, settled a generous sum on his family. I have no idea if his remains were ever found." He looked around the table and saw that they were finished. "Would you like to linger and talk, or would you prefer to ride out and see the rest of the estate?"

Cam and Niki practically jumped up together. Outside, they mounted their horses and rode off to the edge of Wynwoode that bordered Breconbridge. "By the by," Wynford said as they rode, "I was on the other side of the estate yesterday and happened to see someone in your far pasture, the one with the old barn in it, and went to investigate. It was your brother, Robbie, searching for treasure."

Niki laughed. "He's going to have the entire forest dug up if he continues. I thought he was getting disgusted and had decided it was fruitless."

"Perhaps." Wynford smiled at her. "But that wasn't the important thing I wished to mention. After I talked to him, I started back to my own lands, and saw that there were tracks around your barn. Naturally, I went to investigate as I hadn't heard that you had been pasturing any horses there." He paused as Cam and Niki were afraid to breathe. "I hate to tell you this, but I think poachers or horse thieves may have been using your barn."

"Really?" Niki tried to appear innocent. "What makes you think that?"

"Tracks. The fact that someone had tried to clean up things in a way that would appear that no one had been there. The fact that you haven't been using the barn yourself. Several things."

"I'm certainly glad you told us," Cam said, not looking at Wynford. "I'll tell the men to watch."

"I think it would be a good precaution. As you know, I had

a horse stolen from me a while back. If I'm not mistaken, I heard that Ayers over at Lisway had one stolen as well—a prize he'd just bought at Tattersall's."

Cam shook his head. "It's becoming epidemic. I heard that there had been several stolen from Madford, and you know what a small town it is. You'd think the penalty would deter thieves."

"If I catch the thief who took Comet, I certainly intend to see that the law is enforced to the limit." Wynford looked grim.

Niki shuddered. "What's over there?" she asked to try to distract them.

They rode here and there around the estate, and Niki had to admit that it seemed well cared for. It was perplexing. She had expected to find everything in a state of disrepair, and there were some things—unmended fences here and there, some fields that needed clearing of brambles, but overall, things were in good shape. Even the horses they saw seemed to be quite sleek and contented. By the time they returned to the main house, she knew no more than when she had left it.

"Come in for refreshment. I know you must be thirsty," Wynford said, as they rode up to the house. Niki tried to decline, telling him that she needed to get back to Breconbridge to entertain Sarah, but Wynford insisted. She and Cam finally accepted.

Wynford helped Niki dismount again, and again held her much too long. She was compelled to put her hands on his and move them. She looked up at him, right into his eyes, and forced herself to smile. Granted the man was handsome, granted he was charming, but there was something about him that made Niki want to shudder every time he got close to her. It was difficult to smile at him and pretend.

"There you are!" They turned as someone called out from the house. Mrs. Keene was standing in the door, Sarah right behind her, looking miserable. "Naughty girl, you ran off and left us! We had to come over by ourselves. Of course"—she smiled archly up at Wynford as he came in, escorting Niki—

"Sarah would have ridden over herself, but I did so want to come along, so we had to come in the barouche."

"Of course," Wynford said. Cam started to make his apologies and leave, but Mrs. Keene nabbed him and drew him in the little drawing room. "Naughty boy you are, too," she said, "to have gone off and left Sarah. She was so looking forward to riding with you."

As Wynford's cook had the midday meal ready, they all went inside to eat. How Mrs. Keene did it, Niki would never know, but poor Wynford was seated with Sarah on one side and Mrs. Keene on other. Niki couldn't say that she was displeased with the arrangement. The same could not have been said for Wynford.

# Chapter 9

Niki was persuaded by Sarah and Mrs. Keene to ride back to Breconbridge in the barouche with them. When it was time to leave, Wynford escorted her out and helped her in. Rather than just hand her into the barouche, he held her hand and squeezed it, his thumb slipping familiarly over her palm and up her wrist. She couldn't stop herself from looking at him in surprise. "I hope to see you tomorrow, Miss Owen" he murmured with a smile. "Your brother offered to show me around Breconbridge. I'm particularly interested in getting a good look at the horse your guest, Mr. Sheridan, brought in. I saw him yesterday, of course, but I didn't get to examine him up close."

"What horse?" Niki asked, trying to keep her voice level, wondering if he knew about Comet. She was afraid she was going to turn pale and collapse.

"Traveler, I believe he said the name was."

Niki sat down hard in the barouche, and Wynford closed the door. "Yes, I believe that's it. He seems to be quite a horse. Mr. Sheridan was fortunate to find him."

Wynford raised an eyebrow. "Quite. I'll see you tomorrow, Miss Owen. Miss Keene, Mrs. Keene." He waved as they left.

"You seem to have made a conquest," Sarah said with a smile.

Niki looked at her in surprise. "Whatever do you mean, Sarah?"

"I'm talking about Wynford." Sarah looked relieved.

"Of course, it would be to Wynford's advantage to marry into the family whose land marches with his," Mrs. Keene said.

"That eliminates me, then." Niki smiled sunnily at her. "After all, I stand to inherit nothing. I'm merely a stepchild."

"I'm sure," Mrs. Keene said, looking at Niki shrewdly, "that Lord Larch will provide generously. After all, I have noticed that you seem to have become a part of his family quickly."

Niki glanced over at Cam riding alongside and smiled at him. "Yes, she has," he said with a grin. "And, of course Papa will do everything possible for my dear sister." His grin was innocent, but Niki could read the devilment behind it. Mrs. Keene was oblivious to Cam's other meaning and immediately began quizzing him about Wynford.

Niki paid no attention to the conversation, confident that Mrs. Keene would get nothing from Cam. Instead, Niki fell quiet, thinking her own thoughts. She almost shuddered as she thought of Wynford's thumb on her wrist. Mrs. Keene didn't notice her shudder or the silence from both Niki and Sarah.

Halfway to Breconbridge, Niki broke her reverie and turned her attention to the conversation. Mrs. Keene was still quizzing Cam about Wynford, and the entire conversation seemed to center on how wonderful Wynford was. Mrs. Keene was obviously trying to scheme a way to match Sarah and Wynford. Sarah deserved better, Niki thought, no matter what Mrs. Keene wished. Niki decided that she would warn Sarah immediately. Wynford was not a man to marry.

No matter what they had thought to discover from Wynford, Sheridan was right—it wasn't worth it. Wynford was not only dangerous, there was something else about him, and Niki tried to identify just what it was as the well-sprung barouche rocked along the road, but she couldn't. She knew only that something about Wynford wasn't quite right. Every time he got near her, she felt as though she had gotten beside something particularly evil and malevolent. As they neared home, she tried to shake off the feeling. She had promised Cam and Sherry to find out what she could—and she owed it to them to try. She owed it to Comet.

Niki sought out Cam when they were back at Breconbridge, and they walked out to the stables to talk. Private conversation seemed easier there than in the house. They found Robbie and Jem again attending to Comet, or Comment, as they were supposed to call him now. Quick Comment was looking like a thoroughbred now, his coat was healing nicely, and he was beginning to act frisky. Jem and Robbie were soaking his foot again.

"He'll never race, I don't think, but he's still a good horse. Shy, though. I walked through here with a whip in my hand— not to use on him, understand—I was just taking it to the tack room, and the poor lad cowered back in the corner. It was partly my fault, I hit my palm with the whip just as I passed by him. He was terrified." He reached up and stroked Comment's neck. "That you were, boy." The horse pawed at the ground and nodded his head as though he understood.

"Did either of you learn anything today?" Robbie asked.

"Nothing of use," Niki said, sitting down beside Robbie on a short bench.

"I met the jockey and the trainer," Cam said, folding himself down on some hay. He squirmed and straightened his legs out in front of him. "The jockey's name is Sid Ford, and, to be the hottest thing out of London, he didn't seem to know a great deal about horses. He looked more like a slimy stable rat to me."

"From the stews, probably," Jem said. "Boys there are always hanging around the stables looking for work, hoping either to pick some pockets or make some money riding." He moved Quick Comment's foot from the bucket and tossed the water away. Then he turned the bucket upside down and sat down on it. "So you think he's no rider."

"I didn't say that. He's probably a jockey, all right. I just didn't think he had any feel for horses. He didn't seem to care about anything except winning."

Jem nodded. "I've seen that. Those lads never get much of anywhere. They beat their horses and think the whip is the way to get to the finish line. Anyone who cares a whit for his horse won't let one of those jockeys within a quarter mile of it." He looked down at his crippled hand and tried to flex his fingers, but they didn't move. "I knew one of those years ago—the very worst."

Niki reached over and patted him on the arm. There seemed nothing to say, so she changed the subject. "What about the trainer, Cam? I don't remember meeting him. How did you manage it?"

"Oh, I wandered off to the stables while Wynford was strolling around the gardens with you right before breakfast. Remember that I said I wanted to check on my horse? I thought you might be able to handle Wynford for fifteen minutes or so.

Niki scowled at him. "He was polite then."

"Then?" Cam sat up straight. "Did he overstep his bounds?"

"No." Niki frowned and then shrugged. "I don't know what it is about the man, Cam. He does little things—holding my hand just a fraction too long, not turning loose when he gets me from my horse. Just little things, but they make my skin crawl."

"Stay away from him then, Niki. Nothing's worth having to put up with that."

She smiled at him. "If Mrs. Keene has her way, no one else will be allowed near." She laughed. "Poor Sarah. It must be terrible to have a mama like that." She laughed again as Robbie and Cam made faces. "Now, what about the trainer?"

"Creevy? Well, he's . . ."

"Did you say Creevy?" Jem asked, his face suddenly furious.

"Yes, that's the man. Fairly short, stocky. Black hair, heavy eyebrows." Cam spoke quietly. "Do you know him?"

"A scar on one side of his face and another on his arm?"

Cam looked at him curiously. "I didn't see his arm, but, yes, he did have a scar on the side of his face. Ran from here to here." He ran his finger from high on his left cheekbone down in front of his ear. "Looked like an old scar."

Jem got up and turned his back to them. They stayed silent while he composed himself. He held up his broken, useless hand. "He gave me this."

"Is he the jockey you meant—the worst one?" Robbie asked.

Jem turned around, his face carefully set. "Yes." He sat back down. "Tell me about him."

Cam was devastated, and it showed on his face. "I'm sorry, Jem. I had no idea that you knew him or that he was . . . he was the one."

"Tell me about him."

Cam sighed and rumpled his hair even more than Niki could have believed possible. "He's at Wynwoode and evidently has been for a while. From the way Niki and Robbie described the man, he's the one who beat Com . . . Comment so. The man strikes me as capable of anything."

Jem got up and turned away again, looking not at the lush greenery of Breconbridge, but at years gone by. "That's true, he is." He paused and looked down at his useless hand. "I was riding for old Lord Aynsley at the time, and he had the best stable in the south. I was winning every race I rode in. Aynsley was more than pleased with my performance and had promised me that he'd give me a share of a particular horse." He turned and looked at them, the controlled expression on his face slipping. "You can't imagine what that would have meant to me—a boy from the slums who'd started by mucking out stables. It was my chance to have something, to . . ." He broke off and turned his back to them again. In a moment, he continued, his voice hoarse with emotion. "Creevy heard about what Aynsley had promised me. He told me that I'd never get it, but I put that down to just talk." He stopped again for a minute. "I was going to ride the horse at the Derby races, and he was the favorite. I thought my piece of him was assured. I was called away for a few minutes right before the race by a boy who said that Aynsley wanted to see me. I hunted him up, but he said there must have been some mistake, he had merely sent someone down to wish me luck. I got back to the stables just as the horses were being led out and didn't check the horse. He was skittish, but I thought that was nerves. As soon as I mounted, I knew something was wrong, but I didn't have time to check. I should have gotten off right then, forgotten about the race, but all I could think about was owning a part of him, finally having something. So I didn't.'' He stopped and gripped the top of a fence post with his good hand. His crippled hand flopped on top of the fence rail. ''To make a long story short, the horse went wild—he plunged and reared, taking down another horse and breaking his own leg. He rolled over on me and pinned my hand backwards. I jerked it without thinking and another horse galloped over it.'' He looked down at his hand. ''I lost my hand and my livelihood and my chance. While they took me back to try to patch me up, while they were putting the horse down, I sent a good friend of mine to look over things. He found not one, but three burrs under the saddle blanket. The horse's back had been raked raw before the burrs were put on and it appeared that salt had been rubbed on him. He must have been in agony.''

''Creevy?'' Niki asked.

''I could never prove it, but I knew in my heart that he was the one. He took too much pleasure in my downfall. I heard rumors later.''

Robbie went over and touched Jem on the arm. ''We'll get him, Jem. He's the one who did this to Comment, and we'll make sure he doesn't do it again.'' Jem patted Robbie on the head with his good hand and walked slowly off.

''Another mark against Wynford,'' Cam said.

''Maybe he doesn't know about Creevy,'' Niki said, taking Comment's bridle and leading him to his stall.

''Care to take a wager on that?'' Cam asked, following her. Niki put Comment in the stall and shut the door. ''No. I'm sure he knows. In fact, that's probably the reason he hired Creevy. After seeing what the man did to Comment, I can believe he'd do anything."

Alston returned that night, much subdued, and, much to Sarah's delight, spent much of the evening playing cards with her. Niki and Cam kept listening to the clock in the hall strike, wondering where Sheridan was. He hadn't sent word, and he hadn't returned. "If he doesn't get back by midnight, I'm going out looking for him," Cam whispered.

Niki twisted the embroidery she had picked up to pass the time. She had made a mess of it. "Do you suppose anything could have happened to him?" She could almost see the laughing blue eyes and his smile. Her next vision was of him lying cold in a ditch, killed when his identity had been revealed. "He said someone tried to kill him before, Cam. Could they have discovered him?"

"I don't know. It's possible—anything's possible, Niki." He looked around at everyone gossiping and playing cards. "I can't slip away until everyone goes to bed." He ran his fingers through his hair. Niki was reminded of the way Sheridan's lock of hair always fell down over his eyebrow. "I want to go with you, she whispered.

"No."

"Yes. There's no reason I shouldn't. I can ride as well as you can."

"Dash it all, Niki, you can't do that. You just can't."

"Can't do what, Camden?" Lady Larch came over and sat across from them. "Just what are you two conspiring against?" she asked with a laugh. "Or are you conspiring *for* something? The two of you are getting as bad as Robbie."

"Heavens!" Cam said in mock horror. "You malign me. Has Robbie been talking to you about the Robin Hood project?"

Niki knew an attempt to change the subject when she saw it and decided to help. "Robbie has been after everyone to help him on that. Wouldn't we be surprised if he actually found something?"

"The only things Robbie is going to find are a pile of rocks and some tree roots. I've been dodging him faithfully. The next thing you know, Robbie will have me in shirtsleeves, holding a shovel, and searching for treasure.'' He laughed. ''If you must know, Mama,'' he said to Lady Larch, ''we're trying to think of something to do for Father's birthday. You know it's only a fortnight away.''

Lady Larch put her hand to her head. ''I didn't know! Or, that is, I knew, but I had completely forgotten! Oh, dear. What can we do that would be a surprise? Do you think we need to get him a gift? Or do you think that just a celebration would be enough? How many people should we invite?''

''Stop, Mama!'' Niki found herself laughing in spite of her worry about Sherry. ''One thing at a time.'' She glanced at Cam, partly in admiration for his Banbury tale, and partly in mischief. ''Why don't we leave the entire thing up to Cam? After all, he knows Papa through and through. What better person to plan?''

''Wonderful!'' Lady Larch smiled and looked at her husband to make sure he hadn't heard the conversation. ''Do count on me to do whatever you ask of me, Camden. What a splendid idea!'' She glanced again at Lord Larch. ''I'll leave the two of you to plan so your papa won't be suspicious. Just let me know what you need.'' She stood up, smiling. ''I just love surprises!''

Cam looked gloomy as she left. ''If she expects me to plan something, she'll have a surprise all right.'' He gave Niki an indignant look. ''Why on earth did you suggest I plan anything?''

Niki grinned at him. ''Serves you right for telling such a tale. Although, I do admit that it was almost as inspired as Robbie's Robin Hood story. The two of you must have had years of practice to come up with these bouncers.''

Cam grinned back. ''We have.'' He glanced at his father and thought a moment. ''Why don't we have a race? We could use the track at Ayleswood. The races there would be over, and we could invite everyone.''

''Why not have it at the little track here at Breconbridge?

We could invite all the neighbors and the village. Your father—Papa—would probably enjoy something right here at home. Besides, it would give us an excuse to go to the village and various places nearby without having Mama asking eternally what we were doing.''

"Good idea." Cam made a face and nodded. "Besides, if it were here, we wouldn't have to do very much work to have everything ready. Mama would see to the refreshments, and we could invite everyone by word of mouth. We could say that we didn't want written invitations because it was a surprise.'' He nodded. "Yes, that's it, I think. We wouldn't have to do much at all.''

"Ever lazy, Camden." Niki laughed at him, then jumped as the clock in the hall struck. "It's eleven and he hasn't returned, Cam. I'm getting worried.'' She bit her lower lip as she fretted.

Cam refused to look at her. "I was worried four hours ago.'' He stood. "I'm going to make my excuses and go up. I'll go searching for him in an hour." He circled to his parents, and in a few minutes he was out the door. Niki got up hastily as Mrs. Keene started toward her. She tossed her embroidery down and sped over to her mother. "I'm beginning to get a headache," she said, putting her hand to her head and staring at her feet. She simply couldn't look directly at her mother and tell a falsehood, even one that was socially acceptable. When was she going to learn to bend the truth without looking as guilty as if she had just committed murder? Never, she supposed with a sigh as she left the company.

She went upstairs and knocked on Cam's door, telling him she was going to be in her room. She made him promise to let her know the minute Sheridan returned. He was dressed to go out, his watch open on the table in front of him.

Niki closed the door to her room but didn't change. She blew out her candle and opened the draperies so the moon could shine inside. She looked out the window for a while, worried, thinking of Sheridan and of the dozens of things that could have happened to him. True, he seemed to be a devil and a rogue, and an American to boot, but she realized that she had come to like him. The thought of never again seeing him smile was enough to make her shiver.

She heard the clock strike the half hour and heard the noise of everyone following Lord Larch's lead in keeping country hours. In just a short while, everyone would be in bed. She sat in a chair by the window, listening to the doors shut as maids and valets helped everyone and went downstairs to their own beds. At last the house grew quiet. She flipped open the tiny watch her father had given her and looked at the time. It was five minutes until midnight. She stood and looked out the window again. She stopped and held her breath as she thought she saw a movement at the end of the tree-lined alley leading up to Breconbridge. There had been a flash of moonlight glancing off of something metal, she thought. She waited, peering out the window, and thought there was a shadow that moved. It was large—like a horse. Sheridan was riding back, she thought. She waited, watching, but she saw nothing else. The shadows had swallowed up whatever it had been, and she saw nothing except the moon making strange shapes with the trees and shadows. Behind her, she heard a sound and realized it was Cam's door opening softly. She ran across her room and opened the door. "Cam," she whispered, "come here."

"I've got to go." He glanced up and down the hall which was lit by one candle left burning in a sconce. He moved toward the stairs.

"Come look out my window," she whispered, grabbing his arm. "I thought I saw something." She pulled him inside her room.

"Dash it, Niki, this isn't proper, you know." He tiptoed inside, his boots in his hand. "Actually, I'm not even sure this would be proper if you were my sister."

"Ssshhh." She held a finger to her lips. "I thought I saw something move in the alley out front, then there was a flash of light as something caught the moonlight. I thought it might be Sheridan on Traveler. Look." She dashed to the window, Cam right after her. They looked for a moment but saw nothing except shadows.

"You're imagining things," Cam told her. "I'm leaving. I thought I'd wake Jem and take him with me." He turned away.

Niki looked out again and saw again a large shadow. The horse had broken away from the shadows and moved out into the open space between the alley and the stables. It was Traveler—she would know that big horse anywhere. Her heart leaped with relief. "There he is, Cam. Look!"

Cam looked again, then put his hands on the window and opened it. "What's wrong?" Niki asked.

"I don't know. Sheridan's weaving in the saddle."

"Maybe he's just tired. He's had a long day, after all."

Cam sat down and started to put on his boots, then got back up again. "I can't risk anyone hearing me. I'll see you later." He grabbed his boots, then ran out the door and down the stairs before Niki could stop him. She hesitated a second, glanced back out the window but saw no one there at all. She snatched up a thin cashmere shawl and ran out after Cam.

She hurried to the stables, going at a half run, the moonlight bright enough for her to see. She rounded the corner of the stables and saw Traveler standing there, Jem at his head. Cam was kneeling on the ground. As she came closer, she saw something else. Sherry was sitting on the ground, holding his head. His clothing was torn—one sleeve was pulled from the shoulder seam and was hanging in shreds. "What happened?" she gasped.

Niki stopped and caught her breath as Cam turned to look at her, his face white. That was when she saw that one side of Sherry's head and face was covered with something that glistened black in the moonlight. It took Niki a moment to realize that Sheridan's face was smeared with his own blood.

# Chapter 10

Niki felt her knees go weak, and she had to grab on to the side of the stable to keep from falling to the ground. "What happened?" she asked in a voice she didn't recognize as her own.

Cam looked over his shoulder at her. "He's been shot."

Niki put her hand over her mouth. "Oh, no! Is he . . . is he . . . ?" For the first time in her life, she thought she was going to faint.

"No, he's not dead." Cam turned back around.

"Not dying either," Sherry said faintly, "but damn close to feeling like it. My head has to be the size of a bushel basket."

Niki ran up to them and knelt beside him. She put her hand on the clean side of his face and reassured herself that he was still warm and breathing. "You look terrible," she blurted.

"Thank you so much." Sherry tried to shake his head, then moaned slightly at the pain.

"We've got to get him into the house, Cam," she said. "He needs a doctor."

"No doctor," Sherry said faintly. "He'd see . . . the dye."

He closed his eyes and slumped. Niki put her hand behind his shoulder and held him.

"He's right," Cam said. "No doctor."

"Don't be silly. Is this charade worth someone dying?" Niki glanced down as Sherry leaned into her, the clean side of his head lolling onto her breast and shoulder.

"You heard him—no doctor," Cam said firmly. "Jem, you take care of Traveler, and I'll get him into the house. Niki can open the doors." He put his arm under Sherry's. "Do you think you can stand?"

Sherry nodded, almost imperceptibly, and tried to stand. Between Cam and Niki, he stood up, but he wobbled when they tried to move. "Let me tie the horse and help you," Jem said. "I can come back and stable Traveler in a few minutes. It won't hurt him at all." He moved to step between Niki and Sherry and took part of Sherry's weight on his shoulder. Slowly they made their way to the house. Niki ran ahead to open the door, peering inside to make sure no one saw them. The hallway and stairs were lit, as usual, to find one's footing. Jem and Cam half dragged Sherry up the steps and into his room. They placed him on the bed and took off his boots.

"I'll go see to the horse and then come back. You might need me." Jem touched the side of Sherry's head. "I think it may look worse than it really is. Head wounds bleed a great deal." Jem shook his head, started to say something, and thought the better of it. Instead, he slipped out into the hall and pulled the door closed behind him.

Niki quickly poured water from the pitcher into the bowl and wet a towel. She was surprised to see that her hands were shaking and forced herself to stop and take a deep breath. Then she leaned over the edge of the high bed and began swabbing gently at Sherry's face. The water was red in just a second. Cam held Sherry's head so that she could wash the blood away. "The bullet went here," Cam said, pointing with his finger. "Lucky it didn't do anything except graze him."

"Lucky, you say?" Sherry moaned. "You should feel my head."

Cam chuckled and glanced at Niki. "Can you take care of him by yourself for a minute?" She nodded, and he got up, then paused by the door. "It isn't really proper for me to leave you alone in his bedroom, is it?"

"I'm harmless," Sherry croaked from the bed.

Niki paused in her swabbing and glared at Cam. "Here we are in the middle of all this mess, and you worry about being proper? Really, Cam." She rinsed out the towel and began washing gently around Sherry's temple. Cam went out, chuckling to himself.

"How does it look?" Sherry asked, grimacing.

"Much better." Niki held up the candle and peered.

"Damn, watch out!" Sherry held a hand up to his cheek. Niki looked down and saw that hot candle wax had dripped onto his skin. "Sorry." She blew on the candle wax to harden it slightly and then peeled it up. "Anyway, your wound looks better than I thought it would. Most of it is in your hair and will be covered. Right here above your temple, you'll have a visible place, but I think you might get by with saying that you ran into a limb or some such."

"A limb? Dear heavens, my reputation as a rider will be gone," Sherry moaned, trying to sit up. "Is there a hand mirror around?"

"Don't you have one?" She glanced at his toilet articles arranged on top of a chest. There was only his shaving kit and a brush.

"Inside the shaving kit." He swung his legs over the side of the bed and sat there a minute.

"What's wrong?"

"Nothing," he said between clenched teeth. "I was just waiting for the room to stop going around and around." He blinked. "Could you get me the mirror? I want to see the damage for myself."

"All right, but promise me you won't move. Don't try to stand up."

He put his fingers to his forehead, gingerly moving down

toward his injured temple. "All right. It'll take a while for the floor to stop moving anyway."

Niki opened the shaving kit and took out a battered, but once handsome silver mirror. The initials WSD were engraved in script on the back. Just as she closed the kit, she heard a tapping at the door. She opened the door, mirror in hand, to find Cam standing there. He had a full bottle of brandy and two glasses in his hand. "What . . ." Niki started to ask, then stopped as they heard a door click open down the hall. Cam dashed by her into Sherry's room together and shoved the brandy bottle into her hands while he closed the door almost shut. He left it open just a crack and peered out. Then he closed the door softly and turned around, his finger to his lips. "Papa," he whispered, leaning back against the door. "Thank God I got in here and didn't meet him." He looked at Niki, wide-eyed. "Thank God he doesn't know you're in here. Talk about a mess! There would be the devil to pay."

Niki was standing beside the bed, the brandy bottle in one hand and the mirror in the other. Sherry looked at her and reached over to take the brandy bottle. Without waiting for Cam to pour into the glasses, he pulled the stopper and turned the bottle up, taking a long swallow. He wiped his mouth with the back of his hand and handed the bottle back to her. She, in turn, gave it to Cam, who filled the two glasses and handed one to Sherry. "I knew this was the medicine you needed," he said with a grin.

After the glass of brandy, Niki handed Sherry the mirror and he examined the graze. "To be no bigger than that, it feels like hell," he muttered. "Feels like a whole cannonball hit my head."

"How did it happen?" Niki asked.

Sherry pushed the falling lock of hair back from his eyebrows. "I was trying to find out something and . . ." He paused. "I suppose you could say I was breaking and entering." He gave a weak chuckle. "What's another crime when you're already in for horse stealing?"

"Nothing like a hanging offense to make one feel brave."

Cam laughed. "Breaking and entering? You're coming down in status. Next thing you'll be picking pockets."

Sherry tried to grin back at him. "My respectability seems to have disappeared since I met this family." He glanced longingly at the brandy bottle. "I suppose I'd better start at the beginning."

"Always a good place," Cam said, pouring Sherry another glass of brandy. "Niki told me you went off after a closed wagon with the two horses in it. one a real looker and the other a nag."

"The gray was a thoroughbred if I've ever seen one," Niki said.

Sherry nodded, then grimaced. He propped the pillows up and leaned back against them as Cam pulled off his boots. Then Sherry wiggled his toes and stretched. "I caught up with them and followed them into town," he said. "They were going to the fair at Wilmay. Evidently a part of the Wilmay Fair is a series of horse races. Dozens of farmers there, several with their prize horses. They tried to get a race or two started with the prime horse, which . . ." he paused and looked at them, "went into the wagon as a gray, but came out a black." He waited for their reaction.

"Dye?" Cam asked.

"I suppose so. I didn't get close enough to examine the horse. Went by the name of Dark Star. Anyway, they offered to race anything there, but didn't get any takers for the better part of the day. Anyone who knew horses took one look and decided against running with that one. Finally, one brave soul decided to risk a race—no betting. The gray—or black—lost by a nose."

"Lost? A horse like that against farm horses?" Niki raised an eyebrow.

"Lost. I suspected deliberately, but who knows?" He sipped his brandy. "Anyway, there were a couple of races after that, and the whole time that broken-down nag was standing there looking as if it were going to drop over dead any minute. It was the subject of much laughter, I can tell you. Wynford's men—on second thought I prefer to call him Jackson—Jackson's men were calling themselves Badger and Dunbarton. One of them was really the one named Creevy, I think. I met him the other day.''

Cam nodded. ''We've heard about Creevy.''

Sherry took another sip of brandy and glanced at Cam. ''At any rate, there were two more races until the main race and Jackson's horse—the dyed gray—ran in both of them. He split—took one and lost one. The winnings were a pittance. Then came the main race and there was a tremendous amount of money for a small, farm-town race. Badger had been working the crowd and taking bets on his horse, the broken-down nag. Needless to say, the odds were astronomical, and no one would bet on such a horse, so Badger bet a considerable sum on his horse to win. I'll have to give Jackson's men credit—he did warn everyone that the horse ran like the wind.''

''And he did, I'd wager,'' Cam said with a grimace. ''Just like Comet would do in a race.''

Sherry nodded. ''Took the whole thing. Just got on the track and ran away from everyone, including the thoroughbred. And there wasn't a thing anyone could do. They had been told the horse was fast, and the bets had been legal.''

''Still they'd been taken,'' Niki said.

''Of course.'' Sherry finished his brandy and started to move to put his glass on the table beside the bed. Niki reached over and took it from him. ''I tried to get as close as I could to take a look at the horse, but they collected their money and got out of there as fast as they could. I think most of the horse's injuries were superficial. Some sores, mud smeared on his coat. They even had some blood on his nose—I think that's what put most people off. His coat was dull, but that could have been dye of some sort.''

''How did they tumble to you?'' Cam leaned back in his chair. ''You said you were involved in a little breaking and entering. What happened?''

''Badger and Dunbarton—or Creevy and whoever, if you prefer—stopped at an inn on the road for supper. They were flush, of course, and I gave them time to get a bottle before I went inside. Badger was already in his cups, but Creevy didn't seem drunk at all, although he was drinking steadily. He was looking around, and I kept my back to him.''

''Since you'd met him,'' Niki noted. ''It would have been sticky for you to appear to be following him at the inn.''

''Exactly. Anyway, their meal was brought to them, and I decided to go outside and take a look at the horses. I was inside the wagon when Creevy came out to check on them. He caught me and we got into a fight.'' He tried a grin that wobbled a bit. ''He's certainly strong for a little man.''

''He was a jockey,'' Cam said briefly. ''Jem has always said that jockeys are the toughest men alive.''

''I believe it.'' Sherry grinned again. ''We fought, and I got away from him. I don't think he was able to recognize me in the dark. I ran from the wagon, jumped on Traveler, and we got out of there.'' He touched the graze gingerly. ''He's a good shot as well. He gave me this as a parting gift. It hurt like blazes.''

''I can imagine,'' Niki said, grasping his fingers and moving them away from his wound. His fingers curled around hers, firm and warm. ''You happen to be most lucky, Mr. Sheridan. You could have been killed.''

''Not for the first time either.'' He grinned at her. ''I've had more close calls here in civilized England than I ever had on the frontier. This place is dangerous.''

Niki grinned back at him. She realized that he was still holding her fingers and started to pull away, but it felt so warm and comforting. Perhaps it felt that way to Sherry, as well, she thought. She left her hand where it was. ''Are you sure he didn't recognize you?''

''Fairly sure. It was dark as pitch. That was why I didn't see him coming to the wagon. He must have decided to stop in the middle of his meal and check. Maybe he had a feeling.'' He closed his eyes wearily.

Niki had to force herself not to touch his forehead and smooth back the strands of hair that had fallen again across his eyebrow. "You need to rest," she said.

"Uuummm," he murmured, not opening his eyes. "My head hurts like the devil. I don't know if I can sleep."

Niki and Cam glanced at each other and nodded. Cam slipped out the door while Niki sat beside Sheridan, her hand in his. When Cam returned, he held a glass. "Here, drink this," he said, holding the glass to Sherry's lips.

Sherry roused and drank. "Good Lord, what was that?" He made a face.

"Something for your headache," Cam said, putting the empty glass on the table. He glanced at Niki. "Do you want me to help you undress and get into bed? Unless, of course, Niki wants the honor."

Niki pulled her fingers from Sherry's grasp and stood. "Hardly, Camden," she said. She glanced down at Sherry and again had to resist the urge to smooth his hair. Instead, she smoothed his pillow. "Cam's next door and I'm right across the hall. Call us if you need us."

"Uuummm." Sherry was already half-asleep. Niki left and went to her room. She was still up, brushing her hair, when Cam knocked softly and came in.

"Laudanum?" she asked.

Cam nodded. "But not much. I thought he needed it for his head. And he needed to sleep." He paused at the door, and Niki looked at him, nibbling on her lower lip as she worried. "What do you think?"

"I think he'll be fine. I suspect that tomorrow he'll have a headache most of the day."

"At least. I meant about what he discovered."

"We know how Wynford used—or planned to use—Comet. I just don't know why they had to mistreat him to that degree. It would be a fine line to mistreat a horse enough so that he looked bad but was still able to win races."

"I know. I've wondered about that." Niki put her brush back. "All I could think of was that Creevy realized Comet's racing days were over because of his ankle and was showing the others how to make horses look as bad as possible." She spread her hands wide. "That doesn't seem to make sense, I know, but I can't think of anything else."

"I know. It sounds as good as anything. Perhaps Creevy just enjoyed inflicting pain on something that couldn't fight back. From what Jem told us, that's a good possibility." He put his hand on the knob. "I don't think Sherry will rouse until midmorning. You get some sleep, sister."

She smiled fondly at him as he closed the door. She thought she would never sleep and took a book to bed with her. When she woke up, it was morning, the candle had burned completely down and gone out, and her book had fallen to the floor.

The day was uneventful. To Niki's surprise and Mrs. Keene's great joy, Alston asked Sarah to go riding with him. Sarah came into Niki's room in tears wanting to know what to do. Niki took a chair out into the hall and dropped it with a great crash, then informed Alston that Miss Keene had fallen and seemed to have twisted her ankle slightly. She would still love to tour the countryside with Alston, but would have to do it from the barouche.

"You are such a friend," Sarah said, throwing her arms around Niki. "I would never had thought of such a trick. How wonderful you are." She left to get ready.

"Don't forget to limp," Niki hissed after her, as she went down the hall. Sarah immediately began to hop. "Not that much. Remember that you happen to be hurt only slightly."

Niki closed her door and sat down in the chair. "You're becoming a regular prevaricator, Anika," she muttered to herself. "The vicar will take you in hand if you don't stop this." She had to share her trick with Cam and Robbie when they asked her about Sarah going out in the barouche. Both thought it a famous solution.

"You're getting almost as good as I am," Robbie told her. He and Blazer were on their way to the stables. "Jem's going to let me hold Comment's foot," he announced. "Do you want to help?"

Niki declined and went back upstairs. There had been no

sign of life from Sherry's room, and she was worried. What if Cam had given him too much laudanum? She had always heard that laudanum and spirits didn't mix, and Sherry had drunk a good bit of brandy. What if he had been wounded worse than they thought? She thought of a dozen different scenes, each of them ending the same way—the body of Sheridan Devlin stretched out on the bed, cold and blue. At last, she could stand it no more. She looked up and down the hall, then dashed across to Sherry's door and opened it.

He was still in bed, sleeping heavily. He had been put into the gold bedroom. The draperies were a topaz color, and the bed was hung with a heavy damask the shade of burnished gold. The light filtering through the gold draperies gave the room a strange hue—it looked rather like everything in there had been covered with a light dusting of gold.

Sheridan had evidently tossed a great deal during the night and had pushed the bedcoverings down. The outer spread was almost on the floor, and the sheet was twisted around his waist. Cam hadn't dressed Sheridan in any nightclothes, and he was there, asleep, naked to the waist. Niki stopped and stared for a moment, then reminded herself that she was here on a mission of mercy. She needed to make sure Sherry was all right. Cautiously, she approached his bed and touched his forehead. He moaned and turned, showing her even more of his unclothed body. She jumped back, unable to take her eyes from his chest. He was bronze, as though he had worked out in the sunshine without a shirt on at all. The strange light from the window made him seem like a golden statue, all curves and planes.

There was golden hair on his chest, almost bleached to a white color, that looked strange contrasted with the black dye on his hair. She noticed that the rogue strand of hair that always fell across his eyebrow had covered his forehead. The scar on his eyebrow seemed even more pronounced now, and she noticed that he had another scar, this one on his shoulder. It looked like a saber cut but was now only a thin, white line on the bronze of his skin. His body was well formed and muscular, much more muscular than it appeared when he wore his clothes.

Niki imagined how it would feel to touch that bronze skin, to feel it warm next to her. She caught her thoughts and felt her face burn. She shouldn't be thinking such wanton ideas. She shouldn't be seeing such sights. If she were caught, her reputation would be ruined.

She made herself stop looking at Sheridan's body and instead look at his face, then touched his forehead again. He wasn't feverish as she had feared, although his skin was warm from his being asleep. However, there was a bad-looking bruise on the side of his face where the graze began. His hair covered the worst of the graze, and she thought he would be able to get by with their story of a limb hitting him on the head. She let her fingers trace lightly across the edges of the bruise, then gave in to temptation and smoothed his hair back off his forehead. He mumbled something and clasped her hand in his. Niki tried to draw back, but he kept a firm grasp on her fingers. There was a smile on his face.

Niki tried again to move her hand, but he held it and, to her horror, moved her palm to his lips and kissed it. She got gooseflesh up her arm and down to her toes. She had to get out of his room. She was having trouble breathing. She wiggled her fingers, and Sherry moved his lips and the tip of his tongue up her palm to her fingers, then nibbled on the tips of her fingers. "Mmmm," he mumbled, turning over slightly to face her. He was still asleep.

Then he began kissing her fingertips. "So good," he whispered.

Niki felt herself go scarlet. Worse, there was a noise outside, then a tapping at the door. "Mr. Sheridan," a voice called out. Good God! It was her stepfather! She jerked her hand from Sheridan's and looked around wildly. There was no place to hide except one. She ran around to the other side of the bed and fell onto the floor just as she heard the door open. She rolled under the bed, hidden by the thick damask bedskirt. In a crack of perhaps an inch between the bedskirt and the floor, she could see the bottoms of her stepfather's shiny boots.

"Oh, do excuse me, Mr. Sheridan," Lord Larch said. "Camden told me you were up, or I would never have bothered you. I was on my way to change clothes to go fishing with the boys and wanted to see if you might like to join us.''

"Thank you," Sherry said, as though he had been awake for a while. "I was somewhat ill last night, and stayed in this morning."

"Nothing serious, I hope," Lord Larch said.

"No." Niki could hear Sherry chuckle. "Just a touch of a headache." There was another chuckle. "I hate to admit it, but I was out riding yesterday and didn't pay attention to where I was going. As you can see, I came out on the worse end of an encounter with a tree limb. I'm fine today."

"Good to hear it. I'll tell the boys that you're indisposed." Lord Larch's boots turned slightly.

"I'm just fine, and I'd enjoy a quiet hour or two fishing. If you'll give me time to change, I'll join you downstairs." Niki heard Sheridan move in the bed. It sounded as if he were getting up.

"Certainly. Take your time. You'll need some breakfast as well. We'll meet out by the stables. I have fishing gear there." Lord Larch laughed. "Nothing like wetting a hook, is there?"

"Absolutely nothing."

Niki thought she caught a hint of laughter in Sherry's voice, but he said nothing else. Lord Larch bade him good morning and Niki saw the shiny boot tips turn as Lord Larch walked across the floor. Then she heard the door closing.

What to do now? She certainly couldn't leave her hiding place while Sheridan was in the room. She would just have to stay there until he dressed and left. She shuddered. If anyone knew she had been in here while he was dressing—it didn't bear thinking on.

She heard another noise and, looking under the edge of the bedskirt, saw his bare feet on the floor. She held her breath and squeezed her eyes shut. She had never been in such a predicament.

Then it got even worse. The bedskirt was lifted and Sherry knelt down and gazed under the bed, right into her eyes. He had nothing on except his breeches. He looked at her and grinned broadly, his eyes dancing in his face. "Well, my dear Miss Owen, would you like to come out now, or do you plan to spend the day there?"

# Chapter 11

Instead of just rolling out from under the bed, Niki hid her face in her arms. Never, never in her whole life had she been so mortified. She felt a tug at her elbow.

"Come on out. I promise I'm on my best behavior. I'll even put on my shirt if that will help." There was laughter in his voice as he pulled on her arm.

Niki gave up and crawled from under the bed. Sherry put his hand on the back of her head and laughed. "I do believe it's time to have a conversation with the maid who takes care of this room." Sherry helped her to her feet and pulled a piece of lint from her hair. "Turn around. I can't let you go out in public with lint all over you. What would the neighbors say? Not to mention the family." He chuckled to himself as he plucked lint here and there from Niki's hair. Finally, he turned her around and she found herself looking right at the golden hair in the center of his chest. He looked down at her and laughed again. "Your face, Miss Owen, rivals the sunset at this moment. Do allow me to put on my shirt." Niki tried staring at the floor as he picked up a shirt and slipped it over his head. However, she cheated a little—she kept her lashes lowered, but watched him as he dressed. She had never seen a man do that before. But then, she had never been alone with a man in his bedroom either.

"There," he said, leaning against the door, his shirt loose, not tucked in, with the ties dangling. "Is that better?"

"Quite. Now if I might leave." She took a step toward the door, but he didn't move. She could see the corners of his mouth moving in amusement. "Really, Mr. Sheridan. I merely came in to make sure you were all right. I assure you that I certainly do not make a habit of coming into men's bedrooms."

"Oh, I'm sure of that, Miss Owen. Thank you for being so concerned. I appreciate your worry that I might have a fever. I must say that you have an extraordinarily gentle touch."

Her eyes widened and she stared at him. "You knew! You were awake! You . . . you charlatan!"

He laughed again. "What righteous anger, Miss Owen. I apologize, but I wouldn't have missed that for the world. Tell me if I'm injured again, will you be as solicitous?"

"You can rot for all I care," Niki snapped. "Now, sir, if you'll move, I'll leave you to your laughter." She took another step toward him.

Instead of moving, he caught her hand and pulled her even closer to him. With his other hand, he smoothed her unruly hair away from her ear and ran his fingers down the side of her jaw and onto her neck. "My dear Miss Owen," he began, then stopped as his eyes turned serious. He took a deep breath and smiled again. "Perhaps that speech should wait. Again, I apologize for my behavior. Yes, I should have let you know I was awake. My only defense is that I couldn't help myself." He put his hands on both of her upper arms and moved her to one side of the door. "Let me look before you go barging out into the hall. I don't want you running into Mrs. Keene or your father. It wouldn't do at all for him to insist we get married before nightfall, would it?" He cracked open the door and looked out, then stepped aside and held the door open. "Hurry." He gave her a little push on her back and, as soon as she was safely in the hall, closed the door again. Niki looked at the closed door, then put her hands to her burning cheeks. She dashed into her own room and locked the door behind her, thankful that Shotwell wasn't in there to see her. She was mortified. There was no way she could ever face Thomas Sheridan—no, Sheridan Devlin—again. Never.

Niki gave Sherry an hour to get out of the house before she went downstairs. Mrs. Keene and Lady Larch were busy gossiping and embroidering, but Niki didn't want to do that. In fact, she didn't want to do much of anything. She found herself wandering from room to room aimlessly, thinking one minute of the way Sheridan's body had looked in the golden wash of the room and the next minute condemning him for pretending to be asleep. She only hoped he didn't tell Cam about her embarrassment.

She didn't see the gentlemen until right before supper. She dawdled in her room as long as she could, finding first this and that for Shotwell to do. She changed clothes twice, much to Shotwell's amazement. Ordinarily, she simply put on whatever Shotwell chose and went out without even looking in the mirror. Tonight, though, she fretted over her appearance, finally deciding on a dress of deep rose pink that was one of her favorites. She knew the color flattered her, and she wanted to look her best. If she was going to be embarrassed beyond words and have to face everyone, then she wanted to do it looking as good as she possibly could. Still, she waited until the last minute to go down.

When she finally came down, everyone was already assembled in the drawing room, getting ready to go in to eat. Sherry was there, dressed in blue that made his eyes seem even bluer if that were possible. He was telling everyone how he had been so taken with the scenery that he hadn't seen the limb that was hanging. "It had evidently been hit by lightning," he explained, "and I was right into it before I knew it."

"Fortunate you weren't knocked off," Cam noted.

"True," Sherry said. "I thought I was going to be. If it had been any horse except Traveler, I think I might have been."

"Where did you manage to find that horse?" Alston asked,

and the conversation went in another direction. Niki went over
to sit beside her mother. She wanted to put as much distance
between herself and Sherry as possible. Perhaps, she thought,
as Sarah walked toward her, she could persuade Sarah to walk
in with him. "I had the most wonderful day," Sarah whispered
breathlessly. "Thank you."

"Thank me for what?" Niki turned to look at Sarah. She
was positively glowing, looking better than Niki had ever seen
her.

"For thinking of that story to tell Alston. We went out in
the barouche. Mama didn't feel like going, so she borrowed
Shotwell to accompany me. Didn't she tell you?"

Niki shook her head. "No, I was busy today and didn't really
miss her. This evening, I neglected to ask her about her day."
*No,* she thought to herself, *I wasn't thinking of a thing except
how I hated to come down here and face Sheridan.*

"You were busy? What were you doing?"

Niki fixed her eyes on Sarah's pale green kidskin slippers
and groped for something to say. "Oh, I had letters to write,
and some mending to do." *Do you really want to know?* she
thought to herself. *I was on my bed most of the day, thinking
of how Sheridan looked in the bed, imagining how it would be
to have him in mine. Imagining those hands that touched my
face touching other things.* "There are always a dozen things
to do." She looked at the men standing there, getting ready to
go in to supper. She needed to arrange for Sarah to walk in
with Sheridan. There was no way she could do it herself.

"I know." Sarah put her hand on Niki's arm. "I think Alston
has an interest, Niki," she whispered. "Will you do what you
can?"

Niki looked at her in surprise. "Of course, Sarah. Do you
return his regard?"

"Yes, oh yes!" She smiled broadly as Alston broke away
from the men, came over to her, and offered his arm. "Will
you do me the honor, Miss Keene?"

Worse luck for Niki, Mrs. Keene nabbed Cam, while Lord

Larch gave his arm to his Lady. That left only Sheridan standing there, looking amused. She took his arm stiffly.

"In case you were going to ask, I'm feeling quite the thing," he whispered to her, as she stood beside him, as far from him as possible. Her whole body was rigid. He pulled her closer, and she was forced to step in. Her bare arm snuggled against his side and she could feel the warmth of his body and the slight prickliness of his coat. The feeling wasn't unpleasant.

"I told you that I didn't care." She stared straight ahead.

He chuckled. "Ah, yes, I believe you said that you didn't care if I rotted. A most pithy choice of words."

Niki couldn't answer him as they were in the dining room. The others were already being seated, and she resigned herself to having to sit beside Sheridan for supper. That didn't mean that she had to talk to him. Alston was on her other side. She could always spend the entire meal talking horses with him.

Alston didn't turn her way. He spent the entire time talking to Sarah, turning to Niki only once or twice as politeness demanded. "It seems you're stuck with me as a conversationalist," Sherry said, the corners of his mouth quivering. "What shall we discuss? I'm afraid I know nothing about English politics, the weather here isn't too familiar to me, and as for gossip—if it didn't happen in Richmond or Williamsburg, I don't know about it."

Niki refused to look at him. She spooned her soup carefully. "Did you have a good day, Mr. Sheridan?" she asked. Her mother had instilled that one must always be polite to one's dinner companions.

"That I did," he said. His voice held an undertone of laughter. "Of course, it started off perfectly. It isn't often that I have such a perfect beginning to a day."

Niki choked on her soup.

"Are you all right, dear?" her mother asked as conversation stopped for a moment, and everyone looked at her.

"Fine," she answered in a strangled voice. "Everything is fine, Mama."

Everything wasn't fine, but there was no way she could admit it. The others resumed their conversations in just a moment, and Niki returned to her soup. "It is very gauche of you, Mr. Sheridan, to say such a thing. I would think you had already caused me enough embarrassment."

Sherry chuckled. "Attribute it to my uncouth American ways, Miss Owen. However, I apologize if you happen to feel embarrassed. I certainly don't think you should. I appreciate your concern." She glanced up and met his eyes. "I care very much for my sisters and wouldn't hurt them for the world, but I'm always teasing them. I suppose the same applies here. Shall we call a truce and not mention it again?"

Niki worried at the thought that had been nagging her all day. "You haven't mentioned it to anyone else, have you?" she whispered cautiously.

"Good Lord, no! Do give me some credit, Miss Owen. Some things are meant to be private."

Niki felt herself relax. The soup was removed and the next course brought in. Sherry began telling her about his travels along the American frontier. It was just the kind of conversation one would use with a dinner companion one had just met. Niki should have welcomed his words and tone, but, for some reason, she didn't. The connection they had felt was gone. Wasn't that, she asked herself over dessert, what she had wanted? She didn't know. It was vexing—whenever she was around Sheridan, she didn't know what she wanted.

After supper, while the men were still talking in the dining room, Sarah sat beside Niki and talked about her day. She was convinced that Alston was interested in her. "But then there's my background," she said dully. "That is an obstacle."

"If he cares for you, I don't think it would be."

Sarah looked at her with tear-shiny eyes. "My father's in trade, Niki. You don't know what that's like. I've always been on the fringes of society, no matter what Mama does. True, Papa could buy and sell half the ton and still have money left over, but they discount that. Money means nothing to society."

"From what I've seen, I think you're incorrect, Miss Keene."

Niki glanced up to see Sherry standing behind them. "I didn't hear you enter, Mr. Sheridan."

"I've learned to tiptoe around the savages," he said with a grin, coming around the sofa and sitting across from them.

"And what does that mean?"

"Whatever you think it may mean, Miss Owen." He leaned forward. "As to your comment, Miss Keene, I've noticed that the people in London society who snub others do so because that gives them a sense of power. They have little else except debts and encumbered estates, so they rely on their silly rules about what's proper or rather, *who's* proper." He grinned again. "That observation, of course, is based on approximately five or six hours in London society. However, as an outsider, I think I may have more of a perspective."

"I tend to agree with you, Sheridan." Alston sat in the chair next to Sherry's.

"Tell me then, Alston, do you find some of the rules and regulations that London society imposes as ridiculous as I do?"

"I certainly do. For instance, why should a young woman have to apply to the patronesses of Almack's and be allowed there before being accepted into society? What exactly does that prove?"

"My point exactly. Things are much different in America."

"I have heard," Niki said, "that in America everything is based on wealth. Is that true?"

"Of course not. I like to think that acceptance is based on someone's true worth."

"Horsefeathers." Niki couldn't help herself. "Society is society. If you think London society is restrictive, you should see Spanish society."

"No doubt," Alston said. "Still, London society is all a sham. And my observations are based on innumerable hours in society, most of which were incredibly tedious." He glanced into his wineglass, which was almost empty. "I'm thinking of giving it up for most of the year and retiring to the country."

"I love the country," Sarah said.

"Really, Miss Keene? I'm delighted to hear that. Not many

women do." He gave Sarah a dazzling smile before he turned slightly to face Sherry. "I want to leave the clubs and parties of London and simply come home and raise horses. Do you think there's a market in America for good horseflesh?"

"I think so, but the transportation there would finish off most horses. However, I think you've already gotten a good start on having the premier horse farm in this country. Have you thought of going to all thoroughbreds?"

The talk drifted into horses. Cam came over to join them as Niki and Sarah simply sat and listened. Finally, Lady Larch could bear no more. "Gentlemen, you've had your day of horses and fishing. Isn't it time to cater to the ladies a little?" She rang the bell and had the tables set up for cards. Niki found herself partnered with Sherry, with Sarah and Alston opposite. Sherry was sitting with the candlelight falling over his shoulder, illuminating the side of his face that was uninjured. Niki was unable to concentrate on the cards, thinking how the light looked much as it had this morning, when the light from the sun through the draperies had given his skin that same golden look. She and Sherry were defeated soundly.

Although they kept country hours and went to bed early, Niki excused herself before the others were ready to retire and went up to her room early, thinking that she might go to sleep and forget this day. She had Shotwell brush her hair extra, as that was always soothing. Tonight, however, it didn't work at all, and she couldn't sleep. She thought to try reading, but the only book she had on hand was one she had brought up to use to press some flowers. It was heavy, but certainly nothing to read. About half past one, she got up, put on her dressing gown, and went down to the library to find something that might put her to sleep. Herodotus had done it in the past and maybe would again.

When she went into the library, she saw that the servants had neglected to check the room. There was a candle still burning on the table. She picked it up and went to the shelf, pulled the Herodotus, then started to blow out the candle and leave. "If you don't mind, Miss Owen, I prefer not to have to sit in the dark." She whirled, wary and surprised to see Alston sitting in the large wing chair by the fireplace. He had a bottle of wine on the table beside him and was sipping from a glass. The bottle was almost half-empty.

"I'm sorry, I didn't know you were here." Niki put the candle down on the table where it had been. "I couldn't sleep, so I came down to get a book."

He leaned forward and took the book from her fingers. "Herodotus. Sometimes he can be entertaining, but there are times . . ." He turned the book over and handed it back. "An excellent choice for insomnia, Miss Owen. Perhaps I should try that instead of this." He held up the wineglass, then put it down on the table and put the stopper in the wine bottle. "Since neither of us can sleep, Miss Owen, do sit down and join me. Perhaps we can talk ourselves into sleep."

Niki glanced down at her dressing gown and then at Alston. "I really shouldn't . . ."

He chuckled. "Are you bound by those restrictions we were discussing earlier, Miss Owen? I would have thought you more unconventional."

She pulled up a small chair and sat down across from him. "I'm not sure I'm so bound by convention as others are, but there are certain rules, especially for females. What if. . ."

"What if we were discovered?" He waved toward the door. "Who in the world is going to be wandering around the library at a quarter until two in the morning."

"Well, we are." Niki grinned at him.

He regarded her for a long moment. "You're an unusual person, Miss Owen. I wish things were different. I'd like to get to know you better, but . . ." He let his words trail off and looked at the wine bottle. He refrained from opening it again, Niki noted with approval. "I hope we can be friends," he said unexpectedly. "I think I'd like that very much."

"I'm sure we can." Niki didn't know how to answer.

They sat in silence for a few minutes, then Alston put his elbows on his knees, and, leaning up, put his head in his hands.

"I've made a mess of my life so far, Miss Owen, did you know that? I've been here reflecting on it."

Niki didn't know how to answer him. "I'm sure there's still time for you to redeem yourself, sir. Things can't be that bad."

He looked at her bleakly. "Oh, but they are, Miss Owen. I have to get married immediately. My father's orders, sent straight to me through his solicitor." His mouth twisted slightly. "Father was too busy to attend to it himself. However he was very specific. I have to marry someone with enough money to get me out of the scrape I'm in." He gave a short, harsh laugh.

Niki sat there, wondering what to say. "Parents usually have our best interests at heart," she finally offered.

"My father has his purse strings at heart." He picked up the wine bottle and put it back down. "Still, my problems are of my own making. Mine and Jackson's."

"Jackson? Do you mean Wynford?" Niki was all interest.

He nodded. "Yes. I've always known him as Jackson. Suffice it to say, Miss Owen, that if he chose to collect tomorrow, I'd be forced to flee to the Continent. Or perhaps get directions from Sheridan and head for America."

"What happened?" Niki paused. "I don't mean to pry, but . . ."

"Quite all right, Miss Owen. I have need of a confessor." He looked at her and gave a rueful smile. "You have a sympathetic manner, do you know that? I feel I can talk to you."

"Thank you." She smiled at him. "If you choose to confide in me, I assure you that the particulars of our conversation will go no farther."

He leaned back and closed his eyes. "That's good to know. Too many women do nothing except gossip. It's refreshing to meet one who doesn't." He rubbed the side of his face with his hand. "The wine and the hour make for confidences, do they not?" When Niki didn't answer him, he continued. "I met Jackson several years ago. I began gambling on little things, then bigger things as the years went by. Some months ago, I was taken quite royally, I think. Jackson swore the race was honest, but I have my doubts. To make a long story short, I owe the man more than I can pay. It's necessary that I marry an heiress so I can pay my debts.''

"Sarah Keene?"

He looked at her. "I think so. Her father's in trade and her mother was a cit, but they're rich beyond words and Sarah's an only child." He gave her a crooked grin. *"Nouveau riche."*

"I've never considered Sarah in that light," Niki said carefully. "It's true that her father is a self-made man, but from what I've heard, he's upstanding. He doesn't seem to be the typical newly rich man."

Alston's expression was half smile, half grimace. "Well, Miss Owen, better *nouveau riche* than not *riche* at all. Miss Keene seems to be quite a well-educated, proper young lady. I've learned my lesson and I daresay that I would make Miss Keene a creditable husband."

"I'm sure you would." Niki was uncomfortable with the conversation and tried to turn it back to the topic of Jackson and horse racing. She learned very little, only that Alston's main purpose in coming to Breconbridge was to try to talk to Jackson. It hadn't helped at all, but, as part of the payment, Jackson had insisted that Alston advise him on his horses. Jackson also wanted some of the prime horseflesh that belonged to Alston's father. "That is an impossibility, I told him," Alston said, "but he refused to listen. He's insisting that I produce two prime horses. I haven't even mentioned it to my father. I know he would never agree."

"Perhaps you could offer something else instead," Niki suggested.

"A pound of flesh might do it." The corners of his mouth turned down. "Miss Owen, one hates to admit that he was thoroughly fooled, but I'm afraid I must say so. I thought Jackson an honorable man, but instead, he's proven to be the very worst. Indeed, I'm surprised he hasn't been brought up on criminal charges at some time."

"It might be that no one knows of his dealings."

Alston nodded. "I think you may be right. He's very good at what he does." He shook his head. "Shall we change topics,

Miss Owen? I'm afraid I'll never sleep if we continue to discuss this unsavory character.''

At that point, Alston digressed to horse racing in general and then horses in general. He was surprised at Niki's knowledge of the subject. "Remember," she told him with a smile, "I've been around horses since I was in leading strings in Spain." He questioned her about Spanish horses, and she told him all she knew. "The barbs changed horse breeding forever," he said thoughtfully. "There may be something to Sheridan's marigold theory after all.''

"Marigold theory?"

Alston chuckled. "You'd best have him explain it to you. He has sheets and sheets about marigold breeding. He intends to apply it to horse breeding.''

"Marigolds?" Niki couldn't make the connection.

"Marigolds." Alston paused as the clock in the hall chimed three o'clock, and he looked up. "The candles are guttering, Miss Owen. I suppose we should go up and try to sleep. I hope I haven't kept you from your Herodotus.''

Niki stood and picked up the book. "No." She smiled at him. "But I think I might be able to sleep now. Will you?"

"I think so." He picked up the guttering candle and offered her his arm. "I'll escort you up.''

At her door, he stopped and looked down at her, then blew out the candle. "Thank you for your company, Miss Owen, and for your promise that my confidences will not be bruited about. I needed someone to talk to.''

"I would be glad to listen at any time." Niki smiled back at him and went into her room. She heard his door close down the hall as she crawled into her bed.

As she started to doze off, she remembered that she would be unable to share her information about Jackson with Cam and Sherry. After all, a promise was a promise.

# Chapter 12

Shotwell came into Niki's room much too soon the next morning. Sarah was right behind her, almost in tears. Niki sat up in bed and tried to wake up. "Niki, you've got to help me," Sarah wailed. "You've got to!"

"Help you with what?" Niki was still groggy.

"Alston asked me if my ankle was better and, like a fool, I said it was. He then said that was excellent—we could ride over to the ruins at Bynwith." Sarah threw herself down on the bed. "You know I can't ride, Niki. Whatever shall I do? Say something! Do something!" Sarah put her head down on Niki's bed and moaned.

Niki looked down at her and made a face, then sent Shotwell out for a restorative cup of chocolate. "Do hush, Sarah. I'm sure Alston won't mind if you don't ride. Just take the barouche again." She patted Sarah on the head absently.

"He *will* mind. After all, he's one of the best riders in the kingdom. His father owns all those horses. Niki, you simply must teach me to ride. Right now! Surely I could learn before I had to leave this morning. How difficult could it be? You just get on the horse and say 'Move.'"

"There's a little more to it than that." Niki regarded her. Sarah's face was all red and splotched from crying. "I can't teach you to ride, Sarah. You'll have to learn that on your own." She paused, then a thought hit her. "No, don't try it by yourself. You'd probably break your neck or break down a perfectly good horse. No, we must make up another excuse for today. When you get back to London, have your father hire someone to teach you to ride."

"I can't wait until then! I need to know this morning!" Sarah's wail was anguished. Then she stopped and looked at Niki. "Make up an excuse? What kind of excuse? What are you thinking?"

Niki took a deep breath and let it out slowly. "We'll have to plan something that requires the barouche or a carriage." She sighed again. Last evening, she had decided to try to get Sherry to take her to Wynwoode, but now she realized that was simply out of the question. Creevy might recognize him, or realize that Sherry's injury had not been the result of an encounter with a limb. No, she quickly decided, ignoring Sarah's wails, the best thing was to make sure that Sherry always had either Cam or Robbie with him. At least, Niki thought ruefully, with the two of them hanging onto his coattails, Sheridan wouldn't go haring off by himself and get killed. If he did any looking around or visiting, he would have to take Cam or Robbie with him. She certainly didn't want him traveling alone anymore. He had dodged three attempts to kill him—the next one might actually do the job.

"A picnic," she said slowly over the sound of Sarah's sobs. "We could all go to Bynwith. Surely Sheridan would like to go there and see the Norman ruins, and Cam won't mind. We can even take Robbie and Blazer with us. Robbie loves it there." She nodded her head. "That's it, Sarah. We'll go on a picnic. We'll have to take the barouche to carry Mama and your mother. Naturally, you'll have to travel with them."

"What about you? You'll have to be with us. If you take a horse, then Alston will think I should ride as well."

Niki sighed again. "Very well. Do go downstairs and tell

everyone. I'll have Shotwell take a message to Cook to prepare a picnic for us. I leave it to you to talk Alston into going.'' She remembered last night's conversation with him. ''I don't think he'll protest. I believe he would want to go and further your acquaintance.''

Sarah's face glowed. ''Do you think so, Niki? Oh, I hope so!'' She rubbed at her face. ''He was always the one, you know.''

Niki looked at her in surprise. ''The man for whom you've been moping?''

''Hardly moping, Niki. I was in utter despair, completely hopeless of even making his acquaintance.'' Sarah leaned back and sighed. ''I've adored him for ever so long, since I first saw him in London. At every party we attended, I always looked for him and noted what he was doing, with whom he was talking, when he left. I never thought, because of Papa's trade, that he could ever look at me.'' She stood up and whirled around. ''Now, look at this! What good fortune that we should visit you when he was here! When I saw him, my heart almost stopped. But I didn't dare to dream!'' She paused and looked at Niki with apprehension. ''Do you think he might be really interested in me, Niki? Do you think he could care for me?''

All Niki could think of was Alston's remark that it was *better* nouveau riche *than not* riche *at all.* She couldn't warn Sarah away. ''Anyone who knows you loves you, Sarah,'' she said, and felt like a hypocrite as Sarah's face lit up again.

''You're too good to me,'' Sarah said. ''I'm going to see Alston and then talk to Mama. Do you want me to tell your mother about our plans as well?''

''Please do.'' Niki said this to the closed door. Sarah was already out of the room. It was a relief when a maid came in with hot chocolate. Niki certainly had need of something.

When she got downstairs, she met Cam coming in the door. ''What's this about a picnic?'' he asked. Niki explained the reason, and Cam grinned. ''Alston's in for a surprise one of these days. Still, I'm always ready for a reason to eat.'' He paused and glanced at her a moment. ''Do you have time to help me a few minutes? I'm working on Father's birthday surprise. I've thought about your suggestion for a race and think we should run Com . . . Comment.''

"Don't you think that's too risky? What if someone recognizes him?''

"Who could? I've been talking to Sherry, and we'd love to nick Wynford in the pockets with his own horse. I'd call that poetic justice.''

Niki made a face. "I'm not sure, Cam. I don't want to receive any justice myself. I'd much rather just have some kind of a race with no betting.''

He gave her a disgusted snort. "No betting? Good Lord, Niki, that's no race. That's just a trot around the track. You have to have betting to make it interesting.'' He looked at her sideways. "Sheridan agrees with me. He thinks Comment's ankle will be ready by then. Comment can take the race, Sherry thinks.''

"I can see it now, Cam. Com . . . Comment takes the race and the magistrate takes us away. That would be a birthday surprise indeed.''

"Spoilsport. We'll see.'' He turned to go up the stairs. "We're leaving in an hour for Bynwith. Am I correct?''

"Correct,'' Niki said with a sigh, as she went towards the kitchen to check with cook. Needless to say, Cook was unhappy to be packing a picnic on such short notice. It took all of Niki's stock of soothing talk just to calm her. Making her happy was out of the question. Niki even made arrangements for a carriage with the food to come to Bynwith later, just so Cook would have an extra hour.

The day was overcast, but it wasn't raining, so the trip to Bynwith was made with the ladies in the barouche, while the gentlemen rode beside. Niki would have given almost anything to be mounted on Qadir, riding with them, but she could hardly leave Sarah, Mrs. Keene, and her mother in the barouche while she galloped out front. So she sat in the barouche and chafed. It was a relief to get to Bynwith.

The Norman ruins there were atop a small hill, strewn with

stones from what had once been a proud Norman keep. Lady
Larch and Mrs. Keene spread a blanket and elected to stay at
the foot of the hill while the others went up to explore the
ruins. Jem had driven a wagon behind them that had a folding
table and some chairs for them. Robbie and Blazer had ridden
with him. As soon as the wagon was unloaded, Robbie and
Blazer ran up the hill toward the ruins. Alston offered his arm
to Sarah and they set off, leaving Cam and Sherry to walk up
with Niki. They dawdled, looking at various stones, and the
others were soon far ahead.

"Interesting, but I'd rather be at Wynwoode discovering
something," Sherry remarked. "I feel we're losing time."

"We'll get Wynford at the birthday races," Cam said confidently. "I want him to have some of his own medicine."

"What good will that do?" Niki asked. "What we need to
do is prove that he was the one who tried to kill Sheridan. It's
been quite a path for him to become master of Wynwoode.
First, his older uncle had to die, then both of his uncle's sons,
then his other uncle."

"He doesn't know about me and my brother, or we'd be on
the list, too." Sherry stopped and hit his head with the flat of
his palm. "Niki, that's wonderful thinking! Why didn't that
occur to me?"

They came in sight of Alston and Sarah standing at the edge
of the ruins. "Why didn't what occur to you?" Niki asked,
lowering her voice as they got closer to the others. Robbie and
Blazer were climbing some steps inside the tower that led to
the upper wall. "Be careful, Robbie," she called out. "You'll
fall."

"Here come the laggards," Sarah said, laughing. Her face
was glowing, and it wrenched Niki's heart. Alston certainly
didn't care for Sarah, but just being in his presence transformed
her. Her feelings for him were easy to read.

They walked around the ruins for the better part of an hour,
with Robbie and Blazer leading Cam and Sherry in a chase
around the ruins of the walls. Niki turned her head away part
of the time. She simply couldn't watch—she just knew that

one or the other of them was going to fall from the stairs or the top, right onto the stones on the ground. She was relieved when Robbie spotted the carriage bringing the food. He was, as always, starving, and hurried down to where Jem, Mrs. Keene, and Lady Larch waited. Cam wasn't too far behind him. Sarah and Alston paired off, of course, and Sherry offered Niki his arm for the trip down.

"Do I detect a romance in the making?" Sherry asked with a grin, watching Sarah and Alston walk in front of them. Sarah was almost leaning into Alston.

"If Mrs. Keene sees that, Alston may be banished." Niki looked at them for a minute. "To answer your question, yes, on Sarah's part at any rate. I'm not sure about Alston."

Sherry followed her gaze and watched the pair go down the hill, Alston turning to help Sarah over a particularly slick spot. "I'd say Alston will get what he needs from the relationship." Sherry chuckled. "I tell you this with the understanding that it go no further, Miss Owen."

"Of course."

"Alston told me he had to marry money and do it in a hurry. Cam told me that Sarah's family was well to grass. Very well to grass." He grinned at Niki. "It was a simple matter to add one and one. I'd say an offer will be made within the week. Do you want to make a small wager on it?"

Niki looked at them again. "The odds aren't good enough for me. I think you're right." She skirted the spot where Sarah had almost slipped and had clung to Alston. "This is perfectly dry," she said. "Whatever was Sarah doing? Such playacting."

"That's how it's done by those who know the fine art of flirtation, or so I'm told." Sherry laughed and took her arm again. "What do you know about Alston? He's seems to be a box of contradictions. I wonder just how he feels about Jackson—I can't bring myself to call him Wynford."

"Why don't you ask him? You always seem to be able to get to the point in a hurry. Perhaps you should just discuss with Alston how he feels."

They paused as they watched Alston seat Sarah in a chair next to her mother. "I'll just do that, Miss Owen. Today."

The picnic was almost a success. It would have been a complete success if Blazer had not taken it on himself to leap into the middle of the ham. The human participants were reduced to eating the breads and desserts while Blazer curled himself around the ham and enjoyed it thoroughly. "I don't think any of us could have relished that ham as much as Blazer has," Cam said, watching Blazer carefully bury the remains of his prize. Blazer finished his task, then ran off with Robbie to play in the rocks.

"Robbie is getting adventurous," Niki noted. "Perhaps too much so. Have you noticed that he's been away for long stretches in the woods?"

"I haven't seen him underfoot as much as usual," Cam admitted. "I thought perhaps he was spending all his time with the horse."

Niki shook her head. "No, he told me he was searching for clues in the woods and around the fence that separates Breconbridge and Wynwoode. I told him he wasn't going to find them there. He said he was planning to look elsewhere." She gave Cam a worried look. "I was afraid he was thinking of going onto the property at Wynwoode, and I told him to stay away from there. Perhaps you should mention it to him— he listens to you."

"Since when?" Cam made a face. "The parents haven't been giving him much attention lately, and I've noticed he's been out with Blazer. I'll talk to him." They watched as Robbie rolled across a rock, Blazer right behind him. Blazer wound up on Robbie's stomach as they both fell to the ground.

Cam shifted his attention to the other side of the ruins. "What do you suppose Alston and Sherry are up to? I noticed them wandering away a while ago. They seem to be very deep in conversation."

"Sheridan was wondering just how Alston felt about Wynford. I told him to ask." Niki followed Cam's gaze. "I suppose that's what he's doing now."

"I could have told him that. Alston can't abide the man."
He looked at Niki. "There are some things I really can't divulge,
but suffice it to say that Wynford is pulling the strings."

"Alston told me."

Cam stared at her. "Told you? You and Alston aren't . . .
he didn't . . . ?"

Niki laughed. "No, of course not. I merely happened on him
when he needed to talk. He told me, I suspect, most of what
you know. I can't really divulge more than what you've said,
as I promised not to tell anyone."

Cam shook his head. "He's going to offer for Sarah, I think.
The match is terrible from a family standpoint, but she'll accept
him in a second, and he'll never have to worry about money
again." He paused. "That is, unless her father decides to act
like Wynford."

"I think Sarah is so enamored of Alston and will be so happy
that her father will do whatever she wants him to do." Niki
chuckled. "Sheridan asked if I wanted to wager on Alston's
offering for Sarah, and I told him no."

"No odds there." Cam stood up and offered his hand to
Niki. "It appears the two of them are returning. I see a cloud
on the horizon, and I, for one, don't care to be out here in the
weather. Besides, I need to do some things for the race on
Papa's birthday." He took her arm and walked her back to the
carriage, where he suggested they leave. Halfway to Becon-
bridge, the rain started, and the men were thoroughly soaked
by the time they reached home, so Niki had no time to ask
Sheridan what Alston had told him.

She didn't see Sheridan until everyone gathered for supper
in the drawing room. Then, when she finally had something to
ask the man and hoped he would take her into supper, he
escorted Mrs. Keene in and sat across the table, so that private
conversation was impossible. Later, in the drawing room, Lady
Larch set up for cards almost immediately, so there was no
conversation there either. Niki had to go to bed consumed with
curiosity.

She was able to corner Sheridan the next morning. By design, she came out of her room just as he came out of his. "Good morning," she said cheerfully. She had chosen deep yellow to wear today because of the drizzle outside. The rich color always made her feel better. Unfortunately, the drizzle also made her hair go every which way. Shotwell had tried, but it was no use. Finally, Niki had told her to pin it back. Shotwell had finally managed that, pulling her hair back straight and pinning it into a chignon on the back of her head.

"Good morning, Miss Owen." He stopped and looked at her. "It isn't working."

"What isn't?"

He chuckled. "Your hair." He reached out and touched a tendril that had already worked loose. "But it looks fetching." He stood back and looked at her again. "In fact, you look rather like a buttercup today."

"I like buttercups." She fell into step beside him. "Did you discover what you wished to know from Alston?"

"I'm fond of buttercups myself. Very fond." He paused and grinned down at her. "As for your question, yes, I did." They walked in silence to the breakfast room. As soon as she saw that the room was empty, Niki could stand it no more. "Well, what did he say?"

Sheridan began filling his plate from the sideboard. "Plate, Miss Owen? Would you like a muffin? Eggs?"

Niki snatched up a plate and began putting things on it without even noticing what she was doing. Cam and Alston came in just as she finished and turned around. "Good Lord, Niki," Cam said, eyeing her plate, "are you starving this morning?" Niki glanced down at her plate. It was heaping with one or two of everything on the sideboard. "Yes," she said, putting her plate down with a *thunk*. "Of course I am."

Alston and Cam filled their plates and sat down as well. "Miss Owen was wondering if I discovered what I wanted to know yesterday," Sheridan said with a chuckle. "I've been keeping her in suspense."

"Did you?" Cam asked.

Sheridan nodded. "Yes. I'd wondered about Alston"—he

nodded in Alston's general direction—"and discovered that he cares for Jackson no more than we do. In fact, I was so convinced that I revealed my identity."

Niki almost choked on her coffee. "Oh, and did you tell him the whole of it?"

Sherry laughed. "Are you worried about stretching hemp for horse stealing? No, I didn't mention that."

"I wish you would." Alston looked at them curiously. "That sounds like a more interesting tale than anything I could relate about Jackson."

"Never mind," Niki said hastily. "I'm sure our need to know about Wynford—Jackson is more pressing. Were you able to add to our information?"

Sherry sipped his coffee and drummed his fingers on the table. "I was glad to find out that we had an ally in Alston. The thing that really struck me yesterday, though, was Miss Owen's remark about the list Jackson had to go through to get to the title. It does seem strange that everyone should die one after the other. If we could prove foul play anywhere, we could finish him."

"How could we do that?" Niki asked. "The most obvious attempts have been the ones on your life, and we can't really prove that Jackson was behind them."

"We may be able to." Cam toyed with his toast. "I don't know how, but if all those people met with foul play, there must be a weak link somewhere."

"I wondered about another link—or two." Sherry paused. "How did my cousins die? I heard that the two boys were killed in a carriage accident, but have no details."

"Oh, I remember that well," Cam said. "I found out all the particulars because Robbie was so devastated. He was close friends with young Nigel and was heartbroken when the boy died. That's when I gave him Blazer. Robbie felt his only friend had died, and I thought the dog would help." He glanced around the table. "There were some unanswered questions, I suppose, but Wynford, the boys' father, accepted the verdict of accidental."

"Tell me what you discovered." Sherry's voice was quiet. He pushed his plate away and sipped his coffee slowly as he listened.

Cam sat for a moment and gathered his thoughts. "The boys had been home on a school holiday, and it was the day for them to return to school. They didn't get started on time and had to hurry through some terrible weather. They stopped to eat and change horses at Farleigh, then set off again. The road curves sharply on the side of a hill there, and there's a river below. The carriage was moving along when another carriage came barreling around the curve, forcing Wynford's to the edge. It teetered there a moment, putting terrible strain on the wheels, then one of the wheels snapped. The carriage fell into the river and the boys were drowned. The driver and groom were thrown. The driver hit his head on a rock and was killed. No one ever discovered the groom's body, and it was assumed that he drowned and was washed away." Cam paused. "There were some suspicious tracks and a bush that had been broken badly. It was assumed that someone might have hidden there, but nothing else was ever discovered."

"Did they recover the bodies of the boys?" Niki shoved her still-heaped plate aside.

"Yes. The carriage was a mess, of course, and a part or two of it had washed away. The boys' bodies were found separately—one in the water near the carriage and one farther downstream." Cam stopped and shook his head. "Robbie was completely devastated."

"The groom." Sherry frowned. "Did you say nothing was ever found of him? No trace at all?"

"Nothing." Cam frowned. "No one seemed to think it odd at the time. He was simply presumed dead."

"Was there a magistrate's hearing?" Alston asked, as he poured himself more tea. "Was anything said about the groom there?"

Cam knotted his brow as he concentrated and ran his fingers through his hair. "There was a hearing," he said slowly, "but I recall nothing about the groom. Not a mention at all."

"Do you think the man could have been implicated? His disappearance raises more questions than it answers."

"He could have. I don't know. I think he was a local man."

Alston sipped his tea and looked over the rim of the cup. "What about the driver of the other carriage? What did he have to say?"

"He was never identified. In fact, he may not have existed at all. The magistrate attempted to reconstruct the accident from the condition of the boys' carriage. The side was scraped and had touches of green paint on it. When it left home, it was black and without a scratch."

Alston raised an eyebrow. "And where was Jackson during all this?"

"I don't know. The focus was on the boys. After all, with the heir in America, Jackson didn't stand to inherit. Also, there was the possibility that Lord Wynford might remarry and father other children."

Sherry paused and thought for a minute. "There's something else I've been thinking about," he said slowly. "As I told you, Uncle Richard wrote my father several times. Father realized Uncle Richard was grieving, but he thought he detected a note of hope. Then there was the news that Uncle Richard had died. My father wondered if there was a possibility of suicide, and that was one of the things he sent me to discover." He looked around at them. "Now I think my question may be: Was there any possibility of murder?"

"Murder?" The three of them said the word together and looked at him.

"Yes, murder. That's what we've been discussing here, isn't it? The driver of that other carriage murdered those boys, the driver, and perhaps the groom as surely as if he'd hit them with a bullet. The consensus seems to be that Uncle Richard died as a consequence. I've discreetly asked as many servants I can, and they all tell me that Uncle Richard died from an overdose of laudanum."

Cam nodded. "That's true. Everyone thought he was so distraught that he didn't know what he was doing."

"Perhaps, perhaps not." Sherry paused for effect. "Uncle Richard's death could easily be murder, either by his own hand or someone else's." He paused. "I know it's difficult to think that anyone would be capable murdering a man's children, and perhaps the man himself, but I think we should try to investigate further."

"We need to find out something about the groom," Niki said, nodding. "Didn't you say he was a local man, Cam?"

Cam chewed his lip and ran his fingers again through his spiky hair. "I'll ask around. Someone here will know a name and possibly where to find out something about him. It's a small place. I'll do that today. Want to join me, Alston?"

Sherry stood up. "I've got an errand that will take all day. I plan to go to the Silbury track, where the racing officials are meeting this week. Two of them have agreed to talk to me. I want to find out if they know anything about Jackson and his practices."

"What shall I do?" Niki stood up as well. The three men looked at her, puzzled. "Well, you certainly don't expect me to sit here all day doing embroidery while the three of you are off doing exciting things, do you?"

They looked from one to the other. "I'll tell you what you can do, but you won't like it," Cam said. "You can go see Mrs. Elton."

"The vicar's widow?" Niki frowned. "Whatever for?"

Cam laughed. "Mrs. Elton has been around since the scandal that rocked the Wynfords. What she doesn't know about the family isn't worth knowing. See if you can discover anything about Jackson's background that might be useful."

Niki sighed. "All right. I'll take Sarah with me to help." She made a face. "A whole day sitting and listening to gossip." She sighed. "You men get to do all the good things."

# Chapter 13

Niki's visit to Mrs. Elton was a success.

"Why," asked Sarah as they were riding over in the carriage, "do you want to know about Wynford's family? I thought you didn't particularly care for the man."

"I might change my mind," Niki said vaguely. "I need to discover something about my neighbors. After all, everyone here already knows everything about him. Since I happen to be new to the neighborhood, I felt I should know."

"Why didn't you just ask Cam?" Sarah could be maddeningly logical at the worst times.

"Cam was busy today. Weren't he and Alston going somewhere?"

Sarah sighed and, as Niki had hoped, the mention of Alston's name distracted her. The rest of the way she enumerated Alston's many virtues. Niki asked her baldly if she would accept Alston if he offered. The answer, as expected, was yes, with no hesitation.

Mrs. Elton, a widow with few visitors except other village widows, was excited to see them. Niki had seen her at church, but had never talked to her at any length. Mrs. Elton was as interested in finding out about Niki and her family as Niki was in finding out about the Devlin family and Jackson.

"A bad match, it was," Mrs. Elton said over tea, shaking her head. "But Captain Jackson was a charmer and handsome, oh my! The boy has a touch of it, but nothing like his father." She smiled as she remembered. Soon Niki had learned all there was to learn about the family. It seemed the late Mrs. Jackson had been a bosom bow of Mrs. Elton's when they were children. "I hated to see her marry the captain," Mrs. Elton said, her curls bobbing. "She was taken in by his good looks. I knew better. I knew the man was a charlatan, but she just wouldn't listen to me." She plied Sarah and Niki with more tea and continued. "He led her a terrible life. Her only joy was her son, and he took after his father in temperament." She clicked her tongue against her teeth. "Terrible, terrible."

Out of nothing but curiosity, Niki quizzed Mrs. Elton about the Devlin family. Everything Mrs. Elton told her matched the things that Sherry had told her about his background. "Ah, the second son," Mrs. Elton said with a sigh. "What a handsome man! Just like a blond Greek god he was! Shame on Lord Wynford for letting him take the blame for Richard's indiscretion. It broke Lady Wynford's heart, it did. She never saw the boy again after he left for the Americas. In fact, no one has ever seen him." She poured herself another cup of tea. "I heard he'd married and had a family." She paused and a horrified expression crossed her face. "My goodness, I hadn't thought of it, but they all must be dead or why would Jackson have inherited the title. Poor things. The natives must have killed them." She lowered her voice. "All sorts of strange things happen over there in America, I'm told."

"Without a doubt." Niki smiled and put her cup down. "We really must be leaving. Do come to Breconbridge to visit us, Mrs. Elton. I'm sure Mama would love to have you visit." She tucked her flyaway hair up under her bonnet. She had felt her hair falling down as they rode over in the carriage, and, as the drizzle of the morning had turned to rain, her hair had gotten worse as the day progressed.

"I think our visit made her day," Sarah observed, as Mrs. Elton waved to them from the door as they left. "Do you know enough about Wynford now?"

Niki made a face. "I'm not sure what I learned today. I'll have to go home and write some of it down and try to make sense out of it. She kept jumping around from person to person as though I knew them."

Once back at Breconbridge, Sarah joined Lady Larch and her mother in doing some mending. Sarah was quite an accomplished needlewoman. Niki excused herself and went on to the library to try to write down her impressions of her conversation with Mrs. Elton.

To her surprise, Sheridan was there, sitting at the desk, going over some notes in front of him. "I thought you were going to Silbury to talk to the racing board," Niki said, walking over to the small fire in the grate and holding out her hands. In spite of her warm cloak, she had gotten cold and damp during the carriage ride home. The fire felt good.

"I did." He stood and pulled a chair up next to the desk. "Sit down here, and I'll show you what I discovered." He pulled his papers toward him. "I like to make notes of everything. As I told you once, Mr. Jefferson impressed on me the necessity of accurate records." He shuffled the papers. "Here are the results of horses entered under Jackson's own name. As you can see, about half have won and about half have lost. About what could be expected." He pulled another paper toward him. "I thought I was at an end until I happened to think about the names those two men used at the Wilmay races." He pointed to one column of figures. "Look at this— Dunbarton has won over three-quarters of the races he's entered horses in." He tapped the ends of his fingers against the paper. "That's certainly not normal, especially for someone who really isn't in the horse business. And these are just the races there are records for. Who knows how many small races have been run? The races at Wilmay aren't on this list, for instance."

"So you think something's wrong?"

"I know it." He pulled a small, flat book from the side of

the desk, folded the papers, and inserted them. Niki reached over and picked up the book. It was curved, as though he had carried it next to his body and the book had shaped itself to him. "What is this?" she asked, opening it. The paper she picked up was worn and appeared to have been opened many times. "I'm sorry," she said, catching herself and putting the paper back inside the book. "I certainly didn't mean to pry into anything personal. Do forgive me."

He laughed and smoothed the paper out. "Think nothing of it. This, my dear Miss Owen, is about marigolds."

"Marigolds? You've mentioned them before. Are you fond of marigolds?"

"I can't abide the things, but Farnsworth loved them. Do you remember that I told you about Farnsworth?"

"The man who was killed?"

He nodded. "Yes. I had persuaded him to come to Wynwoode with me, so I suppose I'm responsible for his death in one way. That has certainly bothered me."

"He chose to come, didn't he?"

"Yes, but I still asked. I owe it to Farnsworth to discover who killed him. At any rate, I met Farnsworth on my journey from France to England, and we fell into a conversation. I told him about my attempts at horse breeding, and he told me about his marigolds. You see, Farnsworth was attempting to breed a white marigold. He had the idea that he could find the seed from paler marigolds and plant it, then eventually wind up with a white one. He kept all these meticulous charts on his marigolds. Look here"—he pointed with his finger—"he told me that he was well on the way to a white one. He had taken this marigold and crossed it with this one listed in this column. The resulting flower was much paler than usual." He leaned back. "I thought I might be able to apply the same thing to horse breeding. Take the horses that exhibit winning traits and breed them. It's been done for years, but never with careful records to find out which traits will be passed on."

"And you were going to do that?" Niki smiled at him as she looked at his ink-stained fingers and the careful charts.

He nodded. "Of course. I asked Farnsworth to come with me to Wynwoode and help me begin some charts. I planned to chart the background of each horse there, then keep breeding and racing records on each horse, eventually breeding only the winners. As I said, every breeder in the world has been doing the same thing for years. I merely hoped to refine it and list the traits that made up the ancestors of a winner. That way, I could consistently breed proven winners."

"Do you think it can be done? I remember my Papa talking to Uncle Webster about that very thing. Uncle Webster seemed to feel that the things that made up a champion couldn't be analyzed."

"Possibly. What made Caesar great? What makes Napoleon the way he is? On a closer-to-home level, what makes my father's friend Jefferson so learned? These things have to be some inherited traits that can be applied to all living things. For instance, Sorcerer never won either the Derby or the Epsom Oaks, but yet he sired Smolensko, who won the Derby"—he paused and looked at his notes—"as well as sired Morel, Maid of Orleans, and Sorcery, all of whom won the Oaks. There has to be a reason. Maybe Farnsworth's marigolds will help me find it." He grinned and folded the papers. "Don't get me started on the subject, Miss Owen. I'll talk all evening if you do. Tell me, what did you discover today?"

Niki had just finished relating her day with Mrs. Elton when Cam and Alston burst into the library, dripping wet. "Let me at that fire," Cam said, shaking his head. Water went flying everywhere. He held his hands out to warm them. "Cursed job we had today, wasn't it, Alston?"

Alston removed his coat and handed it to a servant who left, taking Alston's coat as well as Cam's. "Yes, but I think we made headway." He sat down near the fire and stretched muddy boots out in front of him. "The name of the groom was easy to come by–Benjamin Touchstone. His sister still lives here in a house furnished by Wynford's estate."

"That's not the best of it though," Cam said, dragging a

chair to sit where he could be in front of the fire and still look at Sherry.

"That's right." Alston frowned. "The woman was very guarded and seemed afraid to say anything. She stumbled in her story a time or two."

"We pressed her for a while and found out some news." Cam paused, smiling.

"All right," Niki said, "tell us. I can't stand any more suspense."

"Touchstone's alive." Cam smiled in triumph.

*"Alive?"* Sherry stood up and began to pace the floor. "What did she say? Where is he?"

"There's the rub." Cam sighed. "As soon as she let that slip, the woman was terrified. We had to swear by all that's holy that we'd never let them be hurt in any way."

Alston poured each of them a glass of wine. "She was afraid to say very much, but she did say that Touchstone came to see her right after the accident and said he was leaving the country. I don't think she knows anything about the accident, but she's worried about him. I gathered that he sends her a bit of money as he can, but she hasn't seen him since that day."

"She said he was scared out of his wits, and that was very unlike him." Cam stood and turned to warm his back. "He told her that he hit his head. If anyone asked, he told her, she wasn't to tell them a thing. Then he left."

"There has to be a way to find him." Sherry looked from one to the other. "Any suggestions?"

"If he sends his sister money," Niki said, "he probably does it through the post or through a friend. Since you've fairly well ruled out a friend, that leaves only the post. There should be some kind of return address, or a bank draft with an address. If we had that, at least we would know where to start."

Sheridan bowed his head in her direction. "Miss Owen, I commend you. You always get right to the heart of things." He pushed back the lock of hair that had fallen over his eyebrow. Niki noticed in the firelight that the stubble on his face was glinting blond. "Gentlemen, I believe another visit to Touchstone's sister is in order."

"Good thinking, Niki." Cam's voice held admiration. "A very simple solution, but I would never have thought of it by myself." Cam frowned. "I don't know if she'll tell, though. She seemed a little skittish to me."

"Why not send Miss Owen?" Alston said. "If anyone can get information from the woman, she can."

So it was settled, and the next day Niki found herself heading out with Cam and Sheridan as an escort to the home of one Mrs. Ebeneezer Goforth, the former Hazel Touchstone. Alston had escorted Sarah and her mother to the village to get them out of the way, while Robbie had been persuaded to come down with a cough that would keep Lady Larch occupied. Robbie's persuasion had, Niki suspected, involved the payment of a sum of money to him from both Cam and Sheridan.

Mr. and Mrs. Goforth lived in a small, neat cottage on the Wilmay Road. Mr. Goforth had been a groom at Wynwoode as well, but had fallen from a barn loft a few years before and was unable to work. He and his wife sat at the table while Niki introduced herself, then unpacked a basket of fruits she had brought. Cam and Sheridan had stayed outside to talk to the Goforths' son, a strapping young man named Timothy. Sheridan and Timothy had immediately fallen into talking about horses. Timothy appeared as horse-mad as Cam.

Instead of trying to discover something, Niki had decided to come right to the point. "I need to find the whereabouts of Benjamin Touchstone," she said. "I didn't want to come here under any kind of pretense."

"We don't know a thing about Ben." Mr. Goforth looked at her from under bushy eyebrows. "Why do you need to know?"

Niki had pondered about this question as she knew it would be asked. She had settled on the truth. "I wanted to find out about the deaths of Lord Wynford's sons. I knew your brother had been there, and thought he could possibly tell us something."

Mr. Goforth wasn't impressed, and asked her again, "Why do you want to know?"

This was the sticky part. Niki took a deep breath. "We have reason to suspect that foul play was involved, even though it was never mentioned at the hearing. We thought Mr. Touchstone could help us."

The Goforths looked at each other. "Ben never told me a thing," Mrs. Goforth said.

"I understand that. We merely wanted to talk to him. I assure you that he's under no suspicion. In fact, from everything we've heard, he was an exemplary groom. I believe Lord Wynford said Touchstone was the best on the place, and that's why he entrusted his boys to him."

"Aye." Mr. Goforth stared gloomily at the table. "That he was. Ben didn't say anything about it, but I could tell that it tore him up awful when those little boys died." He took a deep breath. "There was something, though . . ."

"Ebeneezer," his wife said warningly.

He patted her hand. "Now, Hazel, we talked about this last night, and I thought we agreed that this needs to be said. Ben will never be able to come back into this country until this is settled. You know how much you've missed him." He waited a moment until Mrs. Goforth nodded her head. "All right." She sighed. "I just don't want anything to happen to Ben."

"Nothing will, I promise you," Niki said. "We just want to find out the truth."

"Well, I don't know it, and neither does the missus," Mr. Goforth said, "but there was something havey-cavey about it all. Ben wouldn't say what, but he was afraid to stay around here. He started over to Wynwoode to try to talk to the old master, but came back within the hour. He couldn't have gone close to the house. He left that night and hasn't been back."

"Do you know where we can reach him? It's important, and we'll do everything we can to protect him and bring him back." Niki almost held her breath.

The Goforths looked from one to the other. "Does Lord Larch know about this?" Mrs. Goforth asked.

As usual, Niki was unable to lie about it. "His son, Camden, is outside. You talked to him yesterday and know him. Would you like me to bring him inside so you can talk to him?"

"Yes, I would." Mrs. Goforth was tight-lipped. "I don't want anything happening to Ben."

Niki went out and called to Cam and Sherry. Soon both men were in the small house along with Timothy. Niki explained what Mrs. Goforth had asked. "She wants to protect Ben," she said.

"I understand that," Sherry said, sitting down beside Niki. "Mrs. Goforth, did you know any of the Devlin family?"

She nodded. "I was a maid there before I married Ebeneezer here. He was one of the grooms. That's how Ben got his job— Ebeneezer found him a place." She looked around the small cottage. "We had hoped to stay here for a while, but . . ." Her voice broke.

"Now, Mother." Mr. Goforth patted her hand again. "Don't mind Mother," he said gruffly. "We had planned to try to get a place at the house for Timothy, and us live here until we died, but we're going to have to leave."

"Why?" Niki asked.

There was silence, and the three family members looked uncomfortable. "Wynford's turned us out."

"After all those years of service." Mrs. Goforth's voice was bitter. "I couldn't believe the man. Just came by pretty as you please and told us to move within the month. He cut off Ebeneezer's pittance when Lord Richard died, and if it hadn't been for Ben sending us money . . ." She broke off and put her hand over her mouth. "But that's not to say that I know where he is."

Sherry reached across the table and took her hands. "Look at me, Mrs. Goforth. Imagine my hair is blond. Have you ever seen anyone like me before?"

She looked searchingly at his face, as did Mr. Goforth. "Mr. Wyatt? You're Mr. Wyatt?" she said, her voice faltering.

Sherry grinned. "No, but the next best thing. He's my father, and he sent me here from America to find out what was going on at Wynwoode. I have to confess that I don't usually look this way. I have blond hair like my father, but''—he grinned at her again—''someone tried to use me for target practice, so I thought I should change my looks.''

Mr. Goforth looked at Cam. ''I know you, young sir, as Lord Larch's heir. Is what he says true?''

''Every word of it.'' Cam tried to smooth down his spiky hair but wasn't successful. ''That's why it's so important that we find Mr. Touchstone.''

Mr. Goforth nodded and took a deep breath. He paused for a long moment. ''He's in Fording Dean, living there under the name of Ben Smith. He works as an ostler at an inn there.''

''We'll go talk to him and see if he knows anything that might help us,'' Sherry said. ''I promise that we'll do everything we can to protect him.'' He stood up. ''You've been most helpful.''

The others stood as well. Niki thanked them and asked if they would be offended if she sent them some supplies from the village. She had noted that they hadn't been able to offer tea to the company. ''I'd like to send some things by way of thanks,'' she said, careful not to be offering charity.

Sherry paused by the door, his hand on the small of Niki's back. He turned to look at the three Goforths. ''One thing I can promise you if things work out. If my father is named the new Lord Wynford, I promise that you'll be able to stay here as long as you want. I'll also see that you have your pension reinstated.'' He glanced at Timothy and smiled. ''Even if we can't work things out here, I'd like to hire Timothy to work for me. I'll pay his passage to Virginia. And yours as well,'' he added, seeing their anxious faces. ''I know you want to be near him.''

Mrs. Goforth tried to speak, but burst into tears instead. ''Thank you.'' Mr. Goforth's voice was rough with feeling.

''Thank you,'' Niki said. ''Whether or not we discover what we need, you've helped us with the effort.''

''You did a wonderful job talking with the Goforths,'' Sherry said, helping Niki onto Qadir. "This may be what we've been looking for."

"I hope so." Niki glanced back at the Goforths' door. "That was a very nice thing you did, promising them their cottage and a place for Timothy."

"It was only fair." He swung up onto Traveler and pulled his watch from his pocket. "Cam, do we have time to go to Fording Dean today? Is it close by?"

Cam smoothed his hair and replaced his hat. "We could probably get to Fording Dean by late afternoon, but I don't know if we'd have time to check all the inns. Ben Smith may be hard to find. Of course, we could spend the night."

"What better way to ask questions of an ostler than to be a guest?" Sherry grinned at him as they began their ride back to Breconbridge. "And I may be able to locate him without much trouble. After all, I *am* a former John Smith."

# Chapter 14

Niki had no time to talk further to either Cam or Sherry. As soon as they reached Breconbridge, the two of them packed a change of clothes and left for Fording Dean. "Men have all the fun," Niki said to Blazer. The dog merely looked up at her and flopped down on the rug in the hall.

"There you are, dear," Lady Larch said, coming down the stairs. "Would you mind checking on Robbie? I have such a headache that I need to go to bed." She put the back of her hand to her head and looked faint.

"Of course, Mama." Niki stifled a smile. Her mother had never been able to abide sick people. Robbie must be putting on quite an act. Niki went up the stairs to Robbie's room, calling for Blazer as she went. Blazer ignored her and began to snore.

When she opened the door, Robbie moaned and shivered under the covers. Niki closed the door behind her. "You may stop now, you charlatan. It's Niki."

Robbie opened one eye and looked around, then threw back the covers. He was bundled in three or four layers and had a hot brick at his feet. "Good, I'm about to roast." He peeled off the top two layers and wiggled his toes in the air. ''Mama thinks I have the measles.'' He grinned. ''I've done quite well if I say so myself. What did you discover?''

''Wretch. You've given Mama a headache. I thought you must have been convincing.''

''I was. Thank goodness I can recover.'' He stretched. ''What did you discover today? Where are Cam and Sheridan?''

Niki raised an eyebrow at him. For your information, they've gone off to find the groom who rode on Wynford's carriage. We discovered he lives at Fording Dean. But that's not to be bruited about. Keep it quiet.

''Fording Dean? That's half a day's ride! They won't get back tonight.''

''I know. They're going to spend the night. I think they told Mama that they were going to look at a horse.'' She sighed. ''I don't know who's worse—you or Camden.''

''I am,'' Robbie said. He jumped up and looked out the window. ''Here come Alston and Sarah back from their carriage ride. Sarah looks like the cat that ate the cream.'' He turned. ''Should I tell Alston what a dunderhead she is?''

''Don't you dare!'' Niki came over and looked out the window. Alston was handing Sarah down and she did, indeed, look smug. Alston must have offered for her, Niki decided, or else have given some indication of it. She and Robbie watched as Alston helped her up the steps and into the house. ''Sickening,'' Robbie said.

''What do you mean?''

''Girls.'' Robbie's voice was disgusted. ''Why would anyone make a fool of himself over Sarah Keene when he could have a horse?''

Niki tried not to giggle. ''Young man, mind your manners.''

''I always do in public, but you're family, so you don't count.'' He leaned against the window. ''Who's that coming up the drive?'' he asked, peering. Niki looked down the alley of trees. ''It's Wynford,'' she said shortly. ''Whatever could he want?''

Robbie dashed back into the room and peeled off another

layer. "I've just recovered, Niki. You go down and see what he wants, and I'll listen at the door."

"You'll do no such thing." She hoped she sounded firm. "When he leaves, I'll tell you why he was visiting." She shut the door behind her to stifle his protest.

Niki paused at the top of the stairs to make sure she looked presentable. When she had gotten back home, she had changed into a pale pink dress that she thought looked insipid. It really did little for her complexion or her looks. Still, she was fashionable and looked good enough. She went down the stairs, reaching the hall just as the butler was taking Wynford's hat. "Miss Owen," he said with a bow, "you look charming today. Your presence here makes my trip worthwhile."

"Thank you." Niki gave him the requisite small curtsy and led the way to the drawing room. To her surprise, Lady Larch and Mrs. Keene were there, talking. Sarah sailed into the room right behind Wynford, still looking smug. She went over to a chair, picked up her embroidery, and sat down. Lady Larch showed no signs of a headache. Instead, she was chattering and smiling with Mrs. Keene. She gave Wynford a particularly inviting smile.

"How very nice to see you," Lady Larch said warmly, inviting him to sit and have tea. He sat on the only available space, the sofa, and Niki was forced to sit beside him. Sarah was in the chair to her right and put her embroidery on the table beside the sofa so she could lean forward to talk to Wynford. "What brings you this way, Lord Wynford?" Sarah asked with a smile. "I do hope you will be able to visit with us for a while."

Niki fumed. The last thing she wanted was Wynford around for an hour or more. The longer he stayed, the better his chances of discovering something from a chance word someone could let drop. "I would be delighted to stay, but I doubt that you will find my conversation entertainment enough."

"Oh, I'm sure we would," Lady Larch said, oblivious to Niki trying to give her a meaningful look. Instead, she looked at Niki curiously. "Whatever is the matter, dear? Are you about to sneeze?"

Niki nodded and gave the best imitation of a sneeze that she could manage. "I got wet yesterday when Sarah and I went to the village. I must be catching a cold," she mumbled, looking at the fireplace.

"What you need is a good cup of tea," Lady Larch said, pulling the bell rope. To Niki's chagrin, Wynford had a cup of tea with them, and chatted for the better part of half an hour. Finally, just as Niki thought he would be leaving any minute, he casually asked where Sheridan and Cam were. Lady Larch frowned. "Where did you say they were going, dear?" she asked, looking at Niki.

Niki caught her breath as she saw that Wynford was looking at her intently. Did he know anything? She had never been able to tell a lie without looking guilty. She knocked Sarah's embroidery off the small table and bent down to retrieve it. As she was looking at the floor, fumbling with the embroidery hoop and pretending to search for the needle, she answered her mother. "Oh, I do believe they said they were going to visit a friend and look at a horse he had. I've quite forgotten the name, but I do know that they planned to stay a night or so." She sat back up and placed the embroidery on the table.

"Pity," said Wynford easily, looking at her. Niki had the impression he was looking right through her and knew that she had not told the complete truth. "I had hoped to talk to Camden about the races he's planning here. He had sent word to me that he was going to have a race or two here as part of a birthday surprise."

"Oh, yes." Lady Larch smiled warmly. "I do hope you'll be able to participate, but do be careful and say nothing to Lord Larch. Camden does so want this to be a complete surprise."

"You may trust my discretion." Wynford gave her an answering smile. "Speaking of horses . . ." He turned to Niki. "Would you do me the honor of riding with me day after tomorrow, Miss Owen? I thought we might take a turn around the road that runs by the estate." He chuckled. "I'm assured by those who should know that the weather is supposed to be fine. If your cold hasn't worsened, of course.''

Niki looked around. Everyone's eyes were on her. She felt herself smile at Wynford, and said, ''I'd be delighted.'' She could almost feel her mother's approval.

Wynford took his leave. Lady Larch and Mrs. Keene immediately began expounding on Wynford's merits, so Niki immediately complained of her cold and a headache, saying that she was going upstairs to rest until supper. It was easy for her to say this because it was perfectly true. After hearing everyone tell her how lucky she was that Wynford was showing an interest, she had developed a crashing headache. Her disposition wasn't improved when she got back to her room. Robbie was there and, worse, Blazer was curled up on her bed, asleep.

''What did he want?'' Robbie asked eagerly. ''I thought you'd come right up and tell me.''

''I had to listen to Wynford's praises first.'' Niki roused Blazer and shooed him off the bed. ''Wynford wants me to go riding with him tomorrow. He also asked where Sheridan and Cam were.''

''Do you think he suspects?''

''Suspects what? There's nothing to suspect.'' She climbed up on the bed and leaned back against the pillows. ''I just hope I discover something tomorrow when we go riding.''

''I'll follow you.'' Robbie's head nodded up and down. ''Don't you worry. I'll be right behind you.''

Niki sat straight up. ''Don't you dare! We're going down the old road and into the village, I think. Wynford would see you in a minute.'' She paused. ''Besides, I'll have to have Jem along. You know how Mama is about my riding alone.''

Robbie got his stubborn expression. ''I should go.''

''You heard me. Don't you dare.'' She put her hand to her head. ''Robbie, could you go have Shotwell get me a cup of chocolate? I have a terrible headache.'' Robbie glared at her, whistled to Blazer, and left. Niki waited for Shotwell for a few minutes, then dozed off to sleep. She had barely closed her eyes when the door opened and Sarah began shaking her. ''Niki, wake up! Niki, the most wonderful thing has happened! It was too precious even to share with Mama and Lady Larch. I simply had to tell you first.'' She shook Niki violently.

Niki struggled up and swung her feet over the side of the bed. ''Alston offered for you,'' she said groggily.

Sarah sat down in the small chair Robbie had pulled up and left by the bed. ''How did you know? I haven't told a soul.''

''He offered for you this morning while you were out on your carriage ride, didn't he?'' Niki chuckled at Sarah's expression and smiled wickedly. ''Madam Anika sees all, knows all.''

''Oh, he did, Niki, he really did. I never thought I'd hear those words anywhere except in my dreams. I've waited my whole life for him.''

''Sarah,'' Niki began, but Sarah was too caught up to hear her. ''Alston wants to get married immediately,'' Sarah said. ''I want that, too.'' She looked down at her hands and twisted them together. ''I'm afraid he'll change his mind if we wait.''

''He wouldn't do that.'' Niki thought about Alston's need for money. ''Are you sure you want to do this, Sarah?''

''Oh, yes, Niki!'' Sarah's face glowed. ''I want this more than I've ever wanted anything in my life. You don't know how I've adored Alston forever. Every time I saw him in London, I thought if only he would look at me, I could be happy for the rest of my life. You don't know how I felt when I knew he was here.'' She took Niki's hand in hers. ''Niki, I know what you think. I know he doesn't love me, but that doesn't matter. I love him enough for both of us.''

Niki smiled at her. ''Then marry the man, Sarah. I wish you happy.''

''Alston wants to get a special license. I want you to stand beside me, Niki. Will you?''

''Of course.'' Niki swung her legs over the side of the bed. ''Now I think you should talk to your mama immediately. Alston will want to talk to your father as soon as possible and work out the arrangements.''

''Do you think there will be . . .'' The thought was so terrible that Sarah couldn't finish.

"No, you goose." Niki laughed. "I think your father will see how very happy you are and will agree to anything you wish. You and your mother can talk him into anything."

"Money, you mean." Sarah stood and looked at her "I'm not *that* much of a goose, Niki. I know that money is the reason Alston offered for me. I may be foolish in many ways, but I do know that, and it doesn't matter. I just thank God that Papa has money, even if it did come from trade."

"I don't believe that for an instant." Niki smiled at her again. 'Now, hurry and tell your mother. I'm sure she's near apoplexy wondering what's going on. And," she added as Sarah opened the door, "you're quite wrong about the money. I think Alston is marrying you for other reasons.'

Sarah's face lit up with hope. "Do you really think so, Niki?"

"I really think so. Niki made herself look right into Sarah's eyes. Sarah smiled and left, closing the door behind her, and Niki fell back across her bed.

"Alston must care for her, surely," she muttered to herself. For Sarah's sake, she hoped so. With a sigh, she got up and rang for Shotwell.

As soon as Mrs. Keene heard the news of Alston's offer and acceptance, she hadn't wanted Alston to leave Sarah's side for even an instant, so she dispatched a messenger to fetch Mr. Keene immediately. "Tell him to travel during the night," she had instructed the messenger, much to everyone's amusement. "He *must* be here tomorrow morning."

The messenger returned the next day, exhausted. Mr. Keene hadn't hesitated—he was on his way and was expected to arrive before evening. Mrs. Keene's plan was that Sarah be married before the week was out if the license could be secured. Sarah had every faith in her father's ability to do so, and Mrs. Keene had every faith that Mr. Keene would agree to terms with no quibbling.

The next morning, Niki slipped away from the wedding talk and went upstairs to dress for her ride with Wynford. She put on a bright green habit and topped it with a black hat that was decorated with a green feather. She rather dreaded going with Wynford, but kept reminding herself that she might discover something important. She hoped Cam and Sherry would return soon so she could talk to them. As she dressed, she thought of Sherry and wished she were going riding with him instead. She looked in the mirror and, instead of herself, saw his image— the lock of hair that kept falling over his brow, the intensely blue eyes that usually held a laugh, and the eyebrow that was a little higher than the other one, the tiny scar. It was strange that she could recall everything about his face. And even stranger that she didn't see him as he was now, but rather as he was when she had first seen him, the sun striking his blond hair.

She turned away from the mirror and sighed. Sheridan had never been more than scrupulously polite to her. Well, maybe not scrupulously, but polite. "Pins and ribbons today, Miss?" Shotwell asked.

"Uuumm." Niki wondered whether Sheridan preferred her with pins or ribbons. He had touched her hair when it was falling down, telling her he liked it. Niki's head jerked upright and knocked the pins from Shotwell's hands as she realized suddenly that she wished Sheridan was something more than just a friend. Shotwell picked up the black hat and put it on Niki's head, adjusting the feather so that it swooped down over one side of her hair. "There," Shotwell said with satisfaction. "Doesn't that look beautiful?"

"Yes," Niki mumbled, not really seeing anything. She didn't want to look in the mirror again, she didn't want to see Sheridan's face. He was a friend, nothing more. He certainly couldn't be interested in her when he could have any woman in Williamsburg or Richmond or, when he was lord of Wynwoode, any woman in London. She wasn't fashionable, not with her part-Spanish looks and dark hair. She shook her head slightly to make his image go away. *It was just all the wedding talk from Sarah*, she thought to herself. That was all.

"Don't you like it?" Shotwell asked anxiously. "You could wear the plain black without a feather."

"What?"

"Your hat. I thought it looked just right, but . . ."

Niki smiled at her. "Quite right, Shotwell. It is perfect. I always rely on your taste." She picked up her gloves. "I think I'll hunt up Robbie for a few minutes. If Wynford comes, send word to me down at the stables."

The stables were cool and dark as usual and Niki paused by Qadir's stall to breathe in the familiar smell of the horses. Robbie had announced that he was going to spend the morning in the stables, but he was nowhere to be seen. Jem was busy saddling Qadir. He hadn't seen Robbie anywhere. "I'm taking it that you would like me along," Jem said, opening the stall of his favorite horse, King's Way.

"Yes." Niki sighed. "I thought I might . . ." she stopped.

"Discover something?" Jem grinned at her.

"Exactly."

He shook his head. "Not likely. Men like Wynford cover their tracks carefully. They never tell you anything except what they want you to know." He looked toward the house and nodded. "There he is. Come on, missy, and we'll ride up to meet him. I don't want him around the stable." He looked over his shoulder to the last stall, where Comet was standing quietly. "Certainly don't want him to see that one."

"Definitely not. Jem . . ." Niki bit her lip, wondering how to phrase what she wanted to say. "Could you . . . ?"

"Don't worry. I'll be watching you, but I'll stay well back just in case he decides to say something." He grinned at her, and she smiled back. Then he helped her mount into the sidesaddle and they rode up the gravel to the front of Breconbridge.

"So sorry I'm late." Wynford touched his hat as she came up. He gave Jem a glance, then shrugged his shoulders. "I had hoped to be here earlier, but I had a problem with one of the tenants." He smiled at her as they rode down the gravel between the alley of trees. "I thought we'd take the road I mentioned the day before yesterday." Niki nodded and they set off. Jem stayed rather far back, close enough to keep her in sight, but too far to hear anything. *Not that,* Niki thought grimly to herself

after half an hour, *there is anything to hear.* Wynford seemed
bent on telling her about his good points. He had mentioned
his success in racing, in society, and as a landlord. However
much of a scoundrel and rogue he might be, the man was sure
of himself and confident of his charm.

He was showing her the boundaries of Wynwoode as they
rode by the field that had held Comet. "As I've told you, one
of my horses was stolen from here." He gestured toward the
field. "Creevy thinks he might have shot at the thief or one of
his accomplices and wounded him. It seems the man had the
gall to try to take another horse when my men were stopped
at an inn."

"Surely not!" Niki stared at Qadir's mane. "Do you know
who it was?" She dared a look at Wynford.

"I have my suspicions." He smiled at her, and she felt he
was hiding something underneath his pleasant exterior. "This
is horse country, and people simply will not tolerate a horse
thief. I'm sure I'd be completely justified in shooting anyone
who stole from me."

Niki felt her heart almost stop. "Wouldn't it be simpler to
call the magistrate or a Bow Street Runner?"

"I like to take care of my own affairs. I will not tolerate
anyone meddling with my property or my life." He smiled at
her again, but the smile did not reach his eyes. Instead of
warmth, Niki felt a chill. There was just something about the
man that unsettled her, and now she was sure that he was giving
her some sort of warning. He glanced back to find Jem, but he
was out of sight around the curve. Suddenly, Wynford grabbed
Qadir's reins from her and pulled her off into the woods. He
stopped as soon as they were out of sight.

"And just what do you think you're doing?" Niki turned
on him, filled with fury.

He moved his horse over next to Qadir, then leaned over
and put his arm around her waist, pulling her to him. Before
Niki could protest, he was kissing her, his tongue probing at
her lips and teeth. Niki tried to pull away, but he was too
strong. She thought she was going to be sick. She managed to

kick Qadir and the horse jumped forward, breaking Wynford's
hold. Niki looked back at him, her eyes blazing. "You forget
yourself, sir!"

Wynford gave her a smug smile. "On the contrary, Miss
Owen, I know exactly what I'm doing." He began to move
his horse up next to her and she kicked Qadir again, urging
him out onto the road. When she came out of the woods, Jem
was there, on the ground, looking at the tracks. Niki looked
back at Wynford, who was riding out of the woods as though
nothing had happened. "Qadir shied at something, Jem. As
nervous as he is, I believe we should get back to Breconbridge."
She turned to Wynford. "Jem will see me home."

Wynford smiled and rode up beside her. "I wouldn't hear
of it, Miss Owen. I'll be glad to see that you get home safely.
I need to go that way myself to make sure my problem with
my tenants has been solved. I believe I mentioned it." The
smile was on his face again but it didn't reach his eyes. "The
Goforths. I believe you know them. I understand you visited
them yesterday. A wonderful act of Christian charity." They
rode on in silence for a few minutes. As Breconbridge came
into view, Niki could stand it no longer.

"How did you know I visited the Goforths?"

He smiled again and didn't answer until they were part of
the way up the alley. "I know everything that happens around
Wynwoode or anything that concerns it. I commend you for
taking pity on them, Miss Owen. I'm sure they enjoyed your
gifts." They rode until they stopped on the gravel at the front
door and he helped her dismount.

"The Goforths said you had turned them off." Niki's tone
was accusing.

"And so I did, Miss Owen." There was that cold smile
again. "As I told you, I do not tolerate meddling, and the
Goforths were guilty of that. However"—the smile was back
in place as he swung into the saddle—"I have remedied that.
The Goforths should be gone by now. The son, Timothy,
seemed to have stolen from the house although, of course, he

denied it. I called in the magistrate, but the boy was gone by the time we got there."

"I don't think he would steal."

He lifted an eyebrow. "Oh, yes, Miss Owen. I'm afraid Mr. Creevy found my property in the Goforths' house. I'm a reasonable man, Miss Owen, so I didn't press charges against the boy's parents. I simply gave them the option of leaving within the hour. They were packing as I left them." He touched his hat. "Good day, Miss Owen. I hope to see you tomorrow evening. Your mother has kindly invited me to supper with you then."

Niki watched as he rode down the alley. She had to keep the Goforths from leaving. The charges against Timothy were false, she was sure of it. She motioned to Jem, and he helped her mount Qadir. If they cut across country, they could get to the Goforths before Wynford did. If nothing else, she could bring them to Breconbridge. But what then? Sherry and Cam should be back soon, and they would know. Yes, she thought to herself as she gave Qadir his head across the fields, Sherry would know what to do.

# Chapter 15

Niki nudged Qadir and he responded instantly, heading off at a gallop across the fields. Just as she and Jem came to the fence that marked the boundary between Breconbridge and Wynwoode, Jem shouted something to Niki. She pulled Qadir up and wheeled him around. Jem was pointing to the distance where a small rider on a large, black horse was clearly silhouetted against the sky.

"Comet," Jem said as she moved up beside him. "I'd know him anywhere. Wait for me here." He urged King's Way forward. Niki paused a moment, then nudged Qadir. She couldn't wait unless she knew about Comet and Robbie. She caught up with Jem in just a moment. He merely glanced at her, nodded, and went on, pushing King's Way into a full gallop.

At the top of the hill, they turned into the woods where Comet and the rider had disappeared. It was only a moment until they found him. Robbie was sitting on the horse, grinning. "He's a goer, all right, Niki," he said. "I promised him that I would take him out the first chance I got, and I did."

"You caught Jem away and took him out." Niki's voice

was flat. "What if Wynford had come by, Robbie? He might have recognized the horse. Then what would have happened?"

"But Comet wants to get out, Niki." He patted Comet's neck, and the horse shook his head as if he knew what was being said. "He needs exercise."

Jem dismounted and examined Comet's foot. "Sound as can be," he said, standing. "He does need exercise, but not here."

"Where are you off to?" Robbie asked as Blazer came trotting up and flopped down beside the horse, his tongue lolling out.

"We're going to the Goforths' and, no, you can't go."

Robbie's eyes widened. "How did you know I wanted to go?"

"A good guess." Niki smiled at him in spite of herself. She tried to be severe. "Robbie, you did a very foolish thing by riding here with Comet. I want you to take that horse back and put him in the stable. We have to keep him hidden until we decide what to do with him." She paused. "I want you to do something for me. Watch for Sheridan and Cam. I hope they'll be back from Fording Dean by now. If they are, and you see them, tell them that Jem and I have gone to the Goforths' house because Wynford told me that he had sent them packing. I plan to get them and bring them to Breconbridge." She looked at Robbie. "Will you do that?"

He nodded, his expression like a true conspirator, and rode off, whistling to Blazer to follow. Blazer wasn't overly eager to get up, but loped along after Robbie and Comet.

Jem let out a long breath. "That could have been bad."

"Robbie has no idea how bad." Niki frowned as she watched the boy, horse, and dog disappear toward Breconbridge. "I should have been harder on him, but . . ." She shook her head.

"I know." Jem nodded in agreement. "It's always hard to come down on that boy. He means well." He headed King's Way back toward the road. "I hope we get there in time," Niki said, hurrying Qadir down the slope.

The Goforths' house was already empty, and there was no sign of them. "They've probably gone to Fording Dean," Niki said, disappointed. "I hope they meet up with Sheridan and Cam." She shook her head. "They've just been caught up in this thing with Wynford and haven't had a choice."

"Like Comet," Jem said, turning King's Way into the lane that led back home.

"I know, Jem. If we don't hear from them by tomorrow, I'll see if Sheridan or Cam will go back to Fording Dean and try to find them. It's the least we can do."

Cam and Sherry weren't at Breconbridge when she and Jem got back there, so Niki had no idea what was happening with them. She began to worry in earnest, imagining both men hurt, dying, or dead. Worst of all, she couldn't mention her fears to anyone.

Robbie had indeed stabled Comet, but wanted to exercise him around the yard. Jem was firm in not allowing that, and Robbie, disgusted, had said that he and Blazer were going off to search for treasure and had wandered down the path toward Wynwoode. Niki was left to return to the big house and try to dodge her mother and the Keenes. Most of all, she wanted to get on Qadir and head for Fording Dean to find Sherry and Cam, but that was impossible. The next best thing was just to be alone with her worry.

She wasn't successful. Lady Larch nabbed her as she came in the door. "And how was your ride, dear?" she asked. "Wynford is such a fine-looking man, and"—she lowered her voice—"an eligible as well. Of course, not quite in the league with Alston, but eligible." She slipped her arm through Niki's and headed her toward the small parlor where the Keenes were sitting. "I simply don't know how you could have let Alston escape you, Niki. You must begin thinking of these things." She smiled as they went inside the parlor, and Niki was forced to listen to wedding plans for the better part of half an hour before she could plead that she needed to go to her room and change her clothes.

The rest of the day was a long and dull one. Niki was restless after Shotwell had finished trying to pin up her hair and paced around the house. Every time the clock struck, she became more and more anxious. There was nothing to distract her from her fretting—her only choices for company seemed to be either sitting with the ladies discussing wedding plans over embroidery or placating her stepfather when he discovered his spyglass missing from the library. He had the house in an uproar for a good hour, but the thing was never found. Lady Larch finally convinced him that he had left it in London.

In late afternoon, Niki heard a carriage roll up to the front, and she dashed to the door. To her disappointment, it was merely Sarah's father. Mr. Keene was a small, dapper man who looked as if he spent a great deal of time indoors. His only trips out were to his office and back home, so this trip was exceptional for him. He and Alston got down to business at once. They closeted themselves in the library most of the afternoon, through supper, and afterward. All the ladies except Niki were consumed with curiosity, but heard nothing from them. Niki was forced to sit in the drawing room listening to the others speculating on the arrangements. The only other topic was a discussion of even more wedding plans. Niki finally complained of an all-too-real headache, left, and went up to bed, stopping first to check on Robbie.

He was in bed, and she could see that he was pretending to be asleep. She shook him and he pretended to snore. She shook him again. "I know you're not asleep," she said, sitting down in the chair beside the bed. "I wanted to remind you again not to get Comet out. The last thing we need is for Wynford or Creevy to recognize him."

"No one could recognize him. He's a different color. And he's all well now."

"Jem recognized him all the way across the field."

Robbie sat up, his eyes wide. "He did? I thought he recognized me." His face crumpled. "Do you suppose anyone else saw Comet? All kinds of things were going on over at Wynwoode." He clapped his hand over his mouth.

"What do you mean?" Niki leaned forward and put her hands on the edge of the bed. There was something very hard under the covers. She pulled back the bedclothes, and there was Lord Larch's spyglass, clutched in Robbie's hand. "Just what did you do this afternoon?"

Robbie slid the spyglass under his pillow. "I just went to the hill at the back of Wynwoode and looked at things. I thought someone might have seen me once, but no one did." He looked at her defensively. "I was just looking." He leaned toward her. "I think something must be going on there, Niki. They were packing up things from the house and putting them into wagons. The wagons went down toward the London road. All the horses seem to have been pulled from the pastures and put into the paddock behind the stables."

Niki made a face as she thought about this. Then she thought about something else Robbie had said. "What makes you think someone saw you?"

"Oh," Robbie said airily, "Wynford has a spyglass, too, and he was looking around. He looked right at the place where I was hiding. He motioned to one of his men, and the man seemed to head my way, but then he took off to the right, so I wasn't worried. No one saw me." He paused. "There was one thing, Niki." His voice sounded small. "I saw them cover two horses with dye. Turned them as black as Comet."

Niki frowned. "I don't know why they would do that. If Wynford owns the horses, there's no reason for him to hide them."

"If he owns them," Robbie said, looking at her. His eyes were huge. "Do you think, Niki . . . ?"

She shook her head. "I don't have an opinion on that, Robbie." She pulled the covers back up and stood. "We're both going to bed now. We need our rest. If Sherry and Cam haven't returned by tomorrow evening from Fording Dean, you and I and Jem will go there and try to find them."

"We will?" Robbie's eyes were shining. "Perhaps they need rescuing."

"I'm sure that . . ." She stopped as the words of reassurance died on her lips. "I hope not," she finally said.

"Sherry can take care of himself," Robbie said confidently.

"And he can take care of Cam, too." He curled up in the bed, the spyglass by his pillow. "Good night, Niki."

She paused at the door and smiled at him. "Good night."

Niki went to her room and tried to sit for a few minutes. Then she got up and began to pace the floor. All evening, she had tried to sound as if she wasn't worried about Sheridan and Cam. At supper, she had agreed when Lady Larch had mentioned that the two had probably stumbled on a good horse and had stayed a second night. Niki wasn't so sure. What if Ben Touchstone was still in Wynford's employ and had done something to the two of them? What if Wynford had sent one of his men to try again to kill Sheridan? It wasn't to be borne. Niki paced around her room until after midnight, restless, wandering to the window every few minutes to see if she could see anything in the dark. She finally fell asleep in her chair and was only roused by a sound from outside in the middle of the night. Her candle had burned low, and she pulled it to her, flipping open her locket watch. It was almost three in the morning. She tried to stand up but almost fell and had to sit back down. She had curled her feet and legs up under her when she had gone to sleep, and now they were numb. She heard another door close stealthily before she was able to stand. Finally, she stood and hobbled to her door, her feet still tingling.

The hall appeared empty, but there was a light under the edge of Sherry's door. Niki didn't know if he was back or if someone else was in there. Without giving herself time to think, she slipped across the hall and turned the knob, then pushed the door open. It opened silently for a second, then the hinges creaked softly. The sound was enough to make Sherry wheel and grab the person in the doorway. "I'm not . . ." Niki tried to gasp as he shut the door and leaned her against the wall, his body pressed against hers. He put his hand over her mouth. She didn't feel fear, only a strange sensation as she realized that his body was pressed against the length of hers and his bare chest was warm against her. He smelled of sweat, horses, and a peculiar man smell that she found pleasant.

"Uuummmm," she muttered, her mouth under his hand.

He moved his hand, but didn't move his body. He was pressing her into the wall, and his presence was doing strange things to her. He looked down at her and smiled, the corners of his blue eyes crinkling. "Well, Miss Owen, I trust there's a reason for this nocturnal visit. I do hope it's the one I want it to be."

Niki had to breathe. She couldn't even speak with him this close to her. Her mouth felt dry and there was a strange sensation in her chest and stomach. She pushed him back. "I came to ... I wanted to ..." She stopped and started again. "I was worried when you didn't return. I wondered what had happened, that is, what you'd discovered."

Sheridan gave her a rueful smile. "And I had so hoped you were here for another reason." He laughed and tied his shirt over his chest. "Forgive me if I'm informal."

"It's to be expected." Niki moved to a chair. The farther away from him, the better. She took a deep breath as she sat down. "Did you see Ben Touchstone? Did you see the Goforths?"

"The Goforths? Why should we have seen them? We went to Fording Dean."

Quickly Niki told him about her conversation with Wynford and that the Goforths were gone. "They must have gone to Fording Dean to see Touchstone," Sherry said, frowning as he thought. "Perhaps I can send for them first thing in the morning and get them back here. I certainly don't intend that they should lose anything because they've confided in us." He looked at her and smiled. "I'll take care of it."

"I'm so glad." Niki let out a breath in relief. "They seemed so nice, but so frightened. Did you see Ben Touchstone?"

Sherry pulled up a straight-backed chair and sat facing her. He dragged the little stool by the bed over with the toe of his booted foot and propped his feet up. "Yes, we saw Touchstone. We even brought him back with us. He's with Jem. We thought that was a good place to keep him until we were ready."

"Ready for what? What did you find out? Really, Sheridan, you're the most maddening person."

"It's a gift, my sister says. She swears my mission in life is to send her to an asylum." he grinned. "I'm glad to know I haven't lost my touch."

"Ben Touchstone?" Niki tried to be firm. She had much rather look at his face in the candlelight and watch the shadows play across it, but she needed to know what had happened.

"He was most helpful." Sherry leaned forward. "It appears that the deaths of my cousins was murder." He waited for Niki to catch her breath and went on. "A carriage came out of nowhere and forced them off the road into the river. Ben was thrown into some bushes and knocked unconscious for a while—he doesn't know how long. When he came to, he peered out and saw Creevy and another of Wynford's men, Miller, he thought the man's name was. Touchstone started to call for help, but just then Miller came from the edge of the river, carrying one of the boys—Nigel, I think Touchstone said. The boy wasn't dead. Creevy picked up a rock and bashed Nigel's head in. Then Miller threw the boy back into the river. Creevy looked around then and asked Miller if he'd seen any trace of Touchstone. Miller told him no, that he was sure Touchstone had drowned and been washed down the river. Then they left. Touchstone stayed where he was for several hours, then crawled out of the bushes and made his way at night to the Goforths. He didn't want to tell them anything for obvious reasons, and he went off to Fording Dean. The reason it took us so long was that he was there under another name." He grinned. "Not Ben Smith. Touchstone thought that wasn't original enough." Sherry's smile faded and he paused. "I've promised Touchstone protection and a position for life if he tells the magistrate his story."

"Won't Wynford just deny that he knew what Creevy was doing?"

Sherry grimaced. "That's what I'm afraid of. Creevy's a hard nut to crack, according to everything I've heard. I don't think he'll give Wynford away." He pushed the lock of hair from his forehead. "Still, the main suspicion will fall on Wynford. I know Uncle Richard was still alive when the accident happened, but his whole life was those boys. Anyone would have known he wouldn't want to go on living without them.''

"Or suspicion could fall on you. Your father is next in line.''

"I wasn't here." He leaned back against the hard back of the chair and closed his eyes. "Wynford tried to have me killed, Niki. He may not have done it himself, but he's responsible for having my cousins killed. And he killed Uncle Richard as surely as if he'd pulled the trigger himself. I intend to see that he pays for that.''

"How?" He looked so weary that Niki's heart almost broke for him. She hadn't missed the fact that, in his exhaustion, he had slipped and called her by her given name.

He opened his eyes and looked at her. "I just don't know. I wish I did. I'm almost afraid to let Touchstone talk to the magistrate tomorrow, afraid that Wynford will be warned and go to the Continent, where he can't be touched. I want him to have to pay for his crimes.''

"Could you wait a day?"

"Cam and I talked about that. It would give us time to try to find out something else about Wynford." He leaned toward her and ran his fingers through his hair. "A day isn't much, though. I don't know that we could force anything.''

His face was gray and lined with exhaustion. She touched the back of his hand. "You need to sleep, Sheridan," she said softly. "Tomorrow, things will appear differently, and perhaps we can all put our heads together and think of something.''

To her surprise, he looked at her and captured her hand between his. He didn't say anything, just looked at her, and his eyes looked dark sapphire in the candlelight. Niki looked back at him and almost felt that she was drowning in those eyes. A strange feeling came over her, and she felt as if she were floating somewhere not on earth. "Niki," he whispered, and she closed her eyes, coming back to reality. She was at Breconbridge, in a man's room, alone, after three o'clock in the morning. She would be ruined if anyone knew of this. Worse, if anyone else knew, Sheridan would be honor-bound to offer for her, and she knew he was the kind of man who would. She wanted him, she was sure, but not that way. She wanted him to want her as well, not be forced to take her. She jerked her hand from his clasp and stood up. "I've got to go." She slipped by him and reached the door. "We'll talk tomorrow."

She opened the door and was in her room in just a few seconds. She leaned against the door and breathed heavily. Whatever was wrong with her? She had never felt this way before. She took a deep breath and tried to steady herself, but it was no use, no use at all.

She undressed slowly, because her fingers were trembling, and crawled into bed, still wondering what was happening to her. She slept fitfully, plagued by dreams. They were dreams like ones she had never had before—dreams about a man with laughing blue eyes pressing against her. The warmth and the golden hair were so real that she could almost feel him with her. She awoke exhausted and with a strange longing. Tossing back the covers, she slipped from the bed and drew back the draperies. Outside, day was just breaking, and the sky was gray streaked with pink. She watched the sun come up, but she wasn't thinking of the beauty of early morning. Instead, in her mind, she could still hear Sheridan speaking her name. "Niki," he had whispered, with a rough edge to his tone. He had wanted her, she knew. She had been sheltered her entire life, and even though she was three and twenty, she was inexperienced in flirtation and the ways of men, but she knew desire when she saw it. She thought of Wynford's kiss yesterday and how it disgusted her. Last night in Sheridan's room, she had wanted nothing more in life than for him to kiss her. Only the thought of his being forced to marry her had saved her. She closed her eyes hard and kept them closed. Still, all she could see was Sheridan's blue eyes in the blackness. Was this love? She didn't know, and there was no one she could ask.

With a sigh, she went back to bed, unsure whether to dream or cry.

When Niki heard the tapping on her door later in the morning, she opened her eyes to sunshine streaming into her room. As she roused, the door opened, and Sarah stuck her head inside the room. "I can't believe this," she said with a laugh. "I never get up before you. For the first time in my life, I can call you a slugabed."

"I didn't sleep very well." Niki leaned back against her pillows and closed her eyes against the brightness of the morning. "Would you mind closing the draperies and ringing for some chocolate?"

"Of course." After Sarah ordered the chocolate, she came over and sat beside Niki. "What's the matter? You've had more headaches in the last week than you've had in the whole time I've known you." She paused. "I know I've been wrapped up in my own happiness, but I've sensed something amiss with you."

"It's nothing." Niki opened her eyes and sat up, pushing her unruly hair from her forehead. The very movement reminded her of Sheridan unconsciously pushing back his wayward lock of hair. She closed her eyes again. She didn't want to think about him.

"You're in love, aren't you, Sarah?" Niki asked suddenly.

Sarah paused as a maid came in with a pot of chocolate and two cups. She dismissed the maid and poured cups of chocolate for herself and Niki. "Yes, very much in love." She regarded Niki for a moment. "Are you?"

"I don't know," Niki said miserably. "I think about him all the time. I dream about him. I dream about . . ." She paused as she felt a blush creeping up her cheeks. "Things," she finished lamely. "I worry about him. I want to be around him, but I don't."

"You're in love," Sarah said firmly. "Congratulations."

"Congratulations? Not that at all It's . . ." She looked at Sarah. "It's terrible, Sarah."

"I know." Sarah poured the rest of the chocolate in their cups. "I felt that way about Alston all last year. Now I could never be happier. Alston and Papa came to an agreement last night, and we're to be married tomorrow." She smiled. "That's what I came to tell you this morning."

Niki smiled back. "Congratulations to you. I'm really happy for you, Sarah, and I hope you're as happy all your life."

"I plan to be."

Niki looked at her and suddenly realized that she and Sarah were more different than she had realized. Sarah would always be happy in her own way. It truly didn't matter to Sarah that Alston didn't actually love her. Niki knew that she could never live like that—she would have to be in love and be loved in return.

Sarah put down her cup and smiled at Niki again. "There I am again, so wrapped up in my own news that I've ignored yours. Dare I ask about the man—is it Wynford?"

"Good Lord, no!" Niki sat bolt upright. "Never."

Sarah laughed and took Niki's cup from her hand. "Let me have that before it comes crashing against my thick head." She put the cup back on the tray. "If it isn't Wynford, then it must be Sheridan."

Niki didn't answer, but didn't look at Sarah either. She wasn't going to lie, and if Sarah looked in her eyes, she would know the truth. Sarah patted her hand. "He seems a wonderful man, Niki. I'm glad you're in love with him, and I think he may care for you as well. I've seen the way he looks at you across the room when he thinks you're not watching him."

"That's just because he thinks I'll do something foolish or say something I shouldn't."

Sarah shook her head. "No, this is different. Has he made any move or said anything?"

"No." Niki pushed back the covers. "This is foolish, Sarah. He doesn't care for me at all, and if I feel anything, it's probably just a passing fancy. I'm going to hunt up Robbie and go for a ride. That should clear my head and get rid of this foolishness."

Sarah laughed and went to the door, pausing there for a moment. "Foolishness, is it? Would you care to make a wager on that, Anika Owen?"

Niki raised an eyebrow at her. "You'll see, Sarah. This is foolishness, and I'll be over it by tomorrow. Just wait and see." She ignored Sarah's laugh and rang for Shotwell to help her with her habit. She would, she decided, never be alone with Sheridan again. She would never think of the man again either. With that end in mind, she bolted down a muffin and a cup of coffee for breakfast and went to find Robbie. He and Blazer were always good for a ride across the fields.

# Chapter 16

Robbie was nowhere to be found. "He probably went behind the house to search for treasure," Cam said, yawning. He was on his way. "Sherry told me about the Goforths. We're going to ride toward Fording Dean to try to find them. Sherry talked to Touchstone about where they might go. It seems there's a relative not too far away, and Touchstone thinks they might have gone there. If we're successful in finding them, we'll bring them back here."

"Then what?" Niki glanced around to see if Lady Larch was in earshot. "What do you plan to do with them? They can't go back to their house."

"No." Cam glanced out the door to see if Jem was bringing the horses to the front. "Sherry and I plan to take both the Goforths and Ben Touchstone to one of our tenant houses. The Bricklens went back to York, you recall, so their cottage is empty. Everyone will be safe there for a while."

"Is Touchstone going with you to find the Goforths?"

Sherry entered the hall and caught the end of the conversation. He looked as if he had slept the entire night. "No, I'd rather Touchstone waited here with Jem until we return. He certainly doesn't need to be seen in public right now." He turned to Cam. "Did you tell her we plan to take them to a safe place?"

Cam nodded. "She's worried about Robbie. She can't find him."

Sherry looked at her and smiled as Jem brought Traveler and Cam's horse to the front and held them by the mounting block. "He's probably out with Blazer. Is he still into the search for Robin Hood's treasure?"

Niki paused a second, then decided to tell them about finding Robbie out on Comet. Sherry looked grave. "I'll have a word with him when I get back. I agree with you—Wynford could recognize that horse, even with the dye." He smiled at her and touched her hand briefly. It was only the lightest of touches, but Niki felt a jolt all the way up her arm. "Don't worry about him."

"Heavens, no. Don't worry yourself about Robbie," Cam reassured her. "He's like a cat with nine lives." He grinned at her as he put on his hat and went outside to mount his horse. Sherry had the audacity to wink at her as he left. He was a scoundrel, she thought to herself, as he swung easily into Traveler's saddle and went off down the graveled path in the alley. Lord, the man could ride! He looked so at ease on the big horse. Niki looked down at her hand where he had touched it. To her surprise, it looked just as it always had. She shook her head to get rid of her thoughts. Sherry certainly had no intentions toward her. Besides, she had to find Robbie. No matter what Cam and Sherry thought, Niki was worried about him.

She walked to the woods behind the house and saw no sign of Robbie or Blazer. No one seemed to have seen either of them since Robbie had cadged some bread, cheese, and two apples from Cook. He had tied the supplies up in a napkin and Cook thought he was planning another day of treasure seeking. Niki wasn't so sure.

The stables were next. There was no sign of Robbie there either. Niki told Jem she wanted to go for a ride, then walked down to Qadir's stall as a groom followed her to get him and saddle him. Qadir's stall was next to Comet's, right on the end, where it was darkest. Niki glanced over the high wall and saw nothing, but Comet was difficult to see in the gloom since he had been dyed black. She looked again and screamed for Jem. Comet was gone, but there was a napkin filled with bread, cheese, and two apples lying on the hay at the edge of the stall.

"Robbie," Niki said as they viewed the empty stall. "I should have given him what for yesterday. I told him not to go out again on Comet, but I wasn't emphatic."

"He knows better." Jem's voice was grim. "Do you think he's gone to the same place?"

Niki nodded. Jem wheeled and ran to the other end of the stable. "I'll saddle King's Way and go get him."

"I'm going, too." Niki looked down to the center of the barn, where Qadir was almost ready for her to mount. "How long do you think Robbie's been gone?"

Jem shook his head. "He was here underfoot early this morning. I'd say two or two and a half hours ago." He thought. "I went to the carriage house to . . . We've got our guest stashed in the carriage house. I went with Mr. Sheridan to see him. I'd say that Robbie took Comet out then. That was almost two hours ago."

Niki sighed. "I hope Robbie's had the good sense to stay hidden. I hope . . ." She couldn't finish. Instead, she waited by Qadir until Jem got King's Way saddled, and then they rode out.

Robbie wasn't in the woods, he wasn't in the fields, he wasn't on the road. "He told me last night that he watched at Wynwoode from the hill behind the house," Niki said. "I hate to go there, but that's the most likely spot left."

Jem nodded and they turned their horses toward Wynwoode. "I hope Wynford hasn't seen him. There'll be hell to pay if they find Comet there. Those men know a dyed horse when they see one. He caught himself. "Pardon me."

"An accurate description, Jem. Let's go." She urged Qadir to move faster and within a half an hour, they were on the hill behind the big house at Wynwoode. There was no sign of

Robbie. Jem dismounted and helped Niki down. "Nothing," he said in disgust. "Just nothing."

"He must have been here," Niki said. "This is where he was yesterday, and I have a feeling that he came back." She started walking around. There was grass on the top of the hill, ringed with bushes. Niki kept well back so the people in the yard at Wynwoode couldn't see her. She didn't want to have to explain her presence. She was almost ready to give up the search and leave when a glint of metal in the grass caught her eye. She motioned to Jem, crouched, and crawled behind a bush. The grass had been beaten down behind the bush. Niki reached down and touched the glinting metal almost hidden in the grass. It was Lord Larch's spyglass.

"He could have left this yesterday," Jem said, opening it.

Niki shook her head. "No, he had it last night when he was in bed." She took the spyglass from Jem, parted the bush, and peered through the glass. "Robbie felt something was going on at Wynwoode. I think he was right. Look down there. Everyone seems to be packing."

Jem peered through the glass, then turned it slightly to look at something off to one side of the house. "Comet!" he whispered hoarsely. "There!" He pointed and handed the glass back to her. "Look what they're doing."

Niki held the glass with both hands and looked. Below she could see the stableyard clearly, as well as two small sheds. In the middle of the yard were two heavy posts in the beaten brown dirt. Wynford had tied Comet to the posts, using a rope tied on either side of the horse, holding him fast. Worse, Wynford was beating Comet with a whip, and Comet was trying to rear up on his hind legs. He was almost unable to move and pulled and tugged at the ropes, his eyes wild and rolling. "Wynford will kill him," Niki whispered. Her face was white as she handed the glass back Jem. "What can we do? Where's Robbie?"

"I don't know." Jem hesitated a moment. "Why don't I go down there, just as if I was coming over to bring a message. I'll see what's happening."

"I could go."

Jem shook his head. "No, wait here a moment and watch. If all goes well and I leave—I'll go back by the front gate—then you circle around and join me. We'll bring help back."

"And if all doesn't go well?"

"Get out of here and ride to Breconbridge for help. And do it in a hurry." Jem handed her the spyglass and walked away with his horse, circling around the woods to appear to come in from the land joining Breconbridge. Niki positioned herself behind the bush, looking through the spyglass. Wynford stopped whipping Comet, but the horse still tried frantically to get loose. Wynford turned from Comet and seemed to stare right at Niki. She burrowed even deeper into the grass and almost stopped breathing. Wynford moved away and spoke to another man who left, going around the back of the barn. Niki forgot about him as Jem rode into the stable yard. Jem dismounted and walked up to Wynford. Immediately, Niki sensed that something had gone terribly wrong. Creevy came up behind Jem and grabbed him. Jem tried to lash out with his crippled hand, but it was no use. Creevy began beating him savagely, and Jem fell to the ground. Creevy kicked him and rolled him over, then two of the men dragged Jem to his feet. Niki pushed the spyglass closed and crawled backwards, heading for Qadir, so she could ride back to Breconbridge for help. She got to her feet and ran toward the woods where Jem had hidden Qadir, but she couldn't find him. Frantically, she searched the edge of the woods.

"This be what you're looking for?" The voice was low and cruel. Niki whirled around. The man Wynford had spoken to was there, holding Qadir's reins. "You'd best be coming with me."

Niki dashed off into the brush, her heavy habit dragging. Twice she stumbled over it, slowing her down. The man grabbed her from behind and brought her down. He fell lengthwise onto her and held her tightly, his hand moving over her breast. "Nice little baggage, you are. I'd just take you here and now if Jackson didn't care. Don't think he'd want damaged goods, but mayhap old Ned will have a turn later." He cackled and got up, dragging her upright. Niki refused to speak as he dragged her along. Qadir had broken free and run through the woods when Niki ran, and she heard him galloping in the distance. She fervently hoped that he went back to Breconbridge. Ned pushed her in front of him, swearing. "Jackson will have my arse, letting a piece of horseflesh like that slip by." He spat on the ground. "It's all your fault." He shoved Niki again, and she fell. He pulled her up by her hair, tangling his fingers in the unruly mass, and hurried on, pulling on her hair when she faltered. At last they came to the stable yard. Jem was there, on the ground, covered with blood, but conscious.

"Miss Owen." Wynford gave her a small bow. "How nice of you to stop by."

Niki tried to run to Jem, but Wynford grabbed her arm and stopped her. "You don't really want to soil your habit, Miss Owen. Creevy will take care of him."

"What have you done with Robbie?" Niki tried not to let her fright show in her voice.

Wynford nodded toward one of the sheds where Blazer was cowering in front of the door. "Ned, go let Miss Owen see her brother. I regret that she and her brother are going to have to travel with us." He smiled at her and his smile reminded Niki of an unpleasant predator. "I had hoped we could become more familiar socially before we were married."

Niki's eyes grew wide. "Married? Are you out of your mind?"

Wynford smiled at her again. "Not at all, Miss Owen. I was regretting that I had missed that opportunity when you appeared on the hillside. I thought it might be you when I saw the sun glinting off the spyglass. Wonderful things, spyglasses. That was how I discovered Lord Larch's youngest as well." He motioned towards the open door of the shed. "There's the boy. He'll have to go with us, of course. I do hope he doesn't meet with an accident."

Niki looked at Robbie. He came out of the shed, his face bruised and bleeding. He fell to his knees and put his arms around Blazer. "I'm sorry, Niki," he said, trying not to cry. "I'm sorry."

She couldn't go to him as Wynford held her back, but she made herself smile at him. "It's all right, Robbie," she said gently. "Everything will be all right."

Wynford nodded to Creevy. Before Niki could protest, Creevy and another man had picked Robbie up and thrown him back into the shed. Blazer tried to follow Robbie inside, but Creevy kicked him away and shut the shed door. Blazer slunk away, then edged his way back as soon as Creevy turned away.

"You can't do this." Niki tried to sound firm, but her voice trembled in spite of herself.

"Oh, but I can, Miss Owen, and I will. As I said, Miss Owen, I was regretting a missed opportunity with you, but now you're here. I certainly don't intend to let the opportunity pass me by again. You'll come with us, of course, and we'll be married before we leave England."

"I won't."

He turned to Niki, his face completely changed, no longer smiling. "You have no choice, Miss Owen. You and the boy are my ticket to the Continent. Lord Larch will do everything he can to keep scandal down, so I expect help from that quarter. You see, the boy told me that your brother and his friend have found Touchstone."

"You killed those boys, didn't you?" Niki looked at him with loathing.

Wynford shrugged. "I had no real choice in the matter. I wanted the title and estate, and I did what was needed to get them."

"And the heir from America?"

Wynford's laugh was harsh. "A damned slippery one to get. I never really knew what he looked like and kept having to send someone else to finish him. It took three tries before we got him, and I was beginning to think the man was part cat and had nine lives." He laughed again.

Niki had to bite her tongue to keep from goading him with

the truth. Instead, she contented herself by saying, "You won't get away with this. My stepfather will see to that."

"Oh, I doubt that. If you open your mouth, the boy will pay." His fingers dug into her arm. "Do you understand me?" Niki nodded. "That's better." He turned to Creevy and pointed to Jem. "Take him to the pond and finish him. We'll be long gone before he's found."

Creevy bent to hoist Jem up. Niki could stand no more. "No!" she cried, breaking lose from Wynford's grip and throwing herself on top of Creevy. She scratched and bit until Wynford grabbed her from behind. "A hellcat," he said, smirking. "Who would have thought it?"

He pinned her arms and nodded to Creevy. "Do it."

"Nnnooo," Niki moaned as Creevy dragged Jem across the stable yard. Just then, she heard a noise. Wynford heard it as well and tightened his grip on her arms. Niki looked up and saw several riders coming at a gallop across the top of the hill between Wynwoode and Breconbridge. She saw the big horse in front, its rider bent low over the saddle. *Sherry!* she thought, almost in tears from relief. *Sherry has come to save me!*

Wynford took one look at the riders and glanced around at his own men. "Pistols!" he yelled, dragging Niki over to Comet. He held her in front of him so Sherry couldn't use his pistol. Quickly he untied Comet's ropes and mounted, dragging Niki up in front of him. He jerked the reins up and kicked Comet hard. Instead of running, Comet began to rear and fight against him. Wynford was having trouble trying to hold him and Niki was hanging on to Comet's mane. In the background she could hear the sounds of pistols being fired, but she could see nothing except horse and the blue of the sky as Comet reared and plunged. Wynford cursed as Comet bucked and reared, trying to throw them off. Niki felt herself sailing through the air, and she landed hard on the dirt. She rolled over as Comet came down hard, his hooves not far from her. "Niki, this way!" someone yelled, and she moved without thinking, rolling over and over. She saw Comet throw Wynford at last. Wynford come down near her, rolling over onto his back as

Comet came at him. Comet reared up almost straight and came down hard, his front hooves crushing Wynford's chest. Blood gushed from Wynford's mouth as he tried to scream. Comet reared up again and came down again, then one more time.

Sherry ran over to Niki and put his arm under her shoulders. "Don't look," he said hoarsely. "Don't look."

"I'm all right," she gasped. "Get Comet."

Blood spurted again from Wynford's mouth. "Don't look," Sherry said again, turning her so that her head was against his chest. He held her for a moment, and she had to make herself say the words. "Comet, take care of Comet." He looked down at her, his blue eyes full of a strange emotion that Niki couldn't identify, then he gently lowered her to the ground. He walked slowly over to where Comet was pawing at Wynford's bloody body. Sherry stood in front of Comet and began talking in a soothing voice. Niki couldn't hear what he was saying, but Comet began to quiet. In just a few minutes, Sherry had calmed the horse and was stroking his mane. He put his hand on the dangling rope attached to Comet's bridle and walked him away from what was left of Wynford. Comet followed, pausing only long enough to nuzzle Sherry's neck. Sherry walked the horse around the corner of the barn, motioning for one of the men from Breconbridge to take him. The man took the rope, then mounted his own horse and headed for Breconbridge, leading Comet behind him. Sherry came back to Niki.

"I was afraid you were going to have to put him down. Comet, I mean." She trembled visibly.

"Comet was just lashing back at someone who had hurt him, Niki. He's not a bad horse, just a mistreated one."

Niki moved to stare at what was left of Wynford. "He's . . ."

"Don't look, Niki," Sherry said gently, kneeling between Niki and Wynford's body. "He's dead. He can't hurt you."

Niki began to shake and couldn't seem to stop. "I knew he was dead," she said, her voice tremulous. "I know he was a terrible man, but no one deserves to die that way."

Sherry put his arms around her. "It's all right, sweeting. Comet's hoof hit him on the head with the second onslaught.

He felt nothing after that." He grimaced. "I hope Uncle Richard's boys were as fortunate." He pulled Niki to him, and she was content to stay there for a minute, wrapped in his arms, listening to the sound of his heart beating steadily. She turned her head to snuggle closer and saw Blazer out of the corner of her eye. The dog was snuffling at the shed door and scratching at it.

Niki sat bolt upright, knocking Sherry on the chin. "Ooofff," he muttered, rocking back and letting go of her. Niki scrambled to her feet. "Robbie," she called. "Robbie." She turned back to Sherry. "Robbie's in there!"

Blazer began jumping up and barking as Niki fumbled with the latch on the door of the shed. Sherry and Cam came up behind her. "Let me," Sherry said, looking at the lock. "Robbie, get back the corner," he called out. "I'm going to have to shoot the lock." Cam and Niki moved behind Sherry in case the bullet ricocheted. Sherry fired and worked the lock loose. As soon as the door was open, Niki slipped by him and into the shed. Blazer was faster—he ran right under her feet, almost knocking her down. Sherry caught her just before she toppled while Cam ran over to Robbie.

Robbie was standing in the corner, his face ashen. "Did you get him?" he asked. "Did you stop Wynford?"

"We stopped him," Sherry said gently, wrapping his arms tighter around Niki.

"I knew we would," Robbie said, bending to put his arms around Blazer's neck. It took Niki a minute to realize that Robbie was trying to hide the fact that he was crying. Cam patted him on the back.

"Yes, we did, and everything's fine," she said softly. "Even Comet."

"Comet's all right? I thought they would kill him." Robbie's voice broke as he tried to swallow his tears.

"He's fine," Sherry said gently. "Wynford doesn't have a claim on him anymore, so he belongs to the estate. On behalf of my father, I give him to you, Robbie. I can't think of a better owner for him."

"Mine?" Robbie hugged Blazer so hard that the dog yelped, then began licking Robbie's face. "He's mine, Blazer." He held the dog and rocked back and forth. Sherry sighed and leaned back against the shed door, pulling Niki with him. "All's well then, Miss Owen, even you." He smiled down at her, his eyes full of a message she couldn't decipher. "I was frantic. I didn't know if I'd get here and discover that you single-handedly dispatched Wynford, or if he had carried you off."

"How did you know where I was?" Unconsciously she reached up and touched his chin with her fingertips. He clasped her hand and kissed her palm.

"Touchstone. He was in the stable, and Jem told him where the two of you were headed. You can imagine how I felt when we found Qadir running alone back to Breconbridge. I thought . . ." He paused and looked at her, catching his breath. "I thought I'd never see you again." He kissed her fingers. "The thought was not to be borne, Miss Owen. I long ago decided that I wanted to see you every day of my life."

"What?" Niki was lost in strange feelings as she looked at him. She felt dizzy and couldn't follow his words.

"Good God, Niki," Cam said impatiently. "The man is telling you that he loves you. He's offering for you. Say yes."

"You are? You really are?" Niki looked at Sheridan, lost in the blue of his eyes.

Sherry grinned at her. "Well, yes. Although I did hope to do this a little more romantically." He released her slightly and she stepped back a step, facing him. "Sweep you off your feet, as it were. However . . ."

"Are you going to do it?" Niki pushed her tangled hair back from her face so she could see every move he made.

"Do what?"

"Offer for the girl, Sherry," Cam said impatiently. "Must I cue each of you constantly?"

Sherry glared at him. "Miss Owen, I truly think . . ."

Niki was afraid he wasn't going to really offer for her. He was going to wait, he was going back to America, she would never see him again, she just knew it. She threw her arms around his neck. "Yes," she said. "Yes."

"Yes? Do you mean it? After all, I'm just an untitled American."

"Yes." She reached up and smoothed his hair back. "Yes."

"Now you're supposed to kiss her," Cam prompted.

Sherry grinned at him, his arms around Niki. "From this point, I can handle things all by myself, thank you." With that, he bent and kissed Niki soundly.

As Cam ushered Robbie out the door beside them, Niki heard Robbie talking as though he were very far away. "Why did he want to do something like kiss her?" Robbie asked in a disgusted tone. "Who would ever want to kiss females?"

"Just wait," Cam said, shutting the shed door so that Sherry and Niki were alone.

Sherry drew back and smiled down at her, his indigo eyes warm in the gloom of the shed. "Just wait. Oh yes, Miss Owen. You're going to have me around day and night forever. Just wait."

Niki smiled at him and snuggled against his chest as he tightened his arms around her. "I've been waiting for you my whole life, Sheridan."

## Author's Note

Hello, I'm Juliette Leigh and I hope you've enjoyed *Sherry's Comet*. I am happy to tell you that Zebra will be issuing another of my Regency novels in December, 1998. The title of that book is *A Touch of Magic* and it's an exciting story about espionage, a circus, a crusading miss who owns a pet leopard, and, of course, a handsome hero.

If you enjoyed this book or have a comment, please write to me. A SASE would be greatly appreciated. My address is:

> Juliette Leigh
> Box 295
> Pineola, NC 28662.

Or, if you prefer, e-mail me at romance@sff.net

You may also want to take a quick look at my web page if you're on the Internet. The address is http://www.sff.net/people/romance

Since I'm learning about the internet as I go along, that page is always under construction, but I plan to post any news I may have, as well as my publication list and information about my newest releases.

I hope to hear from you soon
Happy reading!

# BOOK YOUR PLACE ON OUR WEBSITE
## AND MAKE THE
## READING CONNECTION!

We've created a customized website just for our very special readers, where you can get the inside scoop on everything that's going on with Zebra, Pinnacle and Kensington books.

When you come online, you'll have the exciting opportunity to:

- View covers of upcoming books
- Read sample chapters
- Learn about our future publishing schedule (listed by publication month *and author*)
- Find out when your favorite authors will be visiting a city near you
- Search for and order backlist books from our online catalog
- Check out author bios and background information
- Send e-mail to your favorite authors
- Meet the Kensington staff online
- Join us in weekly chats with authors, readers and other guests
- Get writing guidelines
- AND MUCH MORE!

**Visit our website at
http://www.zebrabooks.com**